CEMETERY LODGE

PAULA HILLMAN

BLOODHOUND
BOOKS

Copyright © 2024 Paula Hillman

The right of Paula Hillman to be identified as the Author of the Work has been asserted by them in accordance with the Copyright, Designs and Patents Act 1988.

First published in 2024 by Bloodhound Books.

Apart from any use permitted under UK copyright law, this publication may only be reproduced, stored, or transmitted, in any form, or by any means, with prior permission in writing of the publisher or, in the case of reprographic production, in accordance with the terms of licences issued by the Copyright Licensing Agency.
All characters in this publication are fictitious and any resemblance to real persons, living or dead, is purely coincidental.

www.bloodhoundbooks.com

Print ISBN: 978-1-917449-20-5

CHAPTER ONE

DECEMBER 2022

Cherie

The train clears the station and immediately, the coast comes into view. I huddle in my seat and press my forehead against the window. It is a white-cold afternoon, but I had to get out of the cottage. It's not so much that I am missing David: his final actions were hardly endearing. It's more that items I'd brought with me from the home we once shared can cause distress.

Today, it was our address book. It is a benign object, the cover decorated with a twine of honeysuckle and roses on a creamy background. He'd thrown it at me as we were packing up, scorn dripping from his voice and onto the names of my *snotty-nosed* academic friends. They hadn't liked him, either.

The coast is a bleak mix of salt marsh and cloudy water. It eventually bleeds into something more agricultural. Grey stone farmhouses; horses gathered around winter fodder; sheep huddled, breath frosting the air.

When the landscape of misty fields falls away, the ruin appears. It rises from the grass, a huge tumble of sandstone and stories. With my passion for local history, I should have visited before now, but this is the first time I've seen the reality of the place. I track it as we pass, craning to hold the sight for as long as possible.

Then it is gone. The vista changes as the town appears. Neat pockets of housing blend into brick terraces and archways, a wall of graffiti judders by. There is a reputation attached to this place. Distinctive Victoriana and claustrophobic community morals. Keeping that in mind will be vital while I'm working here. I have to make a success of this job; it will cancel out my failures. Finally, the train pulls into the station. It's the terminus of the line. End of the road.

I zip my parka and step onto the platform. A few passengers follow, breath steaming. I glance at my watch. There's an hour before the cemetery gates close. In the grounds is a disused chapel. I want a look before its formal assessment by Gillside Archaeological, the company I work for. I'm being nosy: the real *work* starts next week. On a Sunday afternoon, I should be hanging out with friends or family, sleepy from the aftereffects of a well-cooked roast. Breaking up with David ejected me from that kind of life; most Sundays I'm alone.

I hurry across town, but the cemetery gates are shut and padlocked when I arrive. The website for the local council had been clear: gates close at 4pm. It's half past three. There is a lodge house to the side, a pinkish glow coming from behind downstairs curtains. Should I knock and ask for entry? I take a moment to look at the place. It's a Victorian building, a solid stack of grey limestone with a gabled roof. Every corner is sharply edged, every window perfectly arched. I'm a fan of old buildings and this one doesn't disappoint. In the shadowy garden, skeletal shrubs freeze on their shadow; a dilapidated wooden fence shields the rear of the house. Evening is closing in and I wouldn't want to intrude.

I could hurry back to the station and get on the train, forget all about my ridiculous plan... But there's a sandstone wall around the perimeter of the cemetery; there may be another entrance. Eventually, I find a small gate, an iron kissing gate, rusted with age. It leads me onto the western slopes of the cemetery.

The last rays of winter sunlight give the place an eerie beauty. Coloured bouquets are muted; the lawns are silvery-grey. Every grave faces west, towards the sea. In the distance, the chapel is half-silhouetted, steeple glittering. A tingle of excitement skips across my shoulders. This will be my first assignment working independently since I started at Gillside. My new boss has been nothing but kind, and I want to repay him with my best attention.

There is an energy to the cemetery, a sense of lives well-lived and now rested. Bones fascinate me, with their strength and their fragility. They can tell many stories, yet keep quiet about the important ones. Studying them is second nature. Another thing David found distasteful. I push my hands into my pockets, and set off up the slope towards the chapel. No harm will come from taking a quick look; I'm hardly going to disturb anybody.

Pathways wind between headstones. The grass has been neatly clipped; dead flowers removed to waste bins. Standing taps have attached hoses and nozzles; someone cares about this place. It is the first time I've given any thought to the *life* of a cemetery. I'm lucky enough that everyone I love is still alive: my parents up in Carlisle, my sister on the south coast.

I'm not sure if I ever loved David. We liked each other well enough, until I gained my doctorate. Then something changed. He would, with a sneer across his lips, say things like *the doctor will see you now* and *don't expect any common sense from her... she's a doctor*. I gained an archaeology doctorate, not a brain injury. My sister thought his actions pointed towards jealousy; it was more that David and I ran out of common ground. When I did online tutoring through the months of the pandemic, he accused me of giving my virtual students more attention than him. Ridiculous, when he is a primary school teacher and spent a large part of every day in Zoom meetings with his class.

The chapel is encircled by a protective fence. Its windows have been boarded over and the porch door chained shut. I rattle the fence panels a few times to make myself feel better, then turn to take in the view one last time.

The sun is almost gone, leaving the faintest trace of yellow glow along the surface of the sea. Above it is an icy blue sky and the first hint of starlight.

A white marble statue stands just below me: it's a bust of Jesus and is almost life-sized. He is holding open his flowing robes to reveal a sacred heart, a covert smile across his stony lips.

The cold continues to creep. I shiver and huddle into my scarf. There is a distant sound of traffic, an occasional flare of headlights, but the place is deserted. No one would know or care if I slipped between the fence panels and had a quick poke around. In a moment, I am on the inside.

Decaying weeds and nettles clog the base of every wall, and the window boards are crumbling on their edges. I lay my palm against the stone. It is ice cold and slimy with algae. A building like this should be loved and nurtured. It is listed; that much I already know. It was last used as a chapel in the early part of the 1970s, when the multi-faith crematorium opened. Fifty years later and that same crem is falling apart. Despite the chapel's decrepitude, it has a solidity that feels similar to the lodge house. The assessment finally makes sense; I can see why the chapel would be ripe for conversion.

I take a torch from my pocket and switch it on. It will give me a better look at the place where the steeple joins the main body of the chapel. If the flashing is rotted and the lower level of stone slabs have suffered water damage, my assessment might take a different form. I follow the line of the wall, keeping the beam of light pointing at my feet. Grainy darkness spools out from the margins. The cold sets my teeth on edge. My footsteps press.

'What the fuck do you think you're doing?'

A voice comes from the darkness. I gasp, instinctively pointing the torch in the direction of the sound. The flat of a hand comes towards me, and I step backwards, planning my escape route.

Ash

He peers into the darkness. 'I asked what you were doing.'

It's a woman, from what Ash can make out. She is shining the torch beam at his face. When he'd heard the clunk of the kissing gate, he presumed the vandals were back. A pair of teenagers have been taking out their frustration on the graves of babies and toddlers; those loved in a way the teens would never be.

The ever-open gate was a decision made by the local council: grief didn't stick to specific hours; the cemetery should be accessible always. Mainly, there is no problem; recently, one has developed. Ash blames the pandemic. Though it is long over, its mental health impact is still in evidence, especially for youngsters. The person standing before him is definitely not one of those.

'Just looking at the chapel,' comes the reply.

'Looking in daylight would have been better; do you not think?' A sliver of sarcasm has slipped into Ash's voice. No way would anybody be *just looking*. 'Anyhow. The *safety* fence is there for a reason.' He pushes against the torch. 'Come on. Out.'

The fence panels are held together with a special clip, designed to be flexible but stable. Ash has made them this way specifically. Cordoning off the chapel is a visual warning to keep out, but he doesn't want the fence to become a danger. It can be easily breached if the need arises. He pulls at the clips and makes a gap large enough for the intruder to squeeze through. The woman doesn't need to be told twice. She retreats from the dark shadows surrounding the chapel, and makes her way into a pool of moonlight.

'It's okay,' she mutters. 'I can take myself out of here. No need to follow.' Her hand gesture reminds him of the semaphore he'd learnt in the days when youths went to scouts and were encouraged to light fires.

He shakes his head. 'I'm not being funny, but you were trespassing. I'm not interested in why; I just want you gone. So, if I want to follow, I will.'

The woman is small and slightly built. Huddled in her scarf and huge padded jacket, it's hard to put an age to her, but he would guess she's outgrown her graffitiing years. He's had to leave his father half fed, back at the lodge, so his reactions are more curt than usual.

'I'm going, I'm going,' she says. 'No need to stress. Forget you ever saw me.' She scoots away down the slope, leaving Ash wondering about her motives. He's already dismissed everything teens might want secrecy for; what would a solitary and full-grown woman be sniffing out? Perhaps he's best not knowing.

Once she has gone, disappearing into the patch of twiggy hedging at the side of the gate, Ash surveys this part of the cemetery. The gravestones remind him of predatory creatures, hunched silently, waiting for prey that never comes.

It's dark enough now that the townscape below him is

nothing more than twinkling lights and engine-rumble. The sea stretches away, black and glittering and blending into the evening sky. He breathes in the freezing air and lets himself relax. This place is his life. It's a paradox, but someone has to do what he does. People appreciate it. He sees them at their worst, and having someone take charge can help. He often receives thank-you cards, small gifts, kind words. Keeping the crem and the plots looking neat and clean lifts the burden from vulnerable shoulders, and he's happy to do it. His father had the job before him, his grandfather previously. There was never any question that Ash would take on the role.

Back at the lodge, he lets himself in through the front door and hangs up his coat in the hall. His father is moving about upstairs. The fire has gone out in the tiny sitting room he favours, and the supper dishes are on the floor by his armchair. Ash presumes he has gone to bed. It's not yet 6pm, but Hal can no longer handle the cold. It unsettles him; tires him. He is frail beyond his years, and his mental grasp of the world is fading.

'Dad,' Ash calls. 'Dad. It's only me. I'm back from checking the site.'

His father bears the weight of his former responsibility still, seeing Ash as no more than an assistant. Ash smiles: Hal rarely goes further than the garden. Time has become an ephemeral thing for him, a thing with feathers that flits when it is reached for. Very like the jackdaws roosting in the trees around the lodge. His father feeds and tends them, but the slightest attempt at interaction sends them winging away.

The lodge has a tiny but functional kitchen. Ash fills the kettle and sets it to boil. Moonlight has pooled at the far end of the garden, giving Hal's patio a silvery glow. Above the fence, the higher slopes of the cemetery are visible. There is a picture-book quality to the scene, eerie, but homely and familiar.

Why would anyone be poking around in a graveyard on a

wintry evening in December? Should he have called the police about the woman? The cemetery has a twenty-four-hour helpline. He's had to respond to *trivial* call-outs recently, so why shouldn't the police? All council workers have had mental health training, and he's certain the woman wasn't showing signs of a crisis. Nor had he detected the smell of alcohol. Whatever her reason for being there, it won't be weighted equally with the amount of paperwork a police report would generate; he's not going to call the police.

In his office, Ash checks the work schedules for Monday morning. Winter is a busy time. The previous two Decembers weigh heavily, but he tries not to think of them. Though he and his father had been stricken with coronavirus shortly after the first wave, they'd survived. Others hadn't been so lucky. That grim year had been the worst he'd seen. No one wants a crematorium to be busy.

Though he has a full suite of technical equipment: computer, printer, high-speed broadband connection, Ash likes a hard copy of the week's work. Sheets of paper can be folded into the pocket of his overalls, and accessed anywhere onsite. Instead of the neat pile he'd left on his desk, his papers have been scattered on the floor, as though a gust of wind has blasted through. He stoops to pick them up. Something isn't right. There is the faintest noise coming from somewhere in the house, soft, like singing. He tidies the papers, cocking his head towards the sound. It's coming from upstairs.

In the hallway, he flicks on the light. The white glare is disorientating. His father is sitting on the landing. He is peering through wooden spindles as if he's a prisoner, gripping them like they will hold him back forever.

'I don't want her here,' he is whining. Over and over. 'I don't want her here. I don't want her here.'

CHAPTER TWO

Cherie

If I was expecting any sort of welcome at the cemetery, it doesn't come. Though I'm a long way from being *the new girl*, my stomach is bubbling. Having someone to greet me would have helped. When we pull up at the lodge, though the gates are open, no one is about. My boss has driven me from the train station, but is rushing away to another job.

'I feel like a father dropping his daughter at her first date.' He tugs on the handbrake. 'Should I be saying something like "don't do anything I wouldn't do?"'

'You're hardly old enough to be my father, Bill.' I squint into the brightness of the morning. 'And actually, I mean to do everything you *would* do. I won't go far wrong, then.'

He guffaws. 'A fair point, and a kind one.'

'I'm returning your kindness for meeting my train and bringing me down here.'

'No worries.' Bill slaps the steering wheel. 'Happy to help my newest employee.'

My early train journey had been full of brittle sunshine and the press of bodies. Getting on at Cark meant I'd had to stand all the way. When I'd started working at Gillside, I treated myself to a four-wheeled pilot case, a kind of mobile office, meaning I can work anywhere. It saved me on this morning's commute, allowing my free hand to grip the back of a seat as we rattled across the viaduct. I have a tiny rucksack with a cross-body strap for all my other needs: mainly a torch and mobile phone.

'Just leave me here,' I say. 'There's no need for introductions. I can handle it.'

Bill smiles an apology as he climbs out of the car. 'I know you can. The caretaker said to knock at the lodge house when we talked on the telephone. We're– you're expected.' He pops open the car boot. 'I'll get your case then I've got to shoot away. We can catch up later. Give me a ring or something.' His hand gesture mimics a telephone, and it makes me laugh.

I haven't told Bill about my visit to the cemetery on the previous evening. By the time I'd got back to the station, I was seething. More at myself than anyone else. I'd let a random person chase me off, without any argument. I usually stand my ground. It can't have been a policeman or security guard; I wasn't challenged in a formal way, and there definitely wasn't a uniform. I might have disturbed someone up to no good. In which case, I should have informed on them. When I finally meet this caretaker guy, it will be the first thing I tell him.

Once Bill has driven away, I smooth down my jacket and head towards the front door of the lodge. The garden looks different this morning, less ethereal. I leave my case on the tarmac driveway, and let myself through the iron gate. In daylight, the house is less romantic. It has a shabby air, though it is a solid enough building, despite a flimsy plate-glass window on the side gable. The curtains that were tightly closed last night have been drawn back, but there is no sign of life. A black granite plaque with letters chiselled sharply in white marks the place out as *Cemetery Lodge*.

I knock on the front door a couple of times, but no one comes. Has Bill given me the wrong information? Perhaps I am supposed to show up at the crematorium building and drop my gear there. It isn't far away, up a slight incline. I'm about to retrieve my case and make my way there, but someone is striding towards me. A youngish man. He's wearing navy-blue overalls under a fluorescent coat.

'Hi there,' he calls. 'Are you waiting for me? Do you have an appointment? There was an intruder last night, and I've been checking everything is as it should be.' He holds out his hand. 'I'm Ash Black. Oh–'

The hand is withdrawn.

A beat of silence passes between us. Is this the man from last night and he's recognised me, or is he miffed that the Gillside person doesn't measure up? He is eyeing my pilot case and saying nothing.

'Cherie Hope. From the archaeological surveyors.' I don't offer my hand. Judging by the expression on his face, Ash Black's brain cogs are in overdrive. 'It was me, last night. If that helps.' I'm not keen on the sort of surveying I'm being subjected to. In return, I do a little of my own. This guy looks about my age, tall and long-limbed. His hair is dark, with the strangest streak of grey halfway along his parting and reaching down to his shoulders. His expression is distinctly sardonic.

'You're the archaeologist?' He frowns out his confusion.

'I am. My apologies for that.'

He runs a hand across his chin. 'So what were you doing nosing round here last night?'

'Pretty obvious, I would have thought.' I give an exaggerated sigh, and shock myself. My teen years are long gone. 'Just wanted an early peek at the place.'

'The gates were closed. I do that for a reason.'

'Not the little side gate. That's where I got in.'

'The chapel has a safety fence and no-entry signs. Can you not read?' Ash is getting cross. He explains, through gritted teeth, about trespassing and the need to maintain security.

When he's finished, I point out that the cemetery is public land and therefore, in law, trespass would not stand up. The pure stupidity of our banter isn't lost on me, and I wonder what is happening. My conclusion is that he doesn't like or trust having his stereotypical crusty academic preconceptions turned upside down.

'Well, you shouldn't have been there,' is all he offers in response.

I've made an effort with my clothing this morning, choosing a dark blue trouser suit and floral shirt rather than my usual walking trousers and sweater. Perhaps the scruffy outfit would have been preferable: I'm feeling like a fake. If Cemetery Lodge is this man's home, he's hardly going to allow what he deems to be a criminal to set up equipment and use the facilities. A criminal, and a *woman* to boot. Perhaps the place has an office, and he will be able to ignore me. Until he says otherwise, I can do nothing.

'Can we go and look at the chapel or not?' I ask, in the end. 'There is a job to be done and I'm being paid to do it.'

He gives me a look that says he isn't convinced.

'I have ID,' I continue, unzipping the top pocket of my case. When I thrust my pass-card towards him, he snaps his gaze to mine.

'I don't need to see that. My dilemma is that there are no facilities for... women... in the house, I mean. I'd presumed–'

'What? That the archaeologist would be a man?' I sigh. 'Again, sorry to disappoint, but I'm pretty tough. If you've a place for me to safely set up laptop and cameras, a kettle, coffee and a toilet, however rudimentary, I'll be fine, I can assure you.'

He nods curtly. 'Follow me, then.'

I drag my case behind me, trying to navigate the front door without crashing against the skirting. The porch is tiny, and cluttered with outdoor clothing. Once we are inside, Ash calls out to someone: his father, from what I can make out. The place is warm and clean but basic. A narrow hallway leads to three rooms at the back of the building. One is a kitchen.

'Feel free to make yourself hot drinks, or whatever,' Ash says as we pass. 'The office is here. My office.' He pushes against a pitch-pine door. 'There's no downstairs loo, I'm afraid.' He gestures towards the stairwell. 'You'll have to share the upstairs one with me and Dad. It doesn't have a lock; I can't trust him with locks.'

'No worries. I'm perfectly used to sharing toilets. Give me a half hour to get set up then I'll be ready to have a look around the chapel. Officially.' I smile wryly, but there doesn't seem to be any humour in Ash. He nods once, then informs me he has jobs he must attend to and will return for me when he can. I suggest he gives me a key and I can get started myself. The only thing I get is the most disdainful of glances. Then he shoves his hands into the pockets of his jacket, and stomps away.

Ash

There is a freezing draft blowing through the lodge. This woman, this *Cherie*, has left the front door open. She'll need to be given some house rules. This particular door needs to be kept closed and locked. His father uses the rear one to access the garden and his birds. It is fully enclosed, fully fenced off so he can't wander. He doesn't usually bother, but if he sees an open door, there's the possibility he will walk through it. A busy road runs in front of the cemetery gates, and with funerals most days, an escapee father is unthinkable.

Ash is more than capable of looking after Hal and doing his other job, if only people would be more tuned in. He slams the door and hopes Cherie hears.

The sun has cleared the highest point of the cemetery, and the lower slopes are losing their coating of frost. Ash shields his eyes and looks towards the chapel. The place has been allowed to rest silently for many years. Better it remains that way, but he is torn. Repurposing it as offices or retail units could mean his lodge is saved; the thought of damaging the chapel hurts his heart. During the long summer of pandemic lockdown, he had made a study of local antiquated structures. When he could no longer meet up with his motorcycling group, academic study kept him sane.

What he hadn't planned for was how emotionally involved he would become. The chapel was one of the many on his list; the Cistercian ruin another. Though he'd never met his mentors, working online was a practice that resonated: the musings of a cemetery caretaker would hardly have been taken seriously in a university setting.

In the pocket of his overalls, Ash is carrying this week's work schedule. He'll be out doing practical things until eleven. Then he has the appointment he's been dreading; with another woman he hardly knows. He has doodled a skull-and-crossbones next to his notes, and is trying to pretend the meeting won't be happening.

Cherie Hope and her needs will have to wait. She'll have made herself at home, no doubt, and be installing her laptop in an inconvenient position. Luckily, his jobs for the next few days will keep him away from the lodge, so he won't need to share the office with her. Once he has let her into the chapel and made sure the place is safe enough for assessment, she can come and go as she pleases throughout the day. He hasn't told his father of these plans: Hal wouldn't understand.

Earlier, when he'd completed the morning perimeter check, Ash had been ready to let the police know about the supposed intruder. Why a professional woman like Cherie Hope had snuck her way into the cemetery on a brutally cold Sunday evening in December, he cannot fathom. The only positive is that he won't need to inform on her after all; police bureaucracy is something he can do without. Along with many other slippages since the pandemic, the online form-filling required to access public services tends to put people off.

There is a graveside service today. Two young men from the council come in beforehand, and use a compact excavator – what Ash calls a *mini-digger* – for the actual grave preparation. His part is to lay a walkway for the mourners and make the area look tidy. There is nothing worse, in his opinion, than unkempt graves. He doesn't get involved in cremations: they are the preserve of properly trained council officials.

His friends think Ash's job is morbid, that he must be, by association, a little dark himself. It is far from the truth. Caring for Hal has taught him many things. Ash doesn't dwell on the past or future.

The past is an interesting place, but fixed and rigid; the future is so insubstantial, it can be altered in an instant. His aim is to live optimistically within the present. If people don't like this about him, he doesn't much care.

He's had relationships, but nothing that engaged his attention. Those women were delightful but too focused on some point that lay ahead. The way he lives isn't unlike how he rides his motorcycle: the thrill comes from soaring through the journey, not from arriving at the coffee stop.

Though the roads will be icy, he makes up his mind to have a blast on his bike as soon as circumstances allow. Ash makes his way up to the crematorium outbuildings, the main storage facility for his tools. From within the texture of the tarmac driveway, frost glitters. It'll need gritting if people are to park and walk safely. Leaf litter has collected at the edge of the walkway. A crow is rifling hungrily. There's a tranquillity to the scene that steals his breath. The distant sea is a glassy blue, hazy at the horizon and blending into the pastel sky.

When he reaches the side of the building, Ash realises the lid of his plastic grit box is frozen shut. He kicks at it, but it won't budge. From the shed where he stores chemicals, he retrieves a can of de-icer. His fingers are numb, so everything is taking longer. By the time he has freed the lid, filled a wheelbarrow with grit and treated the slope, the sun is high.

He looks at his watch, then curses himself. It's gone eleven. She will have already arrived. His heart jolts. He sidesteps the barrow and shovel and hurtles down the slope towards the lodge. Ash doesn't believe in fate. In his opinion, everything is created in the moment. Which is why he's going to stop this blessed woman before she starts.

CHAPTER THREE

Cherie

While I'm stirring my tea, a jackdaw flies at the kitchen window. The jangle of beak against glass sets my heart juddering. The creature settles on the sill and peers in at me. I don't know much about birds, but recognise this one with its white eyes and pinprick pupils. The silvery feathers at the side of the head cinch it. Two other jackdaws wait on the bird feeder, swinging boldly. My Canon camera is in Ash's office. It is set up with a zoom lens, ready for my shoot at the chapel. I bring it into the kitchen and take a few photos of the birds through the window. I'm examining the back of the camera, when there is a shuffling of feet behind me.

'What you got there, then?'

It's an elderly man, wearing a dressing gown and pyjamas though it's almost eleven. He is white-haired, but with the same facial bone structure as Ash. This is the father he mentioned.

I hold out the camera. 'I took a few shots of the jackdaws. What do you think?'

The man moves warily towards me, craning to see.

'I've spotted three outside so far,' I continue. 'Is there a flock nearby? They seem to be raiding your bird feeders. Clever things, aren't they?'

'Oh, aye. They're clever.' The strangeness of the situation doesn't seem to bother him. There is a person he's never met, standing in the kitchen of his home, helping herself to tea. And he's wearing nightclothes. I never let myself be seen in nightclothes. Surely Ash should have introduced us before he gave me full access to the lodge.

'I'm Cherie Hope,' I say, for ease. 'Your son and I are going to work together for a couple of weeks and he's letting me use his office. I hope you don't mind.'

'Right,' is all he says, but I do notice he is eyeing my mug.

'Can I get you a drink?' I ask. 'Some breakfast?'

'Go on then.' He pulls out a chair from the tiny kitchen table. 'Is our Ash coming for dinner, too?'

'Just me, I'm afraid. Cherie.'

The kitchen is immaculately clean, with surfaces free from crumbs and a dishcloth draped over the edge of a deep sink. Two walls are lined with glossy primrose-yellow cabinets, an electric stove crammed between them. Double doors lead onto a garden, and there is an internal porch. I retrieve a loaf of white bread and a tub of butter from the fridge, and set about making toast. From an old-fashioned dresser, I take plates and a teapot. While I work, Ash's father stretches his legs under the table and leans back, as though it's the most normal thing in the world that a stranger has entered his home, and is chatting while cooking breakfast.

When I've set a plate of toast in front of him and carried over a pot of tea, there is a knock on the front door.

'Oh. Looks like you've got visitors,' I say. No response comes. The knock is repeated, louder, like someone is bashing the flat of their hand against the wood. I get up from the table. 'I'll answer it, shall I? Mr Black?'

Ash's father blinks, but says nothing.

The simple explanation for someone hammering on the door could be a parcel delivery. Ash should make arrangements if his father is not able to answer the door.

'Mr Black. Shall I go?' I expect him to intervene, but get nothing more than a light nod.

'Sorry.' I stretch the word as I hurry down the hallway. There are bolts on the top and bottom of the front door. Ash Black must be overly conscious of security. The hammering continues. I apologise again. A woman is standing on the porch step. She is tall and stately in a grey wool coat with attached cape. Her face is flushed with pink, her mop of grey hair askew.

'I'm early,' she says in an unapologetic manner. Then, 'Oh. I was expecting Mr Black. Are you his partner?' Her eyes sweep over me a few times, like she's searching for something she can't find.

'I'm working with... Mr Black. Cherie Hope, from Gillside Archaeological.' Though I extend my hand, she doesn't take it. I am forced to step aside as she pushes her way into the hall.

'Fetch him, would you? I'm pressed for time.'

I've no intention of fetching him. 'And you are?'

The woman huffs loudly. 'Ria Lace. Councillor Lace, actually. I expect you've heard of me.'

'No. But I'm not from around here. Local councillors are only well known on their patch, I would have thought.' The dislike I'm feeling for this woman isn't helping my manners. A slap of footsteps comes from the kitchen, then Ash's father is in the hall with us. Before I have time to register that he's receiving yet another visitor while wearing his pyjamas, he starts shouting.

'Not her, not her,' he cries, his hands pressed to his face. 'I don't want her here.'

I lay my hand on his shoulder. 'Hey. It's okay. Don't panic. You're safe.'

He is trembling, and shouting for the woman to get out. My soothing words do nothing, my hand is batted away. There is no embarrassment in Ria Lace's expression, no compassion; I see anger.

'Where is Mr Black? This is ridiculous.' She folds her arms and leans back. The twist of her top lip implies superiority. Ash's father is becoming more and more agitated. I am about to suggest she leaves, when the front door bursts open, and Ash storms in.

Ash

Ria Lace's stifling presence fills the hallway. The woman was supposed to meet him outside the lodge. Ash had set things up like this for a reason: the protection of his father. Hal's routines need to be as smooth and sleek as the plumage of his beloved jackdaws. Ruffle it, and his dementia is more visible.

The last thing Ash wants is to flag it up in front of people. It's hard enough that he's had to let the Gillside archaeologist into his home. He apologises for being a few minutes late, but is distracted by his father's panicked state.

'Dad,' he says, putting his hands on the tops of his father's arms. 'I can smell toast. Have you been having toast? It will be getting cold.' He locks eyes with Cherie. 'Dad hates soggy toast, you know.'

Cherie nods once, then slides an arm around Hal's shoulder. 'Come on... Dad. He's right. We can't waste good food.'

Relief washes over Ash. It was a mistake to leave this woman in his house without making her aware of the situation with his father. He'd assumed she'd be a rugged male, working from the back of a battered Land Rover Defender, that he wouldn't have to bother himself too much. He resolves to be more open-minded, and is grateful when Cherie leads his father away.

'I didn't expect to find a mentally deficient old man in Cemetery Lodge.' Ria Lace's nasally voice cuts across Ash's thinking. 'You must have to leave him alone, sometimes. That's a tick on the *against* side, if ever I saw one.'

Ash looks at her sharply. 'Can we stop being cryptic. You're talking about sides before the game has even been explained properly. And my father seems to know you. Why is that?'

Ria hesitates. 'Can we please get on. I've no time this morning for sidetracking.' She rummages in her handbag and pulls out a spiral-bound notepad. 'Thank you for agreeing to this meeting. The HAZ have given me lots of questions to ask... well, answers to find, actually.'

Ash hadn't exactly agreed, and he isn't a fan of acronyms. Or people who use them in an arrogant way, trying to wield a bit of power. But he'll have to ask. 'What's the HAZ?'

'Heritage Action Zone. Another little pie I have my finger in. It's a group within the council, a kind of *double-whammy* of power over the plight of our local buildings.' She smirks.

Ash is going to block her in any way he can. 'I see.' He runs a hand over his chin. 'And what has the HAZ group got to do with Cemetery Lodge? I'm not even sure what you're doing here, *Ms* Lace.'

'Can we sit down somewhere and have a proper discussion, *Mr* Black?' Ria waves her hand in the direction of the kitchen. 'Perhaps over a cup of tea or something?'

There is a small lounge at the front of the house. It is chilly but tidy. Ash leads Ria through. She casts around, then perches on a corner of the sofa. He pulls up a side table so that she can put down her writing pad and bag, then excuses himself and goes in search of her tea. He pauses at the kitchen door. Cherie is having a one-sided conversation with his father. She is telling him about her train journey over the Kent estuary, about the birdlife and the scenery. Hal's not saying much, but he's a fan of train travel, so is listening intently.

'Just grabbing some drinks,' Ash says as he steps into the room. 'Sorry you've been delayed. I'm a bit behind this morning.' The teapot is warm. He pours a cup for Ria and one for himself. She'll have to drink it how it comes. If he must entertain the woman, he's not having her get comfortable.

'It's not a problem, honestly.' Cherie holds up her mug. 'Your dad and I are having a nice chat. Will you be long?'

Her tone makes him feel like a schoolboy being berated for late homework: the teacher is kind but seething.

'Not long. But you could go and get some outside photos of the chapel... in daylight... if you like. Dad is fine by himself. He'll need to shower and get dressed.'

Cherie jumps up from her seat and follows him from the room. 'Can I ask you something?' she whispers when they are in the hallway.

He frowns. 'I suppose so.'

'What's your dad's name? I can't keep calling him Mr Black.'

'Harold. Harold Black.' He waits for her reaction. 'We actually call him Hal, if that makes things easier.'

'Hal.' She smiles. 'Thank you. I'll see you shortly.'

When Ash gets back to the lounge, Ria is standing in front of the fireplace, peering closely at a framed photograph. 'Your family have lived in the lodge for a long time,' she says.

Ash puts down the mugs of tea. He would rather she didn't

stare at his private things, especially since her prime motive for being here is to turf the last remaining family members out of the lodge.

'The house goes with the job; my family have always done the job. It's fairly straightforward and not at all sneaky.'

'No. Of course not.' Ria returns to the sofa, selecting a drink without enquiring about which one was made for her. This infuriates Ash further. He throws himself into the rocking chair on the other side of the room, folding his arms and crossing his ankles. Ria blows across the surface of her tea, then spends ten minutes talking about the HAZ and its function. There is a pot of money, it seems, for the remodelling of local buildings. The idea might be a sound one, but the lodge doesn't need *remodelling*.

When Ria pauses, he interrupts her dull over-elaboration. 'I think you will have realised, even from your brief view of my home, that it wouldn't be a suitable building for the new crem offices.'

She coughs lightly. 'It would be far cheaper to convert than that dilapidated chapel. If we're being honest.'

'Is it just about money?' He nods towards her notebook. 'I presume this *HAZ* group is about preserving local heritage. Spend where it's needed then. Not on the lodge.'

'It's not that simple.' Ria's jaw is set hard. 'Nor is it anything but council business. It is a courtesy that I'm here to get your opinion. Had you not realised?' Her head tilts in a conciliatory way.

This woman isn't getting a foothold; Ash is fighting for his life. 'Why not just upgrade the old crem building? That would be the cheapest and most ethical choice, in my opinion.'

Ria presses her lips together and flips through her notepad. She stops at a page that appears to contain floorplan drawings, then holds it out to him.

'Ethical or not,' she says, 'here's what will happen to the crem building. I was at the planning meeting only last week. These are sketches I made. There's a small amount of money to expand the facility, make it a nicer and roomier place for the clientele. And fix the roof.' She shakes her head. 'It's not the crem that's giving us problems though, is it?'

Ash glances at the drawings. He had no idea about this meeting, yet should have been involved. 'It makes no sense. There's already a suite of offices in the crem. I should know, I clean them. Why not upgrade those, instead. Extend the building outwards? Spend money on that, and leave the lodge and chapel alone.'

Ria sighs impatiently. 'It's not what the council wants. Or the HAZ. The lodge would be a much better site for new offices. Right at the cemetery gates and away from the crem itself.' She lifts her shoulders. 'That's the consensus, anyway.'

'So I'd just be turfed out of my home? Would I even keep my job?' Ash makes sure Ria can hear the edge of sarcasm in his voice. Who does this woman think she is?

She gives him an icy glare. 'Of course you'd keep your job. The council are planning to purchase one of those new-build bungalows on the other side of the cemetery. It will be tied to the caretaker position, and would be yours for as long as–'

'What about my father. He'd find it hard to leave the lodge. He's never lived anywhere else.'

'It looks to me like he will be in a care home soon, anyway. Have you considered it? You must have.'

Ash wants this woman out of his house. They were meant to be discussing the sustainability of the three buildings under his care. The key word was *discuss*; there was supposed to be a consensus. It seems she has already made up her mind. He's not sure about the level of power she wields. Allowing her to make an appointment and take up his time, came from a place of hoping she might give insights into the workings of the local council. He'd got that wrong. The comments she is making about Hal need closing down.

'You don't know anything about my father,' Ash mutters, 'so I'd rather you didn't speak about him in such a flippant way.'

'I don't need to know anything about him. His reaction when he first saw me says it all.' Ria folds her arms defiantly. 'That wasn't a normal response to strangers, so don't try to tell me different.'

Ash gets up from his seat and moves to the window. The sun is high and bright now, and he wants to be outside. He draws back the net curtains and the room floods with light. 'My father was responding to you. Personally.' He enjoys Ria's response to being dazzled. 'He's fine with strangers. And just in case you didn't know, he has a perpetuity clause in his retirement package: he can remain at Cemetery Lodge for as long as he chooses. I'm going to ask for the same when I retire.'

'You can ask,' Ria mutters. 'But it won't happen.'

'Oh, it will.' Ash isn't proud of how he must be coming across. He isn't normally loud or aggressive, but this woman is threatening everything he holds dear without any qualification to do so. He changes tack. 'Why does the council need to rejig the site, anyhow? Everything we've got here is adequate. The only thing that needs doing is the crem roof, if we're being honest.'

Ria gulps down the rest of her tea, then stares up at him. 'We've got people wanting to transfer their businesses here. Then there's the ever-increasing admin team needed to deal with–' She waves a hand in the direction of the cemetery. 'Death, I suppose.'

'What businesses?'

'We've had a florist and a stonemason approach us, looking for premises.' She sends a nosy glance around the room. 'This would make a lovely office. East-facing, isn't it? For the morning sun?'

'It's not going to be an office. Besides which, I've already got one at the back of the lodge. If you're looking for units to house funeral suppliers, converting the chapel is what's needed. The place is cavernous. It must be under consideration; I've got Gillside Archaeological breathing down my neck for an assessment.'

Ria jumps up and makes a show of gathering her papers. 'I had hoped for your interest and support. I didn't expect an argument. This visit has hardly been worth my time.' She moves towards the door. 'But I'll tell you one thing. The HAZ group is adamant; the chapel is not going to be touched.'

Why has the local council commissioned Gillside to do an assessment, if the chapel is *not going to be touched*? Ash doesn't get the chance to ask. Ria sweeps from the room, and within seconds the front door slams.

CHAPTER FOUR

Cherie

Ash's back is ramrod-straight, his jaw clenched tight. When I'd heard the front door slam, I was worried he had left me again, but here we are, marching up the slope of the cemetery towards the chapel. It is almost noon. The winter sun has brought people out; a few are clearing away flowers, others fill water jugs; some stand in quiet contemplation at the gravesides. A dark blue hearse trundles by.

'This place is actually full of life,' I say, to break the tense silence. To my surprise, Ash responds.

'Believe it or not, there's quite a community here. Folks need to keep their loved ones close, even if they have passed.' He tucks a hank of hair behind his ear and peers down at me. 'It's comforting, rather than macabre. I love the place.'

We stare across the quiet expanse. The sea is nothing more than a thin strip of silver, glittering in the distance, giving way to wide swathes of sand and salt marsh. If I could choose my last resting place, it would be here. The passion Ash has for the place is understandable.

'It is beautiful.' I hitch my rucksack higher on my shoulder. 'Have you worked here for long?'

'Since I was sixteen. My dad – Hal – had the job before me.' He laughs sadly. 'It's a family tradition, if you will.'

'He seems a lovely old gentleman. Is he... has he...' I want to ask about his outburst in the face of Ria Lace, but my words don't come out quite as expected.

'He has dementia. Alzheimer's to be exact. I apologise for leaving you to deal with him, without explaining.' Ash is terse, so I pry no further, just nod lightly. We walk the rest of the way in silence.

When we reach the chapel, I get an eye roll as Ash pulls back the safety fence. He hasn't asked me much about my escapade on Sunday evening; he hasn't asked me much about anything, really. I explain that taking detailed photographs of the outside is vital for my assessment. He doesn't have time to hang around. We come to a compromise: he will take me inside first and check on the health-and-safety situation. If all seems well, he will leave me and come back to lock up later.

He holds up a bunch of keys. Most look rusty. Some have rotted labels, but any writing has long gone.

'I found them hanging in the porch,' he says. 'They haven't been used for God knows how long. I didn't even know they were there. Keys for the cemetery buildings are supposed to be kept in a cabinet in my office. That's where I thought these were. According to my father, no one has been inside the main body of the chapel since the 1970s. I don't always believe what he tells me, but I think he's right on this occasion. I'll put them on my main key ring for now, so I've got them if needs be.'

'It hasn't been opened since the 1970s? What treasures await us then?' It's clear the place won't be suitable for conversion. It has a grade two listing, although I've found out from my research that it was stripped of its internal features before those kinds of rules were strictly applied. Ash has already pointed this out, but I want to keep him talking, so I pretend to know nothing.

'I doubt there'll be treasure,' he says. 'But the place will be a time-capsule, that's for sure. I've repaired the roof a few times since I started working here officially. Replacing slates, mainly. But that's all. I'm not even sure which keys are right.'

'Only one way to find out,' I say, more jauntily than I had intended. Ash moves towards the double doors of the porch. They haven't been boarded over like the windows. Instead, two metal handles on the thick wood have been chained together and padlocked. I swing my rucksack into a safe corner, then rummage through the zipped compartments for my camera, torch and Dictaphone. I don't want to miss anything.

When Ash has succeeded in undoing the lock, he pulls at the door. It doesn't open. He rattles the handles with a bit more force, but nothing happens.

'We might have to try option two,' he says with a sigh.

'What's that?' This isn't a huge building. It served as a chapel only for burials associated with the cemetery. It is a simple cruciform shape with an octagonal tower and narrow, arched windows. There is no other way in.

'I'll go back for a crowbar and prise off one of the window boards.'

'No, don't do that,' I say as he steps towards the safety fence. 'You could cause damage. Let me pull the door with you. Two hefts are better than one. I'll just offload my stuff again.'

While I empty my pockets, Ash tracks my every movement.

'Don't travel light, do you?' He raises his brows. 'But what do I know about anything?'

'You know a bit about this building. That's something.' I want to tell him about my passion for structures like this, about my genuine concern for preserving heritage, but he doesn't seem even slightly curious about me.

He slides a hand over the rough surface of the door. 'It can't be bolted on the inside. The wood will just have sealed itself over time, I think.' He grips one of the handles. 'Three small jangles then a huge one. On my count.'

'Okie-doke,' I say, and meet his gaze square on. Something passes between us, though I'm not sure what it is. The closest explanation I can find is that we've stopped being at odds. Then he looks away and snaps at me to put some effort in.

On our final pull, one door comes away from its frame, then falls open with a splintering of rotten wood. Ash is thrown backwards. I steady myself while he gets up from where he has fallen.

'I didn't expect that,' he says with an uneasy laugh.

'You okay?' I'm not sure whether to do or say more; he must have hurt himself when he fell.

'Fine.' He runs a hand through his hair. 'Let's get inside.'

The porch recess is a tiny space. A pair of filthy wooden benches run along each wall, with a mess of dirty planking on the floor. It's very dark. I flick on my torch and shine it forward. There is another door, in slightly better condition. It doesn't appear to have a lock.

'Let me,' Ash says as he reaches for the handle. 'If the state of this floor is anything to go by, it could be lethal inside.'

I keep the torch trained on him.

'I hadn't even thought about electricity,' he continues. 'It would have been turned off at the meter when the place was closed up. You'll need it, won't you?'

'No, actually. We have a set of special lights back at base. Battery operated. I'll pick them up at some point.'

His hand is on the door. When he turns the handle, it opens easily, but a gut-churning odour filters out. I gag. Mostly, I'm used to the sights and smells of antiquity, to decaying flesh and crumbling bones. This is something fresh. And dead.

Ash

His hands are trembling as he pushes open the door. Ash doesn't want to alert this woman, Cherie Hope, to the trepidation he is experiencing. It's linked to his father's bad feelings about the chapel. Hal has never been able to explain them, except to say that on the day Ash's mother left, he'd been working outside the place, replacing the MDF window boards with polycarbonate ones. Ash had been seven years old.

The smell inside the chapel catches in the back of his throat. Cherie shines her torch into the hollow body of the building. The vaulted ceiling space is empty, the walls cold veils of darkness. No shadows are cast. When the beam reaches the floor, she gasps. Caught in the arc of light are the decaying bodies of perhaps forty pigeons. Some are freshly dead, wings outstretched at odd angles, but many are nothing more than a desiccated mass of bones and feathers.

'Christ.' Ash steps away, covering his nose. 'The place isn't as secure as I thought. You'll have to come back when I've cleared it.'

'No need.' Cherie has pushed past him and is toeing the carcasses. 'I'll have to bring my lights, obviously. But can we please have a good poke around now? It'll help me to know what I'm up against.'

This is not a good plan. If anything happens to Cherie in the darkness, he would be at fault. What's more worrying is the fact that he is supposed to be pushing for conversion of this building into bright new office units. His heart sinks: there isn't a chance.

'I'm wondering if it's even worth you doing an assessment,' he says. 'We need to just back away and close the place up again.'

Cherie flicks her torch around the upper levels. 'It looks pretty sound to me. Better than some I've seen.'

'Really?'

'Oh, yes.' She tilts her face upwards. 'I can't see any slivers of light. Always a good sign.'

Ash shrugs in disagreement. 'The pigeons have got in somewhere.'

'Pigeons can get through the smallest of gaps. And they will.' She laughs softly. 'They're not smart enough to get out again, that's the problem. Judging by the state of some of those carcasses, they've been getting in for a while. The oldest ones could have been there for five years at least.'

Is the woman some kind of expert? He's not interested in her credentials, only in the length of time this pointless assessment is going to take.

She nods towards the back of the space. 'Come on. Just a little peek.'

'Okay. But then I will have to keep you out of the place until I've cleared the floor and set up your lights. I hope they have good batteries.'

Her expression says *trust me to know my job*. He backs off. The day had started with assumptions about the kind of person an archaeological surveyor would be; by noon, his assumptions have been turned on their head.

Cherie offers him the torch. He takes this as an indication he should lead the way, which unnerves him. She's the expert, and will have done her research. His knowledge of the chapel has come from the clumsy studies of a layman. With the light aimed downwards, he steps forward, across the wooden floor.

The pigeon bodies are amassed in one place. Towards the

rear of the chapel, where the altar would have been, the floor is clear. The tracery of a large circular window is visible on the east-facing wall. From the outside, Ash has only seen this as a square slab of boarding. Its internal shape is a surprise. Cherie confirms it as a rose window, and continues her explanation about its date and significance. Ash is half listening and half focused on the things he should be doing outside, including checks for the graveside service. He's about to herd her in the opposite direction when she sees a door to their left.

'What's in there?' she whispers, though he can't fathom why she has lowered her voice.

'Not sure. We can look another time. Or, you can. When you've got more light.'

She ignores his comment and shuffles her way past. 'It'll be a sacristy, I think. There's not much scope for one anywhere else in the building, but there has to be a changing room, doesn't there?' She lays a hand on the door. 'Just a quick look.'

He sighs. 'Go on then. Though it's probably locked.'

'It's not.' She turns the handle, and the door opens easily. 'See. Pass me the torch.'

Cherie flashes a beam of light into each corner of the room. It is small and square. The torch beam reveals a keyhole under the handle of a built-in cupboard.

'I bet there's interesting bits and pieces in here,' she says, voice softened. 'Don't suppose you have a key? It looks like an old-fashioned mortice lock. It certainly dates the door.'

He holds out the bunch of keys. 'I've no idea. Try a few.'

'Thanks.' She illuminates the keyhole. 'Sorry, won't keep you much longer.'

While Cherie tries some of the keys, Ash thinks back to his meeting with Ria Lace. The woman doesn't think the chapel is viable for conversion to plush office units, thinks Cemetery Lodge would be a safer bet. What it has to do with her, he can't quite grasp. As a councillor, she may well sit on the town planning committee, and this HAZ group rightly wants to preserve and restore local buildings of antiquity. What makes no sense to him is why anyone would pour money into converting the lodge, when it needs no preservation; all monies should be spent on the chapel, surely. Or on the existing crematorium. And he doesn't think Ria Lace is in any way connected to how the council distributes its financial resources; she's certainly never implied this.

Cherie's voice cuts across his thoughts.

'This one fits,' she is saying. 'Are you all right with me unlocking the cupboard? Say if you're not.'

'Knock yourself out.' He steps away, allowing the heavy doors to be pulled back. The smell is there again. 'More pigeons?' Cherie doesn't respond.

The cupboard is like the ones he remembers from high school. Floor-to-ceiling shelves, and filled with the detritus of the geography and history departments. This one seems to be stuffed full of filthy sheets, blankets perhaps.

'No sign of 1970s cassocks,' Cherie is saying as she points a beam of light towards the lower shelves. 'These look more like–'

She doesn't get any further with her explanation. Instead, she jumps back, hand to her chest. 'My God, Ash. What's that?' She passes him the torch then tugs lightly at a corner of decaying cloth. 'Put some light down here.'

What he sees makes his stomach heave. It is the skeletal remains of a hand, and as it falls free, long arm bones come with it. Cherie kneels and prods further.

'This doesn't look good,' she is saying as she carefully lifts the crumbling fabric. 'There's a full skeleton wrapped up here.' She pauses to examine what looks like a dirty piece of string in the area of the wrist bones. 'Oh, my goodness, there's two.' She pulls a mobile telephone from her pocket and passes it to him. 'Get onto the police. Immediately.'

Her tone drags him back to reality. Two skeletons? How is that possible? Cherie barks the instruction again. He swipes at her phone screen and finds the keypad. While he listens to the ringtone, words jump from his jangling thoughts and into his mouth. Should he request an ambulance, too? Is that how these things work? His confidence has vanished.

What he can't clear from his mind is that his father must know something about this.

CHAPTER FIVE

Cherie

Ash paces in front of the chapel door, his shoulders set sharp and his expression a mixture of fear and disgust.

'What the hell is happening?' he says, exasperated.

The police are on their way. We have been told to stay at the scene, but the situation wouldn't be treated as an emergency. The discovery of two skeletons seems like an emergency to me.

'I've no idea. Only that we'd better do exactly what we are told.' I've already thought about how my intrusion and snooping around the chapel on the previous evening might look. It was completely innocent, but an arrogant move if ever I've made one. David always called me intellectually arrogant.

Ash sighs. 'There's a graveside service at two o'clock and I haven't done the checks. It'll be grim for the family if things aren't right.'

'You go then. I'll see the police. Those skeletons have been there for at least fifty years. Nothing is going to change in the next couple of hours.'

'And you know this because–?' He glares at me.

I glare back. 'My qualifications are in bioarchaeology if you really want to know. The doctorate was about the time and ways bodies decay after death.'

His expression slides along with the rigidity in his shoulders. 'Bloody hell. I might have known.'

'Meaning?' Ash Black has a dim view of women, particularly educated ones.

'That came out wrong, I apologise.' He scratches at his scalp, eyes closed for a moment. 'I confused the words *might* and *should*. I *should* have known, as you seem so capable. It's amazing the effect one wrong word can have.'

His comment jolts my memory. Before I can think about it further, two police cars are crawling towards us along the cemetery's driveway. A white transit van follows closely behind. They must have decided this was an emergency, after all. I shield my eyes against the brittle afternoon sun. Ash drags open the safety fence and steps towards the cavalcade. There is something pragmatic about him, self-effacing even. I've worked in a climate of academic vanity for so long, meeting someone who has no need of such a thing feels refreshing. He's also incredibly attractive, with his dark looks and air of nonchalance. I slap myself down for thinking like this; the post-pandemic world is geared towards identity more than biology. I like that; David never did.

'Let me know if I can do anything,' I call. 'Even if it's just minding your father.'

'He doesn't need minding,' is the reply I get.

A total of six people climb out of the police cars. Two are uniformed officers. The rest wear regulation civvies: dark suits, collars, anoraks. The driver and passenger in the van stay in the front seats. The others nod politely, but hurry past. Ash speaks to them at the porch door. Two of the women make a show of covering their shoes with blue plastic bags, then let themselves be led inside. Why doesn't Ash have to put on the foot covering? Perhaps because we have already trampled over what I am sure will become the scene of a crime. From the little I saw of the skeletons, they were wrapped in cloths and put in that cupboard as *bodies*. Which means someone must have put them there. There can't be a valid reason, so my conclusion is that something criminal occurred.

It isn't long before Ash is leading the two women out again. They chat together in a group, excluding me. There will be no archaeological assessment of the chapel now; I'm redundant. My phone is in my pocket. I resist the temptation to get in touch with Bill and tell him what has happened. He'll find out eventually, but the police will want to keep our discovery quiet for now. Waiting around is awkward, so I'm relieved when one of the men walks towards me, smiling out a greeting.

'You were with Mr Black, were you, love, when he found them?' He nods towards the chapel. 'Girlfriend, are you? *Partner*?' He puts the last word between imaginary inverted commas.

'No.' I make the same gesture, adding a head wobble for effect. I want to defend my position, to explain that it might be helpful if he didn't write me off as the love interest of the main character, but we are interrupted by one of the women. She is tall, with beautifully cut silver hair and an edgy smile.

'I'm Detective Chief Inspector Beck.' She holds out her hand. '*Ginny*. I'll be leading the chapel investigation.' Her attention moves to the man who thought I was his *love*. He is young enough to be my little brother. If I had one. 'You've met Dale, I see. Detective Sergeant Dale Scott. Scottie, we call him.' I detect something in her tone. It might have been her slight emphasis of the word sergeant. I won't be calling this guy *Scottie*.

I take her hand. 'Cherie Hope. I'm the archaeologist

commissioned to assess the chapel. I was with Mr Black when he discovered the skeletons.'

Dale Scott scratches at his neatly clipped beard; Ginny Beck peers at me, eyes an icy blue.

'That's interesting,' she says smoothly. 'Why is the place being assessed?'

'For the viability of internal constructional remodelling.' I watch Dale's expression change. 'It needed more than a desk-based assessment. Hence, I'm here.'

'Ah, I see.' She frowns up at the chapel. 'Could you excuse me for a second. I need to make a call.' Dale stares after her.

'That's my boss,' he says, eyebrows high. 'Always on with the next thing.' We shuffle around each other, then survey the scene. The uniformed officers have surrounded the safety fence with police tape, and are now chatting through the window of the transit. As a student, I was once involved in a dig similar to what is happening today. We'd been on our knees for two weeks, searching for a recorded but absent, graveyard at the rear of an isolated medieval church.

When we finally unearthed remains, the tutor could tell the skeleton wasn't from the middle ages, or any era later than the 1950s. Which made him question its appearance. The police were called, and we found ourselves excluded from the site.

The truth emerged much later, causing us to be fascinated and horrified in equal measure. In 1941, the church verger, an elderly man at the time, had laid his sister to rest in the only way resources would allow: an unmarked grave. Knowing it wasn't legal, he hadn't put it down on public record. He died shortly afterwards, the church never returning to full use. My tutor at the time had set us up to research the story, alongside police and forensic evidence. It had been a painstaking walk-through census data, but it taught me much.

Ginny Beck returns from her call. Her lips are pressed

together, and she is frowning. 'Have you a business card or something, Cherie? It might be useful if we could call on you for some of the legwork in this case.' One hand clutches at the neckline of her anorak. 'It's a chilly one, today, isn't it? I could do with talking to you and Mr Black further, but not out here.' She scrutinises the cemetery slopes. 'That's the caretaker's lodge, isn't it? Do you think we'd be welcome there? I could do with a cuppa.'

'It's Mr Black's home, actually. He's the caretaker.'

Ginny grimaces in a way I can't fathom. 'Of course he is.'

Ash is talking to one of the uniformed officers. She seems to be dominating the conversation, and he is peering at his feet. When they walk towards us, he hangs back, staring across the cemetery. A wash of sympathy comes from nowhere. This guy must wonder why his life has suddenly been turned upside down.

'We're going for a cup of tea and a chat,' Ginny announces. 'Courtesy of Cemetery Lodge, if that's okay, Mr Black.' He nods.

She herds us with outstretched arms. 'Let's move.'

'This will be fun,' I mutter. Ash's expression tells me all I need to know.

Ash

Cherie has a lemon-slice of sarcasm in her voice, and Ash wants to escape. It's not that he means to be obstructive, but he has responsibilities. There is no support; the job needs to be done. These professional people have flexible hours and breathing space. He's not highly qualified or highly paid, but he is conscientious. Perhaps others in his position wouldn't be so focused, would see the job of a cemetery caretaker as *low-level*. It is not low-level to him.

'Follow me,' he says to both women, throwing off Ginny Beck's attempt at taking charge. There's something about the woman he dislikes, though he's aware the problem is his.

'You too, Scottie.' Ginny cocks her finger at a young man Ash hasn't noticed before. He has a wispy beard, and his cheeks are lilac with cold.

'Yes, ma'am.' The guy catches up with Ash. 'All right, fella. I'll be glad to get indoors.' He pushes his hands into the pockets of his anorak. The garment is paper-thin. *Thin enough to spit through,* Hal would say.

They walk briskly towards the house. Cherie is ahead of them, chatting to Ginny in a way that makes Ash think they might know each other. He is never at ease with new people. Especially new *women*. For many years, perhaps as far back as he can remember, Cemetery Lodge has been devoid of feminine influence. This is a point of view he feels keenly. He tried, after his mother left, to find out where she had gone, and why. Hal hadn't been able to voice his devastation, let alone give information. He'd leaned so heavily on Ash, there was no space left for contemplation. By the time a year had passed, neither of them mentioned her.

Now, thirty years later, the only emotion Ash can express about his mother is that he has no softer side to his personality, perhaps because of her lack. His motorcyclist friends tease him about this; they've nicknamed him Hard-boiled Black. While he doesn't challenge the name, they've got him completely wrong. He's never had a problem dealing with anything that might be deemed traditionally the role of a female. It's the 21st century; traditionalists are fading fast. His friends are correct in one aspect, however: Ash is not at ease around women.

When they arrive at the house, he leads them inside. A

blast of cold air meets him in the hallway: his father will have left the back door open. Hal's lunchtime ritual consists of feeding himself in twenty minutes then spending three times as long filling up the bird feeders and enticing the jackdaws down. Cherie takes charge, herding the detectives into his kitchen and keeping the small-talk at an easy level. Ash relaxes a little.

'I'll just check on my father,' he says, though no one responds. Hal is, as predicted, in the garden, well-wrapped up in a warm coat and tweedy cap. He is clutching fistfuls of winter-bitten scrub. A pair of secateurs protrude from his top pocket.

'All right, lad,' he says. 'Thought I'd give the borders a spruce up while the weather's bonny. You back for a brew?'

This is his father: up one minute, down the next; to outsiders, a perfectly stable and happy older gentleman.

'I am, Dad. Do you want one bringing out?'

Telling Hal what has happened at the chapel would only upset him. Time enough when he has to face questioning. And he will. If Cherie is correct in her assessment of the skeletons, they will have been put there in an era when Hal was caretaker. There's no getting away from that fact. The exact dates of his guardianship are recorded in the log that Ash now keeps, though his version is digital. Ginny Beck will be digging into it, no doubt.

In the kitchen, while Ginny and Dale hover, Cherie makes a pot of tea and a jug of coffee. Considering she hadn't seen the lodge before this morning, she's certainly *got her feet under the table*. Another of Hal's sayings.

'Is your dad okay?' Her words cut across Ash's thoughts. 'Does he want a drink?'

Why is Cherie trying to integrate herself into his family? Doesn't she have any of her own?

He nods curtly and accepts a mug. 'Thanks. Dad's doing a spot of gardening.'

Cherie catches his gaze. 'Best leave him to it, then.' She winks. It's like they've entered into a conspiracy, the contents of which he is unsure about. Perhaps he's read the situation wrongly and she's just being helpful. Either way, Ginny Beck seems to have sniffed something out.

'I heard Dad worked as caretaker before you, Mr Black,' she is saying. 'When was that?'

'Throughout the seventies, and right up until recently. I got the job officially in 2004. My father worked alongside me in a voluntary capacity after that.'

Ginny narrows her eyes. 'The seventies? What about before then?'

'I have a full record of caretakers, going back to the late nineteenth century, actually. I've already thought about where those documents are, in the loft storage. I knew you'd want to see them.'

'I would indeed,' Ginny says. 'But there's no rush. I will have to pick your brains, though. And Dad's.'

Her way of talking rather condescending. Hal is not her *dad*, and neither of them would choose to have their brains picked.

Ash wants to escape the situation and take a hot drink out to his father. He's about to leave the kitchen and go outside, when Hal comes in. He is flushed with the cold. 'Now then, lad, where's my brew,' he says as he comes to a halt in the doorway.

'It's here, Dad. I was on my way–' Ash gets no further.

His father's gaze flits about, passes over Cherie standing at the sink, and Dale Scott, who is wedged into a seat at the table. It comes to rest on Ginny. He stares, mouth open, chin trembling. 'Get her out,' he cries, pointing in Ginny's direction. 'I don't want her here. I don't want her here.'

'Dad.' Ash charges towards him. 'It's okay. It's okay. Shush.' Ash comforts him with soothing words and distraction, while running through every scenario that might have caused his father to become this agitated twice in one day. Is he eating properly? Has he got a water infection, the scourge of the elderly?

Moments earlier, Hal had seemed settled and happy, chatting in the garden, pottering. The only conclusion to be drawn is that the Alzheimer's from which he suffers is progressing more quickly than expected. Ash resolves to get in touch with his father's dementia nurse. If Hal is deteriorating, things will have to change.

CHAPTER SIX

Cherie

There is an obvious solution for calming Hal down: Ash needs to take him outside. There are overdue graveside tasks, if I remember rightly. Ginny Beck agrees, citing her flexibility about taking their statements. Her discomfort at Hal's outburst is clear. Ash takes his father and leaves, slamming the door as they go.

'I guess the poor old guy is suffering from dementia,' Ginny says, staring after them. 'Should he be here on his own?' She sips her tea, gazing at me in a way I find unnerving. Does this woman see everyone as guilty?

'I don't feel qualified to judge,' I tell her. 'The Blacks and I only met a few hours ago. Hal Black seems fine apart from what you've just witnessed. I'm sure Ash is dealing with his father in the best possible way. Shall we get on with taking my statement? Your time will be precious, won't it?'

Dale jumps up from his seat and carries his cup to the sink.

Ginny makes no move. 'Oh, the forensic team will be ages yet.' She glances around the kitchen. 'I want to get a feel for

Cemetery Lodge and its caretakers. They'll know something about these skeletons, I'll be bound.'

'What makes you say that?' I am cross on Ash's behalf. The shock he expressed in the chapel was genuine, I'd swear to it.

Ginny gives me a half smile. 'The Blacks have been in charge of the cemetery and its buildings for many years; it's common knowledge. Everyone knows them, or knows of them.'

Dale chips in. 'I've never heard of them.' He lifts his shoulders. 'But you're a die-hard local. Anyhow, it's in the police bible that most crimes like this are committed by people close to the situation, isn't it?'

His comment prompts a glare from Ginny. 'Can you not. We don't know that a crime was even committed here; we know very little as yet.'

'But you said the Blacks–'

'I said they would have information, nothing more.' She rolls her eyes at me. 'Sorry. I'm still trying to train him.' Dale's laugh tells me he is used to Ginny's barbs. His youth makes me want to defend him. I tutored a variety of young men through the long months of the pandemic lockdown, and learned that naivety and ignorance are not the same thing. If Dale Scott is already a detective sergeant, he will have skills; they need to be recognised.

'What's your theory then?' I catch his eye and tilt my head. 'You must have one.'

Ginny holds out her hands. 'Go for it.'

Dale rambles his way through an elaborate tale about people-trafficking and the chapel being used as a kind of holding bay. There are a lot of plot holes, particularly when he insists that the skeletal remains we found were from people tied up and forced into that cupboard.

I stop his theorising at this point. 'There was no tying up.

But I did see a kind of bracelet around the wrist of the bigger body when I lifted the blanket remains.'

This comment causes a gasp from Ginny. 'Just how much did you disturb the scene? What else did you see? I thought you called us straight away.'

'I did. Pretty much.' I leave out the bit where I pulled the cloth wrappings higher and had a proper look.

'You know what?' She gets up from her seat. 'We'd better do your statement straight away. I don't want any more said that isn't on official record.' She nods at Dale. 'Have you got the forms? The *pad*?'

'I've got the pad.' He holds up a slim leather case. 'Ma'am.'

'Can we find a room that's more formal?' she asks, peering at me. 'I want to leave the kitchen free. Mr Black will return with his father at some point, and I'd rather not have a repeat performance.'

Ginny seems to think it's my house. I suggest the only other room I know; the office where I've set up a base. We make our way across the hall, with Dale following behind. I don't envy Ash, having his home serve as a workplace. It's a pattern that many have become familiar with in the past couple of years, but this is different: outsiders invade his home without a thought for his privacy. I feel like the worst kind of intruder.

When I start rummaging through my pilot case, Ginny looks at me quizzically. 'I thought you were unfamiliar with this place. Seems like you're quite at home.'

'I think I explained about the archaeological assessment.' I find a packet of mints and offer her one. 'Ash said it would be okay for me to set up my equipment and work from here.' Shafts of afternoon sunshine are slanting through the window. 'That was about six hours ago, but it seems like a lifetime. Shall I close the blind?'

'Yes, do.' Ginny gestures for Dale to sit at the desk, and we take the small sofa in the corner. She doesn't ease me in slowly. I am asked for details of my birth and nationality, family and work history, any criminal convictions, and my personal ethics. I give her every detail of my dealings with the chapel, but leave out my sojourn on the previous evening. What interests her most are my archaeological qualifications.

'Let me clarify this for myself,' she says when I explain about my study of bodily decay. 'You actually visited one of those outdoor laboratories where they leave cadavers in the open and study them?' She shivers. 'How macabre.'

'Macabre but fascinating,' I reply. 'It gave me insights, that's for sure. But I'm not a medical doctor or anything. I've studied bodies only in the context of their archaeological value.'

'You must have seen a few things though.' Dale is swallowing down everything I say as though my words are the most delicious cake he's ever tasted.

'I have.' There will be no salacious details today, but I do have something. 'Which is how I know the longer arm bone I saw, when I briefly lifted away those cloths, had a Romani coin bracelet clinging to the wrist area.'

Neither of them speak.

'I've seen one before,' I continue. 'On a much older body, but in a similar state of decay. Your forensic team will discover the bracelet eventually, I expect. But I'm just giving you a heads-up.'

Ginny taps her lips with her pen then puts it down. She clicks her fingers at Dale.

'Witness Cherie's signature, would you? We're pretty much done here.'

While I sign the bottom of the form, she fluffs up her coat as though she's about to do battle with the cold. Which surprises me, as she hasn't questioned Ash yet, and he is more important than I am.

'You'll be wanting to get off,' she says lightly. 'Not much can be done about your assessment until the chapel is cleared. Once we've taken the remains to the mortuary, the forensic tests will be repeated at the scene. It'll take a while.'

Dale zips my statement into his case. 'Thanks for your help, love. We'll be in touch.'

Ginny glares at him, then turns to me. 'Can we call on your expertise if we need to?' She hands me her card and leaves one on the table. 'There will be a lot of historical stuff to get through with this case. And could you let Mr Black know that we'll be back later to take his statement. If we don't bump into him first.'

I don't see them out; it's not my place. For the first time in a few hours, I get breathing space, and the enormity of the unravelling situation hits me. There can be no lawful reason why those skeletons were laid out in the sacristy cupboard. I'm confident about the timescale of decay I saw. So, Hal Black would have been caretaker of the cemetery at exactly the time when the bodies were first there, though it doesn't mean he would know anything about it. It does mean, however, that either no one has been in the chapel since, or if they have, they're not admitting anything. And as for the bracelet: Ginny Beck did not like me having that knowledge. Probably because if the sacristy becomes a crime scene, I have compromised it.

There is one more thing, though, and it's really tugging at the edges of my understanding. If Hal Black has moderate Alzheimer's, why is Ash happy to leave him unsupervised?

I tidy up my equipment, packing my camera into its case. I need to ask Ash if I can leave everything in his office for now. It will be possible to photograph the outside of the chapel, even with the police cordon. Completing desk-based work while I wait for permission to do more, would be a solution. As long as the lodge has a good Wi-Fi signal. As there is no one in the house, I decide to explore, and hopefully find a lavatory while I'm doing so.

The stairs are steep and thickly carpeted. There's a handrail on both walls. I flick on the landing light and am confronted by six heavy doors, all closed. One has an old-fashioned porcelain sign, white with a floral border. It says *toilet*. I knock, just in case, then let myself in. The room is clean and functional, with a white lavatory and basin, and peach-coloured towels. While I'm washing my hands, I think about Ash and his father, and their life here. Is there a Mrs Black? A mother? A wife, perhaps?

The landing wall is dotted with photographs. They are grainy and lopsided in their frames. Most are of Hal and a younger boy, which I presume is Ash. The dark hair is the same, and the lanky frame. They are pictured at the beach, on a mountain path, and in the garden of Cemetery Lodge. There is no sign of another person. I'm about to have a peek in the other rooms when the front door opens.

'Hi,' I call as I rush down the stairs. It is Ash and his father. They are hanging up their coats as I reach the hallway.

'Oh, hello,' Ash says. 'That was a strange day, wasn't it?'

I glance at Hal. 'It was. Is everything sorted?'

'It is. I'm going to get Dad settled in his room with a drink. He's enjoyed being outside but it's getting dark now, and he's tired.'

I nod. 'Can I leave my gear in your office? There are bits of work I can do this week while the investigation is proceeding.'

He sighs and runs a hand over his eyes. 'I suppose so.'

'Thanks. Ginny Beck said she would be back later to take your statement. She's left you her number. I'm not sure where they've gone.'

'For food and drink, probably.' He sends Hal off to the kitchen. 'I'll have to get on, if you don't mind. The office door is lockable, so I will make sure your stuff is safe.'

He turns away: I am dismissed.

Bill had offered to give me a lift back to the office after I'd finished for the day. He will be expecting a rundown on my first thoughts about the chapel. When I send him a message, it includes some cryptic comments about what has transpired. I pack up the pilot case and wheel it into the corner of Ash's office. He is moving around in the kitchen, talking to his father, creating the sounds of cooking. I'm not sure why he is so cold towards me: his day would have been more difficult if I hadn't helped out. I creep down the hall, not wanting to alert him to my leaving.

Once I'm outside, I walk down the garden path and head for the cemetery gates. It's not the ideal place to be loitering, especially at dusk. If Ginny and Dale are somewhere about, there is no sign of them. Once again, I feel a wash of sympathy for Ash. His home has been trespassed into by three different women today. I'd like to think my intrusion was the softer of the three. The councillor, Ria Lace, was unconventionally rude and Ginny Beck was a double-edged sword.

I push my hands into the pockets of my coat and flip up the hood. If I'm to find a satisfactory explanation of the day for my boss, I'd better keep my opinions of its main players to myself.

Ash

Seeing the back of Cherie Hope comes as something of a relief. Ash catches a glimpse of her through Hal's bedroom window. She is waiting by the cemetery gates. Though he's been thankful for her help with managing his father and the lodge today, her presence has unsettled him. She's too capable, too *clever*.

He hates himself for thinking these things when Cherie has

done nothing but give support. In truth, he is insecure around people who might look down on him and his situation in life. Has Cherie done that? Of course she hasn't: this is *his* problem. He resolves to be nicer when next they meet.

While his father puts on pyjamas and a thick fleecy dressing gown, Ash climbs the next flight of stairs. These lead to a space they call the loft. It is more of a storage room with roof lights and a boarded floor. It contains box after box of cemetery logbooks. One of the caretaker's responsibilities has always been to record day-to-day happenings. Ash has been doing this since he took over the job from his father in 2004. His own records are mostly digital. He selects the boxes that fit with Cherie's estimated timeframe. It is a place to start, at least; something to engage Ginny Beck's trust. Each box contains books that resemble diaries, though they have the stamp of the borough council. He carries the boxes downstairs and into Hal's bedroom.

His father is sitting in an armchair by the window. He's put the radio on and covered his legs with a knitted blanket. 'Any supper going,' he calls as Ash huffs in.

'It's not supper time yet, Dad.' The boxes drop with a thud. 'I've got food in the oven. It won't be long.'

'Tea, then. The fresh air has given me an appetite, and no mistake. I should go on your rounds with you a bit more often, son. I enjoyed it.'

This isn't a good idea. Apart from anything else, Hal has no concept of his frailty. Though he's happy to put on a coat when he ventures into the garden, he can't tell when he's too cold. Last winter, with the sudden drop in air temperature, he'd suffered a chest infection that worried Ash enough to get a doctor involved.

'I'll bring you some tea, Dad, if you give me a minute, and a few biscuits to keep you going. The paper has been delivered so

I'll fetch that up, too. You stay under your blanket.' He puts a hand on Hal's shoulder. 'Promise?'

'Aye, I will.'

Ash manhandles the boxes down the lower stairs and into the lounge. He flicks on the gas fire and closes the curtains. Only a few hours ago, Ria Lace had used this room for nosing into his privacy; Ginny Beck may as well do the same when she comes back.

When Ash lets them in a little later, Ginny and Dale bring with them a waft of cold air. They are carrying brown paper bags and cardboard cups.

'Hope you don't mind.' Ginny holds up a bag. 'We haven't eaten since breakfast. Can we use your kitchen?'

Ash does mind. His home has become public property. He is a council tenant, but that doesn't mean any visitor to the cemetery can have access. Ria Lace might have been right in her assessment of the situation; the lodge would make good offices, and he could have a new bungalow.

'I'd rather you ate while I did my statement,' he says. 'It's been a tiring day, and my father needs his rest.' He points them in the direction of the lounge. 'Let me fetch my tea and I'll be with you.'

When he returns, Ginny and Dale are perched together on the sofa, rummaging through their bags of food, picking bits out and filling their mouths. The room smells of hot meat and coffee. Ash stands in front of the fire and sips his drink, wishing they would take notice of him. Eventually, Ginny looks up.

'Sorry,' she says, brightly. 'You must think we're really unprofessional. In our job, we learn to take whatever breaks we can get, because the hours can beND gruelling. This is going to be a drawn-out case, I think.'

Dale nods his agreement, mouth full.

'Why do you say that?' Ash frowns, thinking about his chances of getting these two out of the lodge as soon as possible.

'The forensic evidence will take time to gather and time to analyse. Nothing is *fresh*. It could be that we never get answers.' Ginny rubs her fingers across a paper serviette. 'So, can we start by taking down your details, then looking at those logs you mentioned.' She turns to Dale. 'Time to get the pad out again. But clean your hands first.'

It doesn't take very long for Ash to outline his life. It's been ordinary, low-key. Nineteen of the years have been spent at the cemetery, keeping things together; the last ten looking after Hal. Ginny raises her eyebrows when Ash tells her about the history diploma he gained recently. Her praise makes him feel like a schoolboy who has turned his back on a fight. When he offers to show her the caretaker's logs from 1970, her tone changes.

'I have to keep an open mind on timings,' she says, giving him a thin smile. 'Until we have a definite date for the remains, I need to know everything. Cherie Hope told you the skeletons have been there for at least fifty years, I believe?'

'She did.'

'Would you mind suspending your faith in her. She's not an expert in any sense of the word.'

There is no reason for Ash to have faith in Cherie, he hardly knows her. But Ginny's comment has annoyed him. If he wants to have opinions, to have *faith*, he will; he has nothing to hide.

'If we're talking fifty years ago, my father would have been caretaker. He was boss from 1971 until I took over, in case that helps.'

Ginny picks up on the change of subject. 'And before that?'

'My grandfather, Thomas Black, was in charge through the fifties and sixties. He died on the job. Also in 1971. I never met him.'

'Right.' Ginny eyes the boxes. 'This is all on record, I suppose?'

'It is.'

Dale has crouched, and is lifting the lid of a box. Ash's privacy is being severely compromised. Shouldn't visitors to his home wait to be asked before they used his rooms, sat on his sofa, *opened his boxes?*

'Where's your mother, Mr Black?' Ginny is looking into his face. His sense of being invaded heightens.

'If you want the truth, I've no idea.' He holds her gaze until she blinks and looks away.

'I find that very odd.'

The story is personal. Ash won't be forced to tell it. 'Odd, but true.' When Ginny gives a smirk, he adds, 'I haven't seen her since 1991.'

'Is she alive?'

He gives a blast of fake laughter. 'You tell me.'

'So they divorced, did they? Your parents.'

'Nope. Still married, as far as I know.' If Cherie's dates were anything near accurate, Ginny must realise the remains in the chapel are not his mother. Even as a small boy, he understood the place had been out of use for years. 'It's not my mother in the chapel. Please don't imply that it might be.'

Dale coughs loudly and Ginny holds up her hands. 'Sorry, sorry. I didn't mean to offend. Until we know exact timings and dates, though, everything is on the table. You must understand that, Mr Black.'

Ash is distracted by his father, moving about upstairs. The last thing he wants is for Hal to clash with this woman again. He runs his hands over his face, wishing he could wipe away this day, start it again. There would be no Cherie Hope and her chapel assessment, no need for new offices and retail units, and his father would be as happy and settled as he had been on the previous evening. Then he remembers the truth. Hal had been agitated by something on Ash's work schedule. Perhaps it is coincidence that his father's condition seems to have deteriorated, or maybe something else is going on. Either way, he could do with getting Ginny Beck and Dale Scott out of his house.

'Why don't you select a few of the logbooks, take them back to the station,' he suggests. 'Choose a range of dates, and have a good read. You'll get used to their format, for when you have a better idea of timeframes and the like.'

Ginny takes the hint. 'That's fine. But we will need to speak with your father, eventually. In one form or another.'

'Meaning?'

'There are techniques we can use when questioning elderly witnesses. We have staff that are specially trained to deal with–' She taps her temple. Dale stretches his eyes.

'Please don't refer to my father like that.' Ash mimics her gesture. 'And I'll expect to be present at any *interviews* you carry out.' He moves towards the door. 'Now, if you don't mind, I'll need to go and check he's okay. Take the logbooks. But do sign the chitty in the boxes, won't you? And put your fast-food bags in the dustbin on your way out.'

Hal

He can hardly look at the brown-paper parcel in his hands. It contains his father's clothing: corduroy jacket, greasy blue overalls; steel-toe-capped boots. Thomas Black is dead. Those words roll around in Hal's head. They are liberating, but frightening. He is an orphan. Never will his parents find out what he has kept hidden.

The meat-and-Jeyes-fluid smell of the hospital is clogging his throat; he has to get out. Matron is eyeing him suspiciously. She is a terrifying woman, height exaggerated by the starched cap she wears. Though he's been at his father's bedside since the heart attack, she's never spoken to Hal. It's clear now, she wants him off the ward.

He steps into the December twilight. The air is bitterly cold and tinged with coal smoke, the moon a bright crescent, too beautiful for contemplation. He makes for home, parcel tucked under his arm, collar turned, trembling violently. Much has happened in the past few days, and he needs time to process.

Visiting the council offices to be interviewed for his own job felt surreal. It was a formality, he'd been told. If the council official, wearing his officialdom as loudly as his polyester suit, knew about Hal, he would have been run out of town. Instead, a new rent book had been placed in his hand, his upper arm patted in a friendly way.

The streets are deserted. It is like they are conspiring together in an attempt to heighten his loneliness. Every door has been closed and bolted against him; every curtain drawn. Hal's need for companionship had been blunted by the constant presence of his father. Where would this leave him now?

From the women who visited Cemetery Lodge since his mother had passed, Hal heard that he was *tall, dark and handsome*, that he would be a *good catch*. He didn't want to be caught, if those women were the ones fishing. He tramps wearily past a parade of shops, closed now, dustbins lined up neatly for tomorrow's collection.

The weight of responsibility hits him again. How had his father been able to keep the larder stocked and the bills paid, yet still manage the day-to-day life of the cemetery? Hal takes some deep breaths, then screws up his eyes. The scene is unaltered when he opens them again. He is horrified: this is his new reality.

When the lodge comes into view, Hal's emotions take on a more tangible form. Tears stream down his cheeks. No lights shine from the windows, the chimney stands hard-edged against the icy sky. Only the dead will keep him company tonight.

CHAPTER SEVEN

Cherie

When Bill asks how I got on with the cemetery caretaker, he's expecting the truth. I'd spent the previous night thinking about Ash Black, his horrified expression in the chapel, and every abrupt conversation we'd had. None of it was particularly polite; all of it made me feel like I was nosy. Yet something about him resonates and I want to know more. When I see Ash again, I'm going to redouble my efforts at appearing *mainstream*. Bill and I are talking in Gillside's cluttered office. On the journey home yesterday I'd given him a sketchy overview of my news. Today, he demands detail.

I lean my elbows on my desk. 'Ash Black is a nice man who has found himself in a bit of a predicament.'

Bill stares, open-mouthed, then he says, 'Nice? When have you ever used words like nice?'

'What do you want me to say? The guy had a terrible day. A detective more or less accused him of being responsible for those hidden skeletons. Ash had more to worry about than looking after me and my needs.'

'Something else is going on here.' Bill leans back in his office chair. 'Aside from skeletons in chapels.' He gives me a knowing smile. 'You're itching to get back there, aren't you?'

'I am. The whole situation is fascinating. The way those bodies had been laid out in the cupboard – like they were being *stored* or something. And I do mean bodies. It was pretty clear the decay had taken place *in situ*, though the detective woman wasn't happy with my judgement.' I pick up a pen and examine it. 'Who am I to know anything, after all.'

Bill gives a long sigh. 'It'll delay our work schedule, though, which means we'll have to juggle clients.' He scrolls through an iPad. 'I can give you a desk-based assessment to be getting on with. An old farm barn in Kendal.'

Although I'm a newbie at Gillside, being given things to *get on with* makes me feel like a sixteen-year-old Saturday-girl again. While I attended the sixth form of my local school, I'd taken a job at a hairdresser's. When it became evident that I had no talent for dressing hair, I was given things to get on with so that there was a reason to give me the £10 wage at the end of the day. An old farm barn in Kendal is the last thing I want.

'I've left some of my gear at the cemetery,' I say. 'So I'll have to go back.'

'Okay.' Another wry smile plays across Bill's lips. It's as ironic as his khaki sweater with the elbow patches.

'I can still do an outside assessment of the chapel,' I add for effect. 'Might as well get on with it.'

'Might as well.' Bill stands up and stretches his back. 'Shall I run you there? If you wait for the bus or train, you'll lose a lot of time.'

He is aware of the situation with my ex-husband, and has been supportive. I didn't get the car as part of my divorce settlement; I took the money and ran. I pick up my anorak and handbag from the cloakroom and we are soon jogging across the main road to Gillside's car park.

Overnight, a bank of woolly cloud has come in, raising temperatures but hiding the winter sun. Headlights flare. From the passenger seat of Bill's tatty old car, I peer into the meagre grey light and wonder what the day will bring.

The skeletal remains should have been removed from the chapel by now; this probably took place overnight. I'd love to have a proper look at them, but realise there is little chance. When I say as much to Bill, he takes one hand from the steering wheel and taps his chin. 'It depends on the circumstances,' he says. 'There has obviously been foul play, as it were. But if no compelling evidence can be gathered and the case is eventually marked as pending, I could apply to the mortuary. In some instances, archaeologists can get involved. Especially ones with your credentials.'

I scrutinise the way he says *your credentials*. It's a hangover habit from the times David called me out over what he considered was my intellectual snobbery. And me a northern girl at heart. I let Bill off the hook; he is the most moderate person I know.

'I did have a little peek at the skeletons before we called the police. One of them had a Romani bracelet around the wrist.' When Bill gives me a side-eye, I add, 'It was very decayed and tarnished, but I've seen one before, so I'm certain.'

'Interesting,' he mutters.

I wait for him to say more, but he doesn't. I watch his hands on the steering wheel. They are large, skin mottled with age spots. He spent much of his youth working archaeological dig sites in Europe. His posture attests to that, as much as his leathery complexion and ability to get-stuck-in. We've worked together on two projects so far and I've learnt a lot.

When we reach the cemetery, Bill pulls up at the gates. 'I

can put you on my insurance, if you like.' He looks through the windscreen at the sky. 'Catching trains and buses is all very well in the summer, but–'

I climb out of the car and duck my head to see him. 'It's fine, honestly. I enjoy train travel. Gives me space to think.'

'Well, think about this then, on your way back to Cark tonight: there was a Romani community over on Walney Island during the seventies. They came every summer to the same place. Marine salvagers, as far as I can remember.' He checks his mirror. 'I'm a mine of useless information, aren't I? See you whenever.'

Walney Island. It's part of the town, attached to the mainland by a Victorian road bridge. I've seen the island's sandy tip from the cemetery slopes, but never visited. If a Romani community popped up fifty years ago, there is a possibility the skeletal remains we found belonged to their people. It's a theory, nothing more. My brain loves theories. I'm sure it won't be welcome though, so I'll keep quiet for now.

The cemetery is empty. Yesterday there had been a quiet whisper of humanity about the place; today there is no one. I pass Cemetery Lodge, but don't knock. It's ten o'clock so Ash will be doing his rounds. When I get to the top of the gently sloping drive, I find the crematorium deserted. Ash must be onsite somewhere, but I can't see him. I've visited this place once before, in the fading light of a winter's evening, but now a shiver creeps across my shoulders. It's not fear; it's more complex. When I'm starting a dig and the geophysics has already given a hint of something buried, I get the same shiver. Beneath a few metres of soil is a world of people and things hidden for many years. But they once had life, and to me, it's an energy that can't be contained.

A charcoal-grey transit van is parked in front of the chapel.

Its rear doors are open. Ash is hovering at the edge of the safety fence.

'Morning,' I call brightly. 'What's happening.'

He swings round. 'The skeletons are being taken away.' His tone dips. 'Can we keep still and quiet for a minute.'

'Sorry.' My cheeks burn with embarrassment. This isn't how I'd planned things to be when we met again. Two men wearing grey overcoats, faces sombre, are carrying a stretcher. On it is a black Ziploc bag. Ginny Beck is walking behind them.

Ash nods, not meeting my eye. 'It's fine.'

Dale Scott is standing with two uniformed officers, faces shadowed. The atmosphere is subdued, and extremely sad. I feel surplus, an intruder at a funeral. This is nothing like what happens when we've found human remains at a dig, though that's no excuse. I haven't ever attended a crime scene, and the gravity of the situation becomes overwhelming. More than anything, I want to know who the people were behind these human remains, want to help give them justice for the way they have been treated.

Ginny walks across to where we are standing. There is no smile. I nod a hello, but she focuses her attention on Ash. A fine rain is falling, and her coat is covered in droplets.

'Can we come down to the house?' she says, glancing at the sky. 'We must interview your father. I have plenty of questions; there needs to be acceptable answers.'

'Meaning what?' Ash's snappy reaction tells me a lot. I can't see how Hal Black could tolerate a formal interview. There must be protocols when working with a dementia patient.

'Calm down, Mr Black.' Ginny tries to take his elbow. 'You must understand your father is a prime suspect in our investigation. He had access to the chapel throughout the period we will be looking at.' She glances my way, then adds, 'The seventies, as you implied.'

Ash presses his fingers to his eyes and shakes his head. His fluorescent jacket casts a sickly green glow over his complexion. Judging by how unsettled Hal was yesterday, Ash will have enough to sort out without entertaining Ginny Beck and Dale Scott again.

'I can go back to the house, if you like,' I offer. 'If you've things to do.'

Ginny cuts me off. 'No.' She makes a chopping gesture with the flat of her hand. 'I absolutely must have Mr Black there when I question his father. You can make the tea, if you like.'

When I raise my eyebrows, her expression softens. 'That came out wrongly,' she mutters. 'Sorry. I meant to say we'd be grateful if someone did the domestic stuff while we worked with Mr Black and his father. Don't worry if you're busy.'

I want to ask if photographing the outside of the chapel in more detail would be permissible, given the current situation. One glance at Ash's expression tells me he would appreciate my support rather than be rid of me.

'It's fine,' I say. 'The chapel assessment can't proceed as normal. I understand that. In the meantime–' I hold up my hands. 'Happy to help.'

Ash mouths his thanks. My belly performs a somersault, which surprises me into the quietest intake of breath. I'm not sure what has caused these primitive reactions, but as he strides away towards the lodge, I can't tear my eyes from his dark hair or wide shoulders.

Ash

Thoughts come from nowhere and can sometimes crowd out rationality. A threat issued by his mother to his father: *there are plenty of questions and you'd better be able to give me answers.* Ash can't have been more than a small boy when he'd heard the menace in her words.

He'd wanted to protect Hal then; he wants to protect him now. If that means shielding him from the police, he will. Hal is innocent of any wrongdoing; Ash would swear to it. His father knows nothing of what transpired in the chapel, nor the police presence. Explaining away the visitors to Cemetery Lodge had not been necessary; Hal's condition means that short-term, his memory has gigantic holes.

Allowing Ginny's questioning will be a problem; Ash is grappling with it. Perhaps he can persuade her there is no need, though there's every need. The minute he tries to refuse, the woman will be suspicious. Ash clicks on the door latch and heads into the house.

Hal is in his favourite room, sitting in the armchair next to a banked-up fire, radiators blasting. The radio is on, his thermos in its place on a side table.

'Hi, Dad.' Ash turns down the volume. 'You all right?'

'I am. What are you up to, then?'

Ash has given him a rundown of the cemetery tasks for today: tidying after the graveside service; cleaning out the guttering on the crem building; removing loose Christmas ornamentation laid out by those who wish to bring the celebration to their loved ones. Hal remembers none of the conversation.

'Just the usual,' Ash tells him. 'But we've got some visitors coming for a chat, if that's okay?'

'A chat with me?'

'With us both.'

Hal frowns up at him. 'Friends of yours?' He glances at the door. 'I've just got comfortable. You see them.'

Ash must be quick with a compromise. 'They can pop in

here if you like. It'll only be for a minute. They're wanting to know about when you were caretaker-in-charge. They like history.'

'Definitely *your* friends, then.'

The front door slams. Indistinct conversation comes from the hallway, a clattering of feet.

'That'll be the visitors,' Ash says. Hal closes his eyes and leans back against his cushion.

When Ash gets to the kitchen, Cherie is standing by the sink, filling the kettle. A film of raindrops covers her hair. Ginny is shaking water from her coat while Dale Scott grapples with finding them seats.

'The heavens properly opened as we got here,' he says. 'You must have missed it, Mr Black. Teeming down out there.'

Cherie glances over her shoulder. 'Is your father okay?'

'Why wouldn't he be?' Ash isn't sure what is making him so twitchy. Cherie's expression slides. 'Sorry. Yes, he's fine. Dozing by the fire, listening to Radio Cumbria. His favourite pastime, after bird-watching.' She doesn't re-engage.

'We must talk to him,' Ginny says. 'Dozing or not. How is his long-term memory?'

'Patchy.' Ash wants to derail her. His father has dementia; he's not a reliable witness.

'I'll be gentle. This isn't an interrogation. But there are things I must have answers to.'

Dale has taken a chair and is unzipping his leather case. He keeps his focus on the table while Ginny is speaking.

Ash tries to engage his help. 'Have you had the chance to look at some of the logbooks?' When Dale opens his mouth in surprise, Ash quickly adds, 'Oh, I don't mean in detail, but if you've looked, you'll realise how thorough they are. Surely an in-depth study of them will yield more than the memories of an elderly man with Alzheimer's.'

'We've only got a loose timeframe at the moment.' Ginny breaks into their conversation. 'I've looked at the logs. They will be useful, and I'll have to take the rest away eventually, but I still have questions.' She scowls. 'Sorry. But we're investigating a potential crime. I have to be ruthless.'

Cherie carries the teapot and mugs across to the table. She makes a huge show of pouring milk and spooning sugar. Ash is grateful for the interruption. He can see no way out of the situation except to allow Ginny Beck to mine for answers, some answers, at least; they may not be what she wants.

'Dad is in his sitting room,' he says, as Cherie passes him a drink. 'Can I at least know what you're likely to ask him?'

A look zips between Ginny and Dale, one that says *we better had.*

Ginny takes a sip of her tea, then puts it down, pointedly. 'Well, for example, I'd like to know how many people would have had access to the chapel keys during your father's time as caretaker. He'll be able to answer that, won't he?'

'I can answer that.' Ash folds his arms slowly and deliberately. 'I can probably answer most of what you ask him, actually.'

'I need his perspective. You weren't around in the seventies.' Tongue-in-cheek, she adds, 'Unless you're a very youthful-looking fifty-something.'

Cherie lets out a harsh laugh. Until now, Ash hasn't thought beyond her interest in the chapel and the remains. Is she trying to show her support for his family too? He tries out his theory.

'As I was explaining to Cherie, only yesterday, keys to anything cemetery related are stored in a locked cabinet in my office. There are no copies. Access is gained via the caretaker, and this has always been the case.' He stares across at her. 'Right.'

'Right,' comes the reply, though it's not the truth. 'I wanted to know why Gillside couldn't just get keys to the chapel from the town hall or something. So as not to bother the caretaker.'

Ginny harrumphs. 'Okay, well, that was just an example. My next question might be about–'

Dale interrupts. 'People who used the chapel, like vicars, for example.'

'Stop.' Ginny slams down her hands. 'Sorry. Sorry. This is not helpful. Can we just talk to Mr Black senior, without this speculation. You can be there, Ash.' She glares at Dale; he looks away.

'Okay. Let's go.' There's a tension in the room Ash can't explain, except to say that he's being evasive, and Ginny Beck knows it. As for Cherie, she saw him pull the rusty keys from his pocket when they'd opened up the chapel; she'd heard him say he found them in the porch. Why she's colluding in his lie, he can't fathom, but he's having to feel gratitude again. Ginny follows him down the hallway and into Hal's sitting room. Ash crouches by the armchair and pulls gently at his father's arm. Ginny looms over them.

'It's warm in here,' she mutters, wafting the scarf looped around her neck. 'Can I open the window a little?'

'No, leave it.' Ash flicks on the lamp.

Hal yawns and sits forward. 'All right, son? Is it lunchtime?'

'Soon, Dad. I've brought you a visitor. She'd love to have a chat about your time as caretaker. This is–' He gets no further.

Hal takes one glance across at Ginny and jumps out of his chair, head shaking violently. 'Not her,' he wails. 'Get her away from me. I'm not doing it. Get her away.'

Ash hadn't predicted his father's reaction. Yesterday's confusion had come from finding the kitchen full of unknown people, he'd thought. There is more to it than that. Hal has become extremely agitated. He is shouting at Ginny and waving his fists. Cherie charges into the room, Dale Scott on her heels.

'What's happened, Ash?' Her eyes scan the scene. 'Shall I take Hal to the kitchen? Give him some lunch?' She holds out her hand. 'Come on, darling. You loved my toast, yesterday, didn't you?' Hal's screeching misses a beat, and it's enough for Ash to slide an arm around his shoulder and get him out of the room. The gratitude he feels for Cherie's presence is an emotion so solid, it catches in his throat.

CHAPTER EIGHT

Cherie

Hal is grasping my hand so tightly, I feel trapped. We are sitting together on the back seat of a police car, while Ash rides in the front with a uniformed officer. An interview at the station, in a booth with two-way windows, was the compromise reached after an awkward negotiation with Ginny Beck. She's already got Hal pegged as guilty of some hideous crime, and would be happy to see him arrested immediately.

Dale Scott is going to carry out the questioning, with Ash's guidance and support. Hal has agreed to what he thinks is a history discussion, though he'd insisted on my participation.

I've never seen the local police station. According to Ash, the place looks more like a swish office block than the traditional brick-and-bars-on-windows place his father might have recognised. The situation doesn't sit well with me; it feels like Hal is being hoodwinked. I hardly know the guy, but I know one thing, he wouldn't be involved in any crime.

Though it's the middle of the afternoon, darkness is closing in. Ash had shown a flash of anger at the suggestion that his father should be taken away from the lodge for an interview. Not least because of the disruption to the cemetery's functioning. In the end, the celebrant conducting today's funeral had been contacted. He'd agreed to come in early and oversee its smooth functioning while Ash was away. He takes his role seriously. It's one of the things I'm growing to like about him, though I don't think he's my greatest fan. He would be relieved if I were to gather up my equipment and get out of the lodge.

Whatever the outcome of the police enquiry, the chapel will hardly be the best place for remodelling. Especially if a murder took place within its walls. Or two murders.

Ginny and Dale are waiting outside the station. When they see the car, Dale waves his boss away, and she disappears inside. The building screams twenty-first century, with its glass-and-stucco frontage, and huge mirrored windows. Behind it is the sea.

'Hi, folks.' Dale greets us as we lead Hal towards the front door. 'Chilly, isn't it?' A bitterly cold wind is blowing in from the water. It smells of seaweed and rotting fish. I gather my coat tightly at the neckline, and hope Hal isn't too uncomfortable. He's hardly robust enough for an afternoon at the seaside.

Once we're in the reception area, Dale leads us towards the lifts, and we're taken to the top floor. Ash's expression is sullen, and he doesn't say anything, but Hal is fascinated by the place. He asks basic questions and points things out, his previous distress completely dissipated. It makes me wonder if he's got something against Ginny, rather than a generalised bad reaction to strangers. He'd acted in the same way when the councillor – Ria Lace I think she was called – came by; perhaps it is an adverse reaction to women, though not to me.

'Can I get anyone a coffee or tea?' Dale herds us into a quiet room and gestures at a table. 'Take a seat, please.'

'Cup of tea for me.' Hal is in his element, an elderly but jaunty man enjoying the attention his status brings. 'Any biscuits?'

Dale gives me a gentle smile. 'I'll see what I can do, matey.'

It feels like we're getting settled in a café, rather than a police interview room. I can only presume Ginny Beck is standing on the other side of what looks like a wide mirror, panelled with stripes of white plastic.

'All right, Dad?' Ash is wearing a thin anorak. It hangs from rigid shoulders.

'I am. When are the history people coming in?'

'It's the man who's gone to get your tea. That's all. No one else.'

Hal seems happy with this response, so we wait. When Dale comes back, he is carrying a tray of mustard-coloured plastic cups, and some individually wrapped biscuits. He has ditched his suit jacket and rolled up his sleeves. The dreaded statement pad is tucked under his arm.

'There you go,' he says pleasantly. 'No radio for you in here, Mr Black. You'll have to put up with my voice droning on.'

'No worries, lad.' Hal slurps his tea. 'Ask me whatever you like about the cemetery, and I'll be able to answer. Then it'll be me droning, not you.'

We all laugh at that. I catch Ash's eye and he smiles.

'Tell me about how you got chosen to be caretaker,' Scottie says. 'Did you always do the job, man and boy?'

Hal launches into his life story, while Ash chips in with amendments. Some of the timings are off. Hal seems a little unsure of his actual age. He doesn't say much about his marriage to Ash's mother. I discover that her name was Cora, and their time together wasn't happy.

'She left when our lad was a teenager,' Hal says, gravely.

'I was seven,' Ash adds, his tone grim.

'Did you have any other job, Mr Black? Was there a time when someone else ran things at the cemetery?' Dale is furiously taking notes, but Hal doesn't seem worried.

'Nope. Hardly had a day away from the place since my father passed on. That was a shock, right enough. Sometime in the sixties that was.' He bites into a piece of shortbread. 'I think.'

Ash raises his brows. 'It was 1971, actually. It'll be in the logs, if you really want to check.'

Dale takes note. 'I'll bet it was a gruelling job,' he says. 'Not for the faint-hearted. How often did you check the site, back in your day? Out there in all weathers, were you?'

'Oh, aye.' Hal doesn't say anything else, and I wonder if he's even processed the question.

Ash answers for him. 'Part of being the caretaker is that you do a daily recce of everything on the site, including checking for break-ins and intruders.' He glances at me. 'Picking up litter that's blown in; looking for faults. It's what I used to help Dad with, when he was the boss.'

'Ah, right.' Dale adds to his notes, then pauses and screws up his eyes. 'That old chapel in the cemetery grounds,' he says, suddenly. 'There's a bloody big padlock on the door, isn't there? How come?'

Hal shrinks down in his seat. The jovial mood shifts. 'It's been closed for a long time, that place. The lock keeps people out.'

Dale nods kindly. 'You'll have seen the inside, though.'

'Course. Had to let the... erm...'

Ash comes to his rescue. 'When the chapel was in use, various members of the clergy officiated at funerals held onsite. Again, it'll all be in the logs, though it's long before Dad's time. I'm not sure what he's remembering.'

'And is it in the logs as to when the chapel was decommissioned and locked up?'

'That's a matter of public record, not a secret.' Ash sighs. 'But yes, it'll be in the logs. I can give you the date, if you like. It's common knowledge for anyone interested in history.'

'When was it?' Dale leans forward as though a big secret is coming.

'1962. That's when the crematorium building first opened. It's a bit of an eyesore compared to the Paley and Austin style lodge house and chapel, in my opinion, but it has served its purpose.'

I stare at Ash. There's a passion for these buildings in his tone, a sharply honed knowledge. His words also point to the fact that Hal's own father was in charge of the disused chapel for many years. Anything could have happened in this time, but the keyword is *disused*. Hal would have had no reason to go inside the place, but the same may not be true for his father. Ginny Beck's case will pivot on timelines for the skeletons. Until then, I can't see what help Ash, or his father will be.

But Dale doesn't let up. 'Can you remember if anyone ever broke into the chapel, Mr Black? You know, smashed windows or jemmied the door? We both know what bloody vandals are like. No respect for property, not even churches or chapels.'

A flash of alarm crosses Hal's face. 'I always kept a good eye on the place. Why are you asking that?' Ash puts a hand on his arm. It is thrown off. 'I don't know about no vandals or yobs or whatever you want to call them.'

'Again,' Ash interrupts, 'that kind of information will be in the logs.'

Dale holds up his palms. 'Yeah, I know. The logs.'

There can be no further use in talking to Hal, not without telling him what has been found in the chapel. It is time for us to go.

'And on that note,' I say brightly, 'we'd better get Mr Black home. Until you've looked at the dreaded logs in more detail, there's not much he can help you with, is there?'

Ash follows my lead. Dale can hardly argue. It seems to me that the police have little idea about what they are dealing with. Understandable, since it has been only two days since the chapel discovery. We help Hal to his feet.

When we leave the interview room, I catch sight of Ginny Beck walking away along the corridor. Dale hurries towards her. Hal is getting agitated, saying he needs to use the lavatory.

'Take him down in the lift,' I whisper to Ash. 'I'll wait for Dale and find out how we are getting back to the lodge.' When he hesitates, I add, 'Go on. Before he has an accident.'

Once Ash has led his father away, I keep Dale and Ginny in my sights. She is holding out a cardboard file and he is peering at it. I'm not sure if they are arguing, but something is going on. The windows on this level give a clear view across the water to Walney Island. I'm reminded of the Romani bracelet and Bill's comment about a community of travellers living on the island during the 1970s. At this time, travellers weren't required to record themselves on census returns. If the remains in the chapel are linked to Romani travellers, identification is going to be even more difficult. Unless the police have a historic record of missing persons in the area during this time. Either way, I won't be privy to that information, which is an annoying but not insurmountable problem.

'Oh, Cherie. You're still here.' Ginny is striding towards me. 'Did you want something? Only, we are very busy.'

When I'm about to tell her we're waiting for a lift back to Cemetery Lodge, Dale pushes his way in between us. 'Have you let on about the newspaper fragment?' he asks, nodding towards Ginny's file.

I watch them both but say nothing. Ginny frowns out her disapproval. 'I have not,' she spits. 'That information isn't for sharing.' There is a slight hesitation, then she adds, 'But it does mean Mr Black senior could be as guilty as hell.'

My feeling is that she's been trying to get something concrete to pin on Hal. I suppose it would make her life easier if he gave her a confession, but why would he? There is nothing to confess. Dale is shaking his head uneasily, tutting.

Ginny barks at him. 'What?'

'Cherie wants to help,' he says. 'She's a professional; she won't say anything. Tell her.'

I'm not comfortable with the way they're arguing over me, but curiosity is overwhelming all my other feelings. I stand, an errant schoolgirl between teacher and parent, and wait. They mutter to each other; Ash is mentioned.

'Well,' Ginny says eventually. 'Mr Scott here has persuaded me to give you our latest piece of information. Please keep it to yourself until I have spoken with the Blacks.'

I nod eagerly.

'It seems that when the skeletons were removed from the chapel by our forensic team, they discovered the shelves had been lined with paper. Newspaper. The date on the sheets was quite clear in some instances: March 14th, 1972. So we are narrowing down our timeframe. Your guess was pretty accurate, as it turned out. Fifty years of lying there.' She sighs. 'Which means Hal Black *must* know something.'

Ash

Lying is never a good idea; particularly to yourself. When Ash examines his knowledge regarding Hal, there has always been a disconnect when the chapel is mentioned. His father will either refuse to engage in conversation about the place, or become agitated and confused. Ash stays off the subject for those reasons alone. But he can't say any of that to Ginny Beck. The woman already has Hal listed as her prime suspect: a man in his seventies and living with a terminal illness. Not that Ash would want anyone to escape justice. Which means he will have to work hard at proving his father is innocent. His first job will be getting the early 1970s logbooks back from the police, and going through them himself.

His father comes out of the gents lavatory, rubbing his hands together. 'The dryers in there don't work,' he says. 'What's wrong with paper towels, I ask you.'

'Not good for the environment, Dad.' Ash points towards the lifts. 'Come on; don't want to keep Cherie waiting.'

'Who? What environment?' Hal's attention has drifted towards a pair of paintings on the wall opposite. He shuffles closer and peers at them. 'Nice, eh?'

'Very nice.' Ash takes his elbow. 'Can we go?'

Hal smacks his lips. 'I could do with a cuppa. Is there a canteen in this place?'

Ash steers his father towards the open door of a lift. He often chooses to ignore Hal's questions and comments. They make him feel tired, invisible somehow. Looking after a person with holes in their brain tissue can manifest in a strange way. The social connect formed when effort is put into a relationship isn't there. It is like talking to yourself in a mirror. It might look like a two-way conversation, but nothing is happening.

Cherie isn't there when they reach the reception area. Ash keeps Hal occupied with low-level chatter about favourite meals and television programmes. His father may have an unreliable memory, but he knows what he likes. It's one of the anomalies of his condition. The dementia nurse had warned Ash not to google Alzheimer's because its trajectory was dependent on the unique characteristics of an individual. The only predictable outcome was that it would kill Hal in the end.

'They're bringing round a car,' Cherie calls as she strides towards them from the bottom of the staircase. She is gesturing towards a young woman standing behind the glass counter. Ash can't help noticing how clean everything looks; how modern: it's the caretaker in him. Smoothly plastered walls are painted in muted colours, creams and sky-blues, furniture co-ordinates. Indoor plants and paintings complete the look. It's nothing like the cosy but shabby interior of the lodge. His father would probably slop coffee onto pastel-blue carpets, and then where would they be?

'Okay, thanks.' He's trying to be pleasant, but Cherie's presence is grating on him. It's like she's become a family member, when they only met yesterday. She links her arm through Hal's and Ash wants to drag him away.

'Hopefully, the police will leave you alone for a while,' she is saying as they move towards the door. 'Dale told me he has all the information he needs, for now. Once they've vacated the chapel, I'll be able to get on with my job. Not that the place will be suitable for recommissioning after what's happened. Though I bet there will be some ghoulish local interest; there always is–'

She chatters on and on, and Ash stops listening. He stares through the front doors of the police station and into the drizzly twilight. Once again, he hasn't completed the job he's paid for, and it doesn't sit well with him. He wants to take back control of his life, work, see his friends, have a blast on his bike. And now Cherie has asked him something and is waiting for an answer.

'Sorry, what?' He stifles a yawn.

'I was just saying about the Romani bracelet I saw. There will be a connection to the travelling community, I'm sure. My boss said a group of them worked seasonally on Walney Island during the seventies. Perhaps I should tell the police that.'

time carer. A multitude of private social care companies have been set up in the wake of the pandemic. It's not something he's considered before. He and Hal have a good routine, and not much has happened to upend it. This business with the chapel has shown how quickly things can unravel. He considers bringing up the subject with Cherie, she seems so well-informed about everything, much more *twenty-first-century* than he is. She is blinking at him through the half-light. He smiles.

'Is there time for me to have a look at one of these logbooks when we get back to the lodge?' she asks. 'Just for my own interest?'

It's the last thing Ash wants. He's ready to get his father into nightclothes, feed and settle him, then give himself a bit of care. There's a migraine pushing up behind his eyes, probably triggered by low blood-sugar. He wants to go over the work schedule for the rest of the week and make sure anything missed can be moved to another slot.

'Would you mind if I say no?' he mutters, not catching her eye. 'It's been a tricky couple of days.'

'Course not. Sorry.' She looks down at her hands but says nothing else. They travel the rest of the way in silence, Hal asleep between them.

Ash can't think of anything to say that would mitigate his abrupt reaction to Cherie's request. The townscape swishes by, nothing more than dark silhouettes and rainy streaks of coloured light. He watches wearily and thinks of home.

As they near the lodge, Cherie asks the driver to pull up, because she has to hurry for the train. She calls a goodnight, then disappears along the street. Ash wasn't expecting this reaction from her, but he understands it, and feels something akin to shame.

Ash is on high alert, now. He's hardly given a thought to the story behind the chapel remains. His focus has been to do with keeping Hal clear of disruption and blame. 'Do the travelling community still venture over to the island?'

'I'm not sure.' Cherie tilts her head quizzically. 'Bill – that's my boss – would probably know. I don't come from around here, but he's local and has all the *knowledge*.' She taps the side of her nose.

Ash knows very little about her, he realises, and has asked almost nothing.

'Oh. I'd assumed... with working at Gillside, you lived nearby.'

She shakes her head. 'I'm staying in Cark. Near Cartmel. But I come from Carlisle, originally. Sixty-miles north, but a world away. I worked in Lancaster for a while, too. But I don't know Furness very well.'

'Lancaster?' His body jolts.

Hal senses something and tugs at his arm. 'I'm starving,' wails. 'Did I have any supper? It looks like midnight out the and I don't think I have.'

Cherie pulls a chocolate biscuit from her handbag. It h vivid red wrapping that Hal recognises instantly. He's gra and wants to share, but Ash has seen a police car pull ont forecourt. The driver is beckoning through an open windov

'Come on, Dad.' He tugs at Hal's arm. 'Time to go hom

Hal gives him a chocolatey smile. They step towar sliding glass doors and out into the damp chill of evening.

It is warm inside the police car. They are guide together in the rear of the vehicle. Ash manoeuv between them. He is soon dozing, head lolling against shoulder. The weight of his responsibility presses he has to admit it helps to have someone like Cherie; t lifts slightly. Perhaps it is time to think about employ

CHAPTER NINE

Cherie

When I'd stumbled out of the police car earlier in the week, I'd vowed to leave Ash Black where he belonged: in a box marked unapproachable associates. I'd come across plenty in my job, though usually they hung out at the top of their profession, casting glacial looks at those beneath them. That Ash had taken on this form was a shock, considering the empathy he showed towards his father. I haven't been back to Cemetery Lodge since.

With just a couple of weeks until Christmas, the weather is in alignment with the festive mood. A dazzle of winter sunshine has dragged me from the cottage and onto the train. It's a Saturday afternoon and the shoppers are heading into town. My carriage is full of couples and families, muffled up in padded parkas and knitted hats, rosy-cheeked and full of plans. I sit by myself.

It's my intention to walk from the station to Walney Island, and explore the place. The last three days at Gillside have been an intense mix of research and copywriting, and I need to do something practical. I haven't looked at anything related to the cemetery chapel, but I've thought about it a lot. As I'd left work yesterday, Bill threw me a titbit of information too tempting to ignore: the island's traveller community returned every year through the sixties and seventies to a site near the village of Biggar. It is to here I am heading.

The station is a half-hour walk from Walney. I set out at a good pace, striding through the brightness of the morning, smiling a greeting to everyone I pass. The locals are friendly, much more than in the village where I'm staying. My cottage in Cark is part of a brightly painted terrace, situated across the road from a small beck. The cottages are stone built, with neat windows and cobbled forecourts, but I'm yet to feel at home. Considering I have close neighbours, I've never met them. It's likely they only visit during their holidays; second-home owning isn't conducive to a community feel.

I cross to the island using its road bridge. There's a sense of history about the structure that chimes with me immediately. I read further information on its blue plaque, then take my phone from my backpack and google Biggar Village. It's on the south end of Walney, about two miles from where I am standing. The water on either side of the bridge is a deep shade of blue today, reflecting the brightness of the sky. I'm glad I made the journey here. It is giving me a deep sense of optimism.

In the early days after my divorce, I wondered if the stress of it had caused a permanent change in me. Though I felt liberated, it was accompanied by a sense of failure. Butting up against Ash Black and his outmoded views is causing a similar feeling; I'd rather avoid it in the future.

Once I'm across the bridge, I pass through a slew of Victorian terraced housing which gives way to something a bit more modern, then I get to the beach. The tide is a good way out, and planted in it, like the paper windmills of my childhood, are more than a hundred turbines, blades turning gracefully. This would not be a seascape familiar to the traveller community. Ahead of me, stretching southwards, is a narrow road. The landscape is made up from flat, scrubby fields and uneven hedges. I can see the attraction for the travellers: privacy and the raw beauty of an unspoilt coastline. It must have been cold in the winter, though.

It takes me another fifteen minutes to reach the village. A first glance shows me its antiquity. Though there are sturdy whitewashed houses huddled together, I also see barns fabricated from slabs of rough-cut sandstone interlaced with beach boulders.

And there is a pub. 'Morning,' I call to a man wrestling with fold-up tables on the forecourt. 'Or is it afternoon?'

He is short and stockily built, leathery-faced and beaming. 'Hiya, lass.' He glances at the sky. 'Not quite noon, but who's counting? You coming in for a bevvy?'

'Not right now. But I like the look of your lunch board. What time are you serving?'

He casts an eye over my walking attire and settles on my backpack. 'Serving now, but it looks like you've got it covered.'

'I haven't, believe me.'

'Come in then. Before the Saturday brigade land.'

I swing the pack into my hand, and follow him. The interior of the pub is all black-painted beams and horse brasses. A huge wood-burner is blasting out smoky heat, spitting and crackling and lighting up a gloomy corner. Above the bar, fishing nets have been hung and decorated with balls of coloured glass. Surfaces gleam.

'Who are the Saturday brigade?' I haul myself onto a bar stool.

'Bikers. They have a blast around the island, then come here for lunch and a beer. Non-alcoholic of course.'

I wink. 'Of course.'

He returns the gesture. 'What can I get you? Drink wise, I mean?' He lays his hands on the bar, and I can't help noticing the tattoos creeping from his wrists to the place where his rolled shirtsleeves start. They have a tantalisingly marine flavour, fish intertwined with anchors, and there's a compass too.

'I don't suppose you serve coffee?'

'I do. Freshly brewed. Large one?'

'Please.' I squint up at the specials board. 'Is it too early for pie and peas?'

He laughs lightly. 'Never too early for pie and peas. Won't be a mo.'

He leaves the bar through a small doorway. I settle back and enjoy the ambience: a country pub with the tang of the sea. Somewhere nearby is the site where the Romani travellers would have set themselves up, perhaps with their caravans and motorhomes. Hardly a traditional image.

My work as a historian has always thrown up anomalies. History is a two-tiered affair: there's popular history and then there's a deeper dive into the truth. When I worked for the university and tutored on digital platforms, it was hard to get this across. Students thought that because one history scholar noted something, it must be reality; not all students, but most.

The landlord comes back quickly. He is carrying a tray with my coffee, and promises the food won't be long. We chat about the weather and Christmas, and finally he asks me if I'm local, and why I'm visiting the island.

'I'd heard there was once a Romani traveller encampment near here,' I explain. 'Wanted to check out the site, that's all.'

He cocks his head and gives me an eye-twinkle. 'Aye. There was. Long time ago, now.'

'Is there anything to see?'

'Not anymore. It's just a bit of flat ground to the east of the village, near the shore. There was a standing tap, once, and some bits of rough concrete, but not now.' He leans in. 'Why do you want to know?'

'I'm just interested, that's all.' I pretend to be the opposite. 'No worries.'

He's quiet for a few seconds, then he says, 'I was only a kid when they were last here, but I remember kicking a football about with one of the gypsy lads, like. Thought I was so exotic, didn't I?'

I don't tell him that *gypsy* isn't a word used nowadays. 'I guess you've been in the village for a long time, then. Did the travellers not fit in very well when they came?'

'My dad ran the pub before me. That's proper old school, isn't it?' He rests his chin on his hand. 'And actually, they did fit in. Especially round here. We looked forward to them arriving at the end of each summer. It stopped us getting cabin fever, as it were. Someone different in the village.'

I take a sip of my coffee. 'That's good, thanks. When did the travellers stop coming by? Can you remember?'

He frowns. 'Hmm. Let me think. Middle of the eighties, possibly. Early nineties perhaps. I went away to college for a bit. By the time I came back, no one talked about them anymore. Shame, really.'

'Daz,' someone calls from beyond the doorway. 'Food's ready.'

'Won't be a mo,' he says.

The newspaper fragment found under the skeletons does give some clue as to their timeframe; the bodies must have been placed after March 1972. What has been puzzling me is why lay newspaper? It's hardly a good protector against bodily decay. And were these bodies being hidden temporarily? Did someone mean to return and remove them? Protecting the shelves in the sacristy cupboard with a layer of newspaper only makes sense in this context. So, why did no one come back? That person couldn't be Hal Black, surely. Hiding a secret like that would unnerve even the toughest mindset. Ash's father is guileless. He can't have the first idea of what was lurking in a building he passed every day.

When Daz comes back with my lunch, I've already decided to find the exact location of the traveller encampment. From experience, I know that walking a landscape can give a better sense of its history than books or documents. I remember having a fascinating conversation with one of my online students about the scholarly historian, W.G. Hoskins and his advice to *get one's feet wet*. The student wasn't interested in archaic documentation. To them, history could only be found in what was *touchable* in the present. I liked that.

'I've just remembered,' Daz says as he sets my plate down. 'Jakka – this guy from the village – actually married one of the gypsies. She's dead now, and he's in his nineties. I do see him sometimes, standing in his front garden, having a crafty cigarette. I can ask him about it, if you like. He's stone deaf, so I can't guarantee anything.' He passes me a sachet of tomato sauce. 'It'll bring you back to the pub, if nowt else.'

I peer down at the steaming pie and huge mound of mushy peas. 'That looks fab. And I would appreciate any information this gentleman could give. This is the phone number of my office; get in touch anytime.' I write Gillside's landline number on a beermat.

'Okie-doke, thanks.' Daz picks up a tea towel and buffs the beer pumps. 'He lives in Turnstone Cottage, down by the green. Jakka, that is.' He gestures in the direction of the sea. 'But there's no point in knocking. Like I said, he's deaf as a post.'

'Great. Well, I'll wait to hear from you, if I don't pop back before then.'

Daz leaves me to my food and turns his attention to the few

other people who have come in. While I eat, I scroll through my phone, pulling up photographs of travelling communities, trying to get a feel for dates and locations. There is a lot of material on the internet, a lot of clarification about the position of Romani compared to other itinerant people. The bracelet I saw was definitely from their culture. I don't think it is a coincidence that Romani travellers were on the island during the seventies, then a piece of their jewellery turns up on skeletal remains from exactly that era.

By the time I finish my food, the pub is busy. I attract Daz's attention and pay my bill. He gives me rough directions to what was the traveller site, but doesn't have time for any more chat. I use the lavatory, wash my hands, and head outside.

At the far end of the village there is an area of flattened grass in the shape of a triangle. Daz had called it *the green*. It has a signpost pointing three ways: back to Biggar; to the nature reserve; to the shore. Narrow roads lead in each direction.

I'm heading to the shore. Though it is almost mid-winter, my route is lined with the thick, tangled bones of a summer hedgerow. It's impossible to see around each twist and turn, so I'm careful to stay on the pitted edges of tarmac. The sun is high, its rays blinding. I shield my eyes as I walk.

A low rumble starts up, a vibration. At first, I think it is the sea, then I remember how far out the tide is. The sound builds. It's a vehicle of some kind, a tractor perhaps, but I can't see anything over the top of the hedge.

Within seconds, a motorbike flies around the bend and heads towards me. Then another; then two more. There is no place to escape the road, no pavement or banking or even the slightest camber. I lean into a jagged hawthorn bush and close my eyes. I count seven bikes as they pass. They don't slow in acknowledgement. When I dare to look again, the taillight of the last one is flashing red. It has stopped.

Ash

Flying along the lanes breathes light into Ash's body. His thoughts are in danger of becoming too dark to handle, especially after the week he's had.

If his father's condition has deteriorated, their lives will change. The idea of Hal living in a nursing home is not something Ash wants to contemplate. Giving up his job to become a full-time carer would be another solution. Already, Saturdays are his only respite. His father enjoys the radio and TV sporting fixtures that accompany a weekend, and another highlight is the Saturday morning grocery delivery. Hal loves to indulge in banter with the driver, and to put items away according to his strict protocols. Which means Ash has a few hours when he isn't required to do anything. He usually spends it with his motorcyclist friends, sometimes feeling confident enough to languish most of the afternoon.

Up until now, Hal has been fine on these Saturdays. Today though, Ash feels uneasy. He'd left Hal as usual, and his father had been bright enough. Perhaps the outbursts earlier in the week had just been a blip. Either way, this excursion is going to be shortened.

The lanes towards the south end of the island are always deserted. When they've completed a couple of circuits, Ash follows at the rear of the short convoy as it heads to the little pub at Biggar. There are only seven bikers today; attendance falls off in the winter months. As they slow down enough to take in a difficult dog-leg just before the village, Ash is surprised to see a walker. The bikes zoom past with astounding grace. When it's his turn, he slows a little.

And there is Cherie Hope, flattening herself against the

hedgerow, a scowl on her face. He stops the bike and jumps off. 'Sorry if we startled you,' he says as he unfastens his helmet. 'There's not usually anyone walking around here. Especially not in the winter.'

Cherie puffs out her cheeks and puts a hand on her chest. 'Startled isn't a good enough word. I was terrified. There's nowhere for a pedestrian to go.' She gives him an exaggerated sigh.

'Are you okay?' He takes in the light brown hair, held back with a fleecy headband, and the glowing complexion. 'Not too shocked, I mean. Am I all right to leave you?'

She looks him straight in the eye. 'Are you joking? We came across the skeletal remains of two bodies on Monday. I don't recall you worrying about my welfare then.'

'Sorry again. I don't mean to sound patronising.' He runs a hand through his hair, thinking about how he must look. 'I'll go.' He doesn't want to, wants instead to spend the afternoon in the company of someone with a different story to tell. 'Or I can give you a lift somewhere?' He tries to smile. 'Up to you.'

'You can't give me a lift.' She points to her head. 'No helmet.'

He gestures over his shoulder. 'I can get you one.' The clothes Cherie is wearing – padded jacket and walking trousers – are suitable, in his opinion. He can borrow a helmet from one of his friends.

'I wouldn't want to break up the party,' she says. 'And your fellow bikers seem to have gone.'

'Only to the pub. It'll take me less than a minute to get there.'

Cherie's hesitation is not lost on him. Bad manners and disinterest are the only side of him she's seen. He wishes it were different. She surprises him by saying she could hop on the back of his bike, and they could go really slowly back to the pub. He's not sure, but doesn't want to risk losing this contact with her, so he agrees. She doesn't have any problem finding his waist and clutching at it as they plod slowly along.

When they reach the pub, she jumps quickly from the pillion seat, checking they have no audience. His friend's bikes are lined up on the forecourt.

'Are you coming inside for a sec?' he asks. 'While I sort out a helmet?'

'I'll wait here, if you don't mind.'

'Fair enough.' Ash pushes his way inside. His friends are leaning against the bar, peering at the specials board.

'Where'd you get to, Blackster?' one of them calls. Ash explains, tone lowered. There are some ribald comments about a secret girlfriend. He's not allowed to get himself entangled with someone who wears a waterproof coat, it seems. The jibes are good-humoured but come from a place where his lack of attachment is joked about, though little understood.

'I'd go out with him,' another shouts. 'He's gorgeous.'

It doesn't take long for Ash to procure a helmet. In a way, he's relieved to have found an escape route from their planned pub lunch. Hal being left alone is worrying him and he wanted a reason to go and check.

When he gets outside, Cherie is sitting on the wall, face turned to the sun. He is still carrying a fragment of shame about the way he got rid of her on Tuesday evening, especially after she'd been so good with his father. He vows to be nicer.

'Here you go,' he says pleasantly. 'Janice is getting a lift back with Tez, so she says you can loan her helmet. I'll return it tomorrow… if she's sobered up by then.'

Cherie frowns. 'They're not drinking, are they?'

He shakes his head. 'Only Jan. It's her birthday.'

'I see.'

Ash doesn't explain further. His friends don't take risks.

Leather jackets and noisy exhausts aren't indicators of danger; his motorcycle group do a toy run each Christmas and sponsored events throughout the year. One volunteers his biker services at the blood-bank. They are ordinary folk with ordinary jobs. Much the same as he is.

'Why are you on the island, anyway?' He adjusts the chin strap on the helmet and helps Cherie slide it over her head.

'It's a long story.' She tightens the strap and gives him a thumbs-up. 'You can drop me at the station if you like. That'd be a help.'

'What's the long story?'

'If you must know, I was going to look at the 1970s traveller site.' She tugs up the zip of her jacket. 'I think I told you my boss mentioned it.'

Ash slides on his helmet. 'You did. Of course you did.' Once again, he is reminded of how little notice he's taken of this woman. 'We can drive past there, if you like? Do you know the exact spot?'

'The guy in there.' She gestures towards the pub. 'The landlord, I presume. Daz? He told me.'

While she explains, Ash looks at her and listens and wonders about the weird effect she's having on him. It reminds him of being told, as a child, that something was off limits. He understood the adult perspective that he was being protected for his own good, but the desire for that very thing was almost irresistible.

'Hop on,' he says crisply. 'I think I know where we're going.'

CHAPTER TEN

Cherie

The bleakness of the site hits me like a punch to my stomach. The place lies adjacent to the shoreline, at the top of a sloping and pebbly beach. There are no dunes to offer protection, no trees or hedges, it is nothing more than a flat patchwork of scrubby grass and cracked grey concrete. The isolation feels overwhelming. A wave of sadness passes over me. Did one of the traveller community die in secret here, with no one reporting them missing? When Ash comes up behind me, I gasp.

'I've left the bike at the end of the track,' he says. 'Goodness knows how they got caravans and things down here.' He stares out at the sea. 'Did they have caravans?'

'Caravans pulled by rag-tag vehicles.' I nod sadly. 'And probably the very first motorhomes as we know them. But if the travellers were Romani, they wouldn't have had those. They were some of the poorest people in the country during the seventies.'

Something has shifted in Ash's attitude. We're having

conversations; he's making eye contact. We chat about the possibility of a link between the chapel skeletons and any returning traveller community. Neither of us has a theory, but where I find the conversation fascinating, he seems uneasy.

I try to lead him. 'Are you worried about the effect the police investigation will have on your dad?'

'I suppose so.' He kicks at a patch of gravel. 'Not that he has any idea of what's going on. Dad was a bit unsettled when you saw him last Tuesday, wasn't he? He's back to normal, now. His normal, anyway.'

'Glad to hear it. What is he doing this afternoon? Does he not mind when you leave him?' As soon as the words are out of my mouth, I regret saying them. It isn't my business to comment about Ash's care of his father. No criticism was intended, but I sense some was felt. 'Sorry. I'm interested, that's all.'

Ash mutters something about Hal being his priority at all times. I press my lips together and nod in agreement. We scan the shoreline once more, then walk together back to the bike.

'Is this your first time?' Ash says suddenly. 'On a motorbike, I mean?'

I nod. 'First time, yep.'

'How have you found it?'

'Great, I think. Ask me again once we've been on the main roads.' I glance at the sky. 'Time's getting on. Just drop me in the town centre if you like. Don't go out of your way.'

He hesitates, sliding his attention to my face. 'Why don't you come back to the lodge. See Dad. Have a brew.'

'Really?'

'Only if you want,' he continues. 'Don't feel compelled.'

'That's a strong word. *Compelled*. Would *obliged* be better? We've had this conversation about wrong words before, haven't we?'

'Put your helmet on,' he orders, with a wry smile.

We drive slowly until we've cleared the sandy track from the beach. I tuck in behind Ash and match his movements. Once the bike wheels hit tarmac, he accelerates. I lean into his back for stability. The landscape zooms by. There's a different view from the one I gained earlier. We flash past dense hedgerows, brittle with winter; open sea and sky; salt marsh edged with houses; the road bridge. At the traffic lights, we pull up. I flex my back. There's an anonymity to riding pillion, identity tucked away inside a crash helmet and bulky clothes. I like it. Ash calls over his shoulder, asking if I'm okay. I pat his arm in response, then the lights change, and we speed away.

There is a small driveway and garage at the side of the lodge. Ash brings the bike to a standstill at the kerbside and lets me climb down.

'I'll just be a minute,' he says as he lifts his visor. 'Let me have Jan's helmet and I'll put everything away, then meet you round the front. The door's locked.' He rummages in his pocket and fishes out a key. 'Unless you want to let yourself in.'

I take the key. 'Won't your dad panic if I just turn up?'

He flings up one hand. 'Who knows? He seemed to like you when you met him on Monday. Not that he'll remember.'

'I'll wait.' I slide off my helmet and fluff up my hair. Ash wheels the bike towards the garage, then lifts it onto its stand. He pulls at the door and leaves the helmets in a dry corner.

'Okie-dokie,' he says as he strides towards me. 'Let's get inside and warm up.'

I'm not sure what has brought this change in him, but I'm enjoying it. We joke about having salt-smeared faces and helmet hair, and he tells me about Hal's love for betting on horse races.

'I do it for him online,' he explains. 'There was a time when he walked down to the bookies himself on a Saturday, but those days are long gone. He puts piffling amounts on, £1.50 each way, daft stuff like that. I never did understand what it meant.

He has an account now, so I don't even have to go and collect his winnings.'

We stand together on the doorstep of the lodge. I'm conscious of Ash's eyes on me. They are a dark hazel colour and catch at the afternoon sun.

'He's lucky to have you,' I say, but I can't hold his gaze, it's too intense. I put my hand on the door. 'Let's get inside. I need a cup of tea.'

Hal is sitting at the kitchen table, peering closely at the inside pages of a newspaper. 'Hiya, lad,' he says. 'Did you have a good ride out?'

'I did, thanks. Cherie's here to see you again.' Ash fills the kettle while I sit down next to his father. Hal doesn't seem to mind my presence, but there's no recognition that we've met before. He's wearing a thick flannel shirt and a pair of jeans today. With his hair combed and his interest in the paper, he could be any other elderly gentleman scanning the racing pages.

'There's not many runners today,' he says. 'I haven't had any winners.' He winks across at Ash. 'Still in credit though, eh?'

'Still in credit.'

Hal is very settled, showing nothing like the agitation he had when he'd first met Ria Lace, and later Ginny Beck. Ash must have a hard time dealing with his father's unpredictable responses. A time will come, I'm sure, when he won't be able to manage Hal by himself; that time seems a while away yet.

While we drink our tea, Ash whispers cryptically about the chapel. There have been no developments, no communication from the police, although their presence remains in the form of a uniformed officer hanging about, day and night. Hal doesn't join in with our conversation, doesn't appear to be listening. I don't want to outstay my welcome, so when the tea is drunk, I get up from the table and state my intention of walking to the railway station before it gets dark.

'Did you not want to look at the logbooks?' Ash stares up at me.

'Oh.' I shake my head. 'Another time. You'll be wanting to get Hal his evening meal, won't you?'

'I'm not an invalid,' Hal chimes in. 'And I can hear you.'

Ash laughs. 'Take no notice, Cherie. Dad picks and chooses what he hears, believe me.' He stands up. 'Come on. A quick peek, then you can get going. I know you were interested. The police have got the 70/71 logs, but there are stacks more. I only brought down the 1970s ones. If they want any others, I'm tempted to say they can go up to the loft themselves.'

'I'd be interested to look at 1972.' The words are out before I remember that Ash won't have knowledge of the newspaper fragments found under the skeletons.

'Why?' His tone drops.

I make a split-second decision not to lie. Ginny Beck isn't keeping him informed about what is happening in a building he's guardian of; it doesn't seem right. But I'm also preserving myself. I want to keep the good opinion of this guy, now that I've got it. Lies, even white ones, are corrosive. There's no better way to reduce a person to their lowest form, than by lying to them.

'Ginny Beck told me a fragment of newspaper relating to March 1972, had been found under the skeletons.' I watch his reaction. 'Which means that's the earliest date for bodies to have been put in that cupboard.'

He frowns. 'Why tell you?'

'I was being nosy, if you must know. Ginny was flapping over a file with that other guy, Dale Scott, so I pushed my way into the conversation.' When his expression slides, I can't stop myself from adding, 'I was going to tell you when we next met.'

'Right.' He turns away.

Ash

There is a certain kind of irony in the way a simple set of words can create the polar opposite of their intention. *I was going to tell you.* He might have known the people who deemed themselves professionals would stick together.

'Sorry,' Cherie says, and Ash has to admit there's sincerity in her tone. Perhaps she's sorry about having to tell him, about letting the information out; she's apologising for the slip-up rather than the omission.

A bitter sigh slides out of his mouth. 'Whatever. Do you want to see a logbook or not?'

'If you've got time.'

Her cheeks are flushed with heat; a consequence of flying through freezing air then coming into a warm house, perhaps. He catches her eye, just once, then turns his back and leads her into the hallway. They climb the stairs and make their way into the small room where Ash has stacked the three boxes he fetched from the loft. She doesn't say anything.

'The ones you want will be in here.' He lifts the lid of a half-empty box and runs his finger along the logbook spines. 'January 1972.' He looks up at her. 'Not interested?'

She shakes her head.

'February, then? March?' He throws down the lid. 'Take your pick. You obviously know what you're looking for.'

'Ash.' She puts a hand on his arm. 'Don't be cross.'

Is he cross? He's not sure. It's more that his guard was down in the presence of someone who had pushed up against it and helped it fall. He should have fought harder.

He pulls away from her grasp. 'I'm not cross. Do you want to scan through spring 1972 or not?'

'I do.'

She sits on the floor with her back against the wall. Ash isn't sure whether to leave her and get on with making his father something to eat. Cherie reaches up and takes the logbook.

'Sorry to be a pain,' she says as she runs a hand over the first pages. 'I just want to get a feel for the format of these things.'

'Why? You're not the police, are you? They're the ones investigating what happened in the chapel. Not you.' He doesn't mean to sound petulant. His anger, if he has any, is directed at himself. Every time his relationship with Cherie falters, turns *scratchy*, he feels like a fool. She ignores his comments and continues flicking through the pages, stroking her hands over the yellowing paper, running her index finger along the lines of script. Ash paces the room, peers through the window then closes the curtains. It's like there is an intruder in his home and he wants to mark his territory. Her interest in the police investigation is irritating. He examines his psyche, probing like a tongue on a sore tooth, and finds there's a certain amount of jealousy to his feelings; he should be more curious than he is.

'Ash?' Cherie has asked him something. He blinks, coming back to reality.

'Can I look at the January log?' she continues, holding out her hand.

'Sure.' He passes her the book. 'Why?'

She is quiet again, flicking through, expression intent. He stares at her hands. They are small and neat, and he can't imagine them rifling through heaps of soil, searching for long-forgotten artefacts. He hasn't taken the trouble to ask her much about this line of work; he's not even sure she digs.

'There's a name; it keeps coming up. I wanted to track it backwards. It's here, in the January logs, too.'

'What name?'

She beckons him over, patting the space beside her. 'Here.

Look.' Her finger trails underneath a few lines of script; his father's script. 'Victor Hale. The Reverend Victor Hale.'

Ash peers, trying not to touch Cherie's shoulder.

'Your dad starts mentioning him in January and is still doing it in March. I guess he was the peripatetic vicar at the time?' She passes him the book. 'Is he still around?'

Though he's never heard of this Victor Hale, Ash can see him as a presence within the wording of his father's day-to-day recordings. It's not a name Hal has ever mentioned; he's not had many friends, not even acquaintances.

'I'm not sure,' he mutters, passing the book back. 'Is it possible to find out?'

'Oh, it's possible,' she says. 'Leave it with me. Could I take these few logbooks home and have a proper look? I'd get them back by Monday. I'm coming by to take some outside photos of the chapel, anyhow. If that's okay.'

Ash is not sure whether he should agree to Cherie's request, but he knows one thing: in terms of finding out what happened in the chapel, she is now ahead of the police.

Hal

An icy wind gnaws at his hands. The knuckles are chapped and raw. Pain keeps him focused. Hal had spent Christmas staring at the white artificial tree in the corner of the sitting room, and looking at *Morecambe-and-Wise* on the portable TV. At his father's funeral he hadn't shed a single tear. Now, he's working in the cemetery, clearing drains and picking up drifts of litter, and wondering if he's destined to spend his life alone.

The low growl of an engine startles him. There is no one on his schedule for today, though there soon will be. January is the saddest of months, death and grief coming in waves through the winter, but not today. He stomps across the grass, wellington boots sloshing, to get a better view. It's a brand-new Datsun Sunny with a sporty look, finished in trendy metallic body paint. Hal knows his cars, knows this isn't what *common people* are driving. He pulls at his cap and hides his face. The car heads up the slope to the crem building, then stops. Hal tracks it from the corner of his eye. The driver's door opens. No one is expected. This was to be a day of quiet contemplation, no visitors wanted. A man is stepping onto the tarmac.

Hal moves quickly, intending a challenge, suddenly aware of his well-worn and shapeless work clothing. The man is wearing a black cassock and pristine white collar. He is tall and lean, and holding a black briefcase nonchalantly between elbow and body. Hal calls a hello. Then he is staring into what he thinks must be the face of an angel.

First impressions foreshadow everything: the Datsun Sunny, with its glittering bronze body; the man with golden hair; a complexion to weep over. Hal checks behind him. Is that dazzle of a smile for someone else?

The man is bearing down on him, hand outstretched. A watch, silver-faced and with a strap of leather, peeks from the immaculate cuff of his cassock. Hal's stomach flips over. He takes the hand. The palm is feather soft against his own. There are introductions; he is Victor Hale, *Vic the vic*.

They enjoy the joke; Hal, more than he should. By the time he has shown the new vicar inside the crematorium building, Hal is a fish on a hook.

CHAPTER ELEVEN

Cherie

The last rays of afternoon sun drop pools of gold onto my patio. It's a south-facing cottage, so I have the best of both worlds. The day has been full of vivid winter texture and colour, of last summer's shrubby remains and frost-bleached grass. Temperatures haven't risen above zero. I've walked fellside paths around the village and had a pub lunch, and thought a great deal about the time I'd spent yesterday with Ash. I'd like his good opinion, but he seems so reactive; I'm never quite sure if I've done something to cause offence.

Once darkness has fallen, I close the curtains, flick on the lamps and settle myself for an evening of research. That name, Victor Hale, has burrowed into my consciousness, and I want more information. My laptop and notebook are on the coffee table. I have log-in details for an assortment of ecclesiastical sites: English church records and parish registers. If Victor Hale was a practising clergyman through the seventies, I will be able to locate him.

It doesn't take long.

Victor, it seems, had been in charge of a large local parish in the late sixties, and had taken on the chaplaincy of the crematorium in January 1971. Its previous clergyman had died in 1970, and for almost a year the crem made do.

What had struck me when I read through the logs was how Ash's father had transformed his recording at this time. There had been scant mention of anyone during the first few weeks of January, but by June, Victor's name was featuring on every page. My presumption is that Hal formed no bond with the temporary clergy who served the crem; then Victor arrived.

I resolve to ask Ash if Hal has any memorabilia that would link him to this man, letters perhaps, an address, anything. My next puzzle is what happened to Victor Hale. I'm sure there would be something recorded in later logbooks, but I don't have access to them. What I do have is a log-in and password for the government register of births, deaths and marriages. There can't be many local people called Victor Hale, surely.

I leave the research and head to the kitchen to make myself a cup of tea. The garden is in darkness, the lawn nothing more than a patch of grainy silver. On the day I'd secured the cottage, David had telephoned, singing the praises of his new life, and delivering his list of the furniture I was entitled to. Our furniture. I'd made a point of telling him I needed very little, that the place came fully-furnished. His comeback had been to ask if there was enough room for all my books.

Sometimes I wonder if it was my academic career that spelt the death of our marriage. Had I kept my status as *pretty-little-wife-with-a-digging-degree*, would we still be together? Whatever the answer to this, there is no place in my life for people – men in particular – who allow their insecurities to become a barometer for their judgement of others. I carry my tea back into the lounge and resume my research.

Victor Hale is very much alive, as far as I can make out,

though it seems he's far from well. I'm fairly confident the Victor Hale I have located is the same one. He's listed as being a resident of Marsh House nursing home, which is about thirty miles west of Cark, on the coast. This man is eighty-three years old, and a retired Anglican vicar. What Ash will have to say when I tell him is anybody's guess. It's clear he doesn't want me nosing around in the chapel investigation. I haven't worked out if it's personal, or because he has information he'd rather not share. Neither option works for me. If he isn't interested in finding out any more about Victor Hale, I'll do it on my own.

By the time I've put away my laptop and had another read through the notes I've made, it is ten o'clock. I've to catch the early morning train tomorrow because I want to arrive at the cemetery before Ash goes out on his rounds. I can hardly push my way into the lodge without his say-so. And I want to tell him what I've found out about Victor Hale.

Overnight, there is a hard frost. I almost change my mind about catching the early train. My rucksack is weighed down with the logbooks I borrowed, and I haven't slept well. Thoughts of Victor Hale poked into those drowsy moments before falling, causing a loop I couldn't escape from. When I get to the station, the platform is deserted. It's just me and the biting cold. I've let Bill know that I will work from the lodge this week and try to get enough data to complete the outside assessment. I'm hoping by then the police will have moved from the chapel and there will be access to the inside. Otherwise, I'll have to return to the Gillside office and get on with less interesting projects.

The train journey takes me across the Leven viaduct. The estuary is almost hidden by a layer of freezing fog. The disorientation is dizzying, and I'm glad when the first town lights break through and ground me. What I've learnt over the weeks and months since I moved to Cark is that on the Furness Peninsula, no two weather days are the same. I like that about the place. I've learnt something about myself, too: human interaction is what I crave. My years as a purist were intellectually challenging and enjoyable, but I want my skills to be active and interactive now. The short time I'd spent tutoring online showed me that knowledge and understanding without a reach, mean nothing. A few students I'd worked with changed my perception of the academic world. Their ideas were new and fresh, untainted by scholarly presumptions. One essay in particular resonated so strongly, I printed it off and kept it.

No one boards the train for three stops. Whilst I am enjoying the tranquillity, it is comforting when the early-doors school children push their way on. Their faces are smudged with sleep, but they chatter in a peculiar kind of half-formed language and giggle over things they are showing each other on their phones. There is a high school in Ulverston, but judging by the regulation stripy blazers and old-fashioned briefcases, these children are heading to the big town and a more archaic style of teaching. I went to a comprehensive school myself. My parents believed education was only as good as the recipient; I was a diligent student.

When we arrive in town, it is almost light. A few more of the stripy blazer brigade have joined the train, along with a group of what I would class as office workers, laptops fired up against the lure of interaction with the world. From my research, I discovered that Victor Hale had once been in charge of the parish church of St James'. It's on my route to the cemetery, so I decide to take a look. What I find is an impressive building with a gothic style of decorative brickwork and latticed windows. The spire must be at least 100 feet high, and I am suddenly in awe of the man. To preach in a church of this size would take a certain type of personality.

When I knock at the door of the lodge, Ash answers immediately. He is wearing navy-blue overalls, and his hair is damp. The grey streak gleams.

'Oh. Cherie,' he says, rubbing a hand vigorously across his parting. 'You're early.'

'I wanted to catch you before you went out-and-about.'

He steps aside to let me in. 'I need to give you a key while you're using my office. Dad won't mind. He seems happy in your company.'

It's not exactly a compliment, but I'll take it. I follow him down the hallway and into the kitchen. Hal is sitting at the table, wearing his nightclothes and buttering a slice of toast. He nods at me, but there is no other greeting.

'It's Cherie,' Ash tells him. 'She's a friend.'

'I am.' I pull out a chair and sit. 'Any tea in that pot for me, Hal?'

There is no hesitation. Hal reaches for another mug and pours. He doesn't miss a beat with his own breakfast.

'It's a good day,' Ash mouths, and I give him a thumbs-up.

While he potters around the kitchen, I sip my tea and wonder how to bring up the subject of Victor Hale. It certainly isn't for Hal's ears. Not yet, anyway.

'Can I walk up to the chapel with you this morning?' I ask as Ash lifts his fluorescent work jacket from the kitchen porch and slips it on.

He stretches his expression. 'Don't see why not. You can't get inside yet, though.'

'I didn't think so. But I can make a start on roof photographs and research. I'll just get my camera.'

Ash relays some instructions to his father and gives him a firm time for their next rendezvous. To an outsider, there is nothing out of the ordinary to their interaction, nothing that would alert worry about an elderly man with Alzheimer's being left on his own. I understand now that there is a huge amount of thought attached to everything Ash has organised for Hal, and a mountain of trust. The slightest change will upend things, and have dire consequences. Ash is living in a tense world of accountability; no wonder the guy is reactive.

We step together into the early morning. Cold air catches at my breath. The cemetery slopes are shrouded in frost, gravestones becoming ghostly sentinels, looking west towards the sea. I shudder. Though there have been many occasions when I've knelt with the dead and excavated their last resting place, there's a presence here today; an aura.

'Spooky when the frost is up, isn't it?' Ash gives me a sideways glance. He feels it, too.

'Not spooky,' I say, dropping my tone. 'More spiritual. A poignancy, a gathering of—' I hold up my hands. 'Oh, I don't know. You tell me.'

He smiles. It's like the weight of responsibility slides away; a glimpse of spring after the drear of winter. 'There don't always have to be words,' he says. 'Some things can't be rationalised.'

'I agree.' My camera is swinging from my shoulder. I lift it away. 'May as well take a photo, though. I like to include something more creative in my assessments. They're a dull read, otherwise.' I'm trying to think about how I can bring the subject of Victor Hale into our conversation, though I'm loath to upset the atmosphere. Perhaps he won't think anything of it.

When I've taken a few shots, I show Ash the back of the camera. As he leans in, our eyes lock. There's a spark of something, though I'm not sure what.

'Nice,' he murmurs.

'You think so?'

'I do.'

His face is close to mine. I search it for meaning. He lets me. Then he says, 'Do you take a lot of photos?'

'In my job, yes.' I back away slightly. 'But not as a hobby. I don't have the flare.'

'This one looks okay.' He gestures at the screen.

'There's a big difference between an *okay* photo and what passes as exceptional. People can be okay at lots of things in this day and age, don't you think? We've got so much information to access, and teach ourselves.'

'True. I–'

He gets no further. He stares over my shoulder, then blinks twice. Someone is stomping towards us, calling his name.

Ash

In a morning full of possibility, Ria Lace's presence casts a long shadow. She's striding towards him, an animated silhouette but he recognises the voice.

'Mr Black. Mr Black,' she trills. 'I've been to the lodge, but no one is there. I really must talk to you.'

Cherie calls a goodbye. Ash was just about to bare a tiny facet of his soul. A sudden urge to tell her about his history diploma had come over him, her good opinion overcoming his fear of her credentials. And now she's gone.

He stares at Ria. There is a dishevelled look about her this morning, like she left her bed only minutes ago. Under her arm is a rolled-up newspaper, *The Gazette*, he thinks. 'I wasn't expecting you.' She is deserving of his flattened tone.

'Have you seen this?' She shakes out the paper and holds it in a considered way. On the front page is a photo of the chapel.

'No, but I can guess what it's about.'

'Can you really, Mr Black.' She narrows her eyes. 'I don't think you know the half of it.'

While he waits, tongue-in-cheek, she rants. There has been foul play in a council-run institution and it's not acceptable; the Black family have to take responsibility; his father specifically is to blame, as the terrible deed took place during the seventies. Her final comment gives Ash a jolt. Has the local rag really got hold of *dates*?

He reaches for the paper. 'Let me have a look at the article.' When she pulls in her chin, he mutters, '*Please.*'

It has taken a week for the chapel story to filter out. There isn't much detail, only that human remains have been found where they shouldn't be. The headline reads *Waking the Dead*.

'I'm wondering why you're trying to pin blame on my father,' Ash says as he thrusts the paper back at her. 'There's no mention of him.' He darts a glance. 'And anyway, why are you here? We haven't got an appointment. I said all I needed to when we last spoke.'

'Don't get shirty with me. I am, in effect, almost your boss.'

She pulls at the collar of her overcoat, clutching in a way that makes Ash think she is very cold. He cannot understand what she's talking about. If anyone is his boss, it's the chief of the borough council. Not Ria Lace, with her elevated sense of herself and her overuse of acronyms.

'You're far from being my boss, actually.' Ash pushes his hands into his pockets. 'Now, if you don't mind, I've got work to do. If you've got issues or comments about the chapel, direct them to the police.'

What he finds disconcerting is that she knows more than has been reported in the newspaper. Which means there is already *gossip* in the town. He thought the woman would be happy, in some kind of macabre way, about what has happened in the chapel; it's ammunition for diverting the focus of her proposed conversion in another direction: towards Cemetery Lodge. And now she is apologising.

'I'm not trying to pin the blame on your father,' she is saying. 'Forgive me if that's how I'm coming across. Could we talk inside for a few moments? It's rather bleak out here.'

Ash sighs. Communication with this woman is the last thing he needs, but he's loath to create any more problems for himself. He's never had issues with the borough council before, and if a *few moments* would smooth things over and get Ria Lace off his back, he can spare them. 'Okay. But can we not disturb my father. He'll be at his morning nap, and he can be a bit agitated if he doesn't get it.'

They walk together through the swirl of freezing fog. Ria talks awkwardly about Christmas and the latest council projects; her painful left ankle. Everything but the subject that is hanging between them, the proverbial *skeleton in the closet*. When Ash unlocks the front door of the lodge, she hangs about in the hallway while he checks that his father is not in the kitchen.

'We can talk in here,' he offers, beckoning her in. 'What was it you wanted, exactly?'

She embarks on a lengthy explanation about the integrity of council buildings. Ash tries to listen for the meaning beneath her words, and from what he can gather, she and her colleagues have been horrified to think that one of their properties has been so badly used. There is nothing new in what she is saying; it is fluff and waffle. Local councillors don't have a monopoly on revulsion at the chapel situation. Ash saw the skeletons; she hasn't mentioned that.

Finally she pauses and takes a deep breath. 'So, Mr Black, my point is, do I have an assurance that neither you nor your father have engaged in any wrongdoing. I must have your word.' She waits. 'Mr Black? Are you listening?'

He wants to tell her that he isn't. It's like being back at school. He remembers silently contradicting every piece of rubbish his teachers said, and wondering what their agenda truly was. There were one or two teachers whose opinion he valued, but they were mainly so condescending, he loathed them. This is how he's feeling about Ria Lace.

'From my point of view, there is nothing to hide.' Ash grimaces. 'I don't know about Dad. You've seen how he is. We mainly don't have access to his past.'

She scowls. 'I see.'

'Surely this is a matter for the police and not the council. I think I've said the same thing before, haven't I? They've interviewed my father, but found nothing of value.' Ash doesn't tell her that Hal is their prime suspect, as far as an elderly man with dementia can be.

'The police?' She coughs in a loud and exaggerated way. 'I want answers now. I want–'

Ash interrupts with an exaggerated sigh. 'There is *nothing* I can tell you about what's in my father's head. I'm really sorry to disappoint.' He thinks about adding *you can't always get what you want*, but makes a split-second decision to match her tone of superiority. 'If my father tells me anything, you'll be the last to know.'

The colour of Ria Lace's face has changed, from an angry pink to something more like sour cream. One hand clutches at the collar of her coat and the other pats her pocket. Without saying anything else, she flings herself out of the kitchen and slams the front door as she leaves. Ash stares at the garden, and tries to process what just happened. He can't. Instead, he creeps upstairs to check on his father, who is snoring softly in his armchair. His hands are in his lap and his feet are bare. This isn't the persona of a killer, Ash is certain. He closes the door quietly and heads outside.

As he follows the perimeter of the cemetery, Ash puts all thoughts of the chapel and Ria Lace from his mind. He has work to do. Monday mornings are the worst time for things being thrown over the wall. Mostly, it's glass bottles and beer cans, though there was once a mattress, stained and torn and far too heavy for him to lift on his own.

He's never been good at understanding what motivates people. His conclusion about the mattress was that for some people, out-of-sight is out-of-mind. And this leads him back to the bodies in the chapel. Cherie had let slip about the newspaper fragment. If the sacristy shelves had been lined with newspaper, it didn't necessarily mean it had been done when the bodies were put there. People lined their shelves with newspaper for other reasons, especially in latter days; he remembers Hal doing the same thing in their garden shed. The papers could have been there long before the bodies. If that wasn't the case, did the perpetrator mean to come back at another time and move them? Double access to the chapel? How was that possible without his father knowing something about it? Ash leans against the wall and takes a deep breath. Normally, the morning air clears his head and helps his focus; today it smells foetid.

When he's finished the perimeter checks and is heading to the compost bins with an armful of dead flowers, his phone rings. Not many people have his private number. There's the motorcycling gang he hangs out with sometimes, and they would know his working hours, as he does theirs. When he pulls the phone from the pocket of his overalls, the screen doesn't show a contact name. He clicks the green button and answers with trepidation. It is Ginny Beck. She wants him to attend the station at his earliest convenience. There are updates, she tells him. And he is to bring the rest of the logbooks pertaining to the 1970s. If needs be, she will send a car.

CHAPTER TWELVE

Cherie

As so often happens when a seed of doubt is planted, its roots and shoots grow thickly in unexpected directions. When I try to photograph the chapel roof, my mind is flooded with picture after picture of the ways the bodies might have got inside. Ash's father is in some of the pictures. If he was anything like Ash in terms of diligence, no break-in or disturbance would have gone unnoticed. So, unless the police turn up something in the remaining logbooks, only someone with access to the chapel could have placed the bodies there. Which is why bringing Victor Hale into the picture is important.

As if he has read my mind, Ash is striding towards me, shoulders tense, expression grave. 'Cherie,' he is calling. 'Cherie, have you got a minute. I need a favour.'

The uniformed officer standing guard raises her eyebrows. Her cheeks and nose are pink with cold.

'What's the problem?' I ask as Ash approaches. He is not the sort of person to look for favours, nor is he particularly gracious when they are given.

'I've to go and see Ginny Beck, apparently. She's *commanded* me.'

The officer coughs lightly. 'She's good at that.'

'And I've to take the rest of the logbooks,' he continues, 'so I can't pop over on my bike. They're sending a car.' He grits his teeth. 'You wouldn't keep an eye on Dad, would you? I'm not sure how long I'll be.'

'Course I will. Give me ten minutes to get the last of the photos, then I can work from your office and be around for Hal.'

His shoulders relax. 'Thanks so much.' He glances at the officer. 'How much longer have you got to stand there?'

'Me, personally?' She puts a hand on the chest area of her padded black jacket. 'Shift finishes at twelve. But this is still a place of interest to us, so we are protecting its integrity for the foreseeable.'

Her old-fashioned word usage surprises me: she can't be more than twenty-five.

'Ah, right.' Ash turns to me. 'Shall I meet you back at the lodge?' When I nod, he adds, 'I'm so grateful. Thanks.' Then he hurries away.

Once I've circled the area and photographed the differing roof lines, I nudge my way through the safety fence. Standing next to the chapel fills me with questions. In that respect, it is like so many problematic sites I've worked on. The difference here is due to a set of restrictions new to me: criminal law enforcement. I've been happy enough within civil restraints, listings, preservation orders; this situation is intriguing yet frustrating. There is nothing to stop me investigating layman-style, though, so that's what I'm going to do. Ginny Beck did imply I might be of some use in the future; that future is now.

At the lodge, Ash has already moved the boxes of 1970s logbooks into the hall. He's swapped his fluorescent jacket and overalls for clean jeans and a sweater. An anorak is in his hand.

'Thanks for doing this,' he says. 'The spare front door key is there, if anything happens and you need to go out.' He gestures towards a rack of hooks under a metallic sign that says *home*. 'It's the one with the flashy *A*.'

I can't see the key, but don't say anything, as he's clearly in a rush. His hair is neatly combed, grey streak shining. There are a few strays across his shoulders; I resist the urge to pick them off. We head to the kitchen.

'Make yourself a coffee or something.' He waves an arm at the kettle. 'Dad is in the garden, doing what he does. I'll have to wait out the front for the car.' He pats me lightly on the arm. 'We'll catch up later.'

I smile a goodbye. Once again, there is a tension to his movements, as though the world is currently not living up to his exacting standards. I take my camera to his office and flick on my laptop. From experience, I have learnt that downloading photographs needs to be done as soon as possible. I have taken more than a hundred, it seems. This is my first independent assessment and I want it to be on point.

When I have a quick look through the photos, it's interesting to see the chapel roof is in relatively good repair, considering the building hasn't been in use since 1962. Some of the slates are cracked and a few have moved slightly. Nothing that might cause alarm about water leaking in. Victorian buildings were made to stand the test of time. Ash said both he and his father had maintained the security of the building, as part of their routine. Did either of them have a reason for keeping the chapel in such an inconspicuous state? Gut instinct is something I've come to rely on heavily, and my gut is saying *no way*.

When I've finished the downloads, I head to the kitchen. It's almost noon, and part of my *keeping an eye on Hal* might mean making sure he is fed. From what Ash has told me, his father is capable of making a sandwich and heating up a pan of soup. He must miss having company through the day, though. During the solitary months of the pandemic lockdown, I'd missed human contact. How much worse must it feel to see it bleed from your life forever? I reach across the sink and knock on the window. In seconds, Hal comes into sight and gives me a wave.

There is a door leading from the kitchen to the rear garden. I close it behind me and walk through a tiny room that serves as a porch-come-scullery. It has a tiled floor and is very cold. There is a row of coat pegs and a boot bench, and a line of rusty hooks hung with even rustier keys. I remember Ash's assertion about the locked cabinet in his office. These keys match the condition of the chapel key, but can't be anything important; diligence seems to be the Blacks' middle-name. On the floor by the porch opening is a plastic tub full of bird food: seed, fat-balls and bags of peanuts. Hal is at the kitchen window, still peering.

'Hello,' I say. 'It's Cherie. Remember me?'

'Course I do. Our Ash said you'd be stopping by, and I was to make you some lunch.'

'Or I can make you some. I can see you're busy.'

He is holding an empty bird feeder. 'Do you like birds?'

'I do.'

He steps towards a pathway made from flagstones. It crosses a small lawn and ends at a concrete patio. Large trees overhang the area. Their lower branches are scattered with feeders similar to the one in Hal's hand. Two metal stands have been cemented into the ground. More feeders crown their tops. Someone has taken great care in creating this paradise for wild birds. Hal explains how Ash set everything up.

'That lad's a great son, you know. Couldn't wish for better.' He gives me a wink. 'He'll be a good fella for you, too, lass. Keep hold of him.'

I'm about to put him right when I realise he probably won't remember if I do. Instead, I ask him about the birds that visit the garden. He talks at length about the jackdaws that roost nearby, about their intelligence and canny ability to dominate the bird feeders.

'They're my favourites, if I'm honest,' he concludes. 'I'm sure they recognise me. They scarper if Ash is out here. When I'm by myself, they'll come down and even take peanuts from my hand. How about that?'

'Clever things,' I say. 'It's all about the food, is it?'

Hal doesn't answer, and I wonder if my turn of phrase has confused him. When I've thought about a way to make my joke clearer, he finds his voice again.

'They've an eye for other things, too. Apart from food.' He laughs to himself. 'We had a bit of a giggle one day, when our Ash was younger. One of them pesky buggers... them jackdaws, stole a bunch of keys from the porch.' He frowns. 'No. That's not right. I told our Ash, but it was before he–' He touches a finger to his forehead. 'I don't know. I'm not sure now. But they're pesky buggers, right enough.'

'Their eyes are strange,' I say, moving Hal back to the present. 'All silvery and staring. How many hang out in your garden?'

He doesn't answer. There's a vacant expression, as though our last few minutes of conversation have been wiped away. In his hand is the bird feeder I noticed earlier. He reaches up to a low bough and hooks it over. I catch his eye and smile.

'You're our Ash's friend,' he mutters. 'Have you come to make me some lunch?'

'I have. What would you like?'

Hal ignores the question. 'He's a good lad, our Ash. You hold on to him.' His voice crackles with emotion. 'I let mine go: my love. Worst mistake I ever made.'

It feels wrong to be quizzing this elderly man about the past. After a few minutes of conversation with Hal, I understand

Ash's dilemma. His father can present as sharp and in complete control, but his loss of *moments* can be frightening. The threadbare national health and social care services are unlikely to offer support when there is a carer coping so well. Which means father and son will be left to fend for themselves.

'Lunchtime,' I say in a sing-song voice. Hal is easily distracted. He mutters about having something more substantial than sunflower seeds on his plate, then follows me inside. What food to make for him isn't my biggest conundrum, though. What I really want to know is what happened to his wife, Ash's mother.

Ash

A high-pitched buzzing cuts across Ash's thoughts. The police driver glances at him over her shoulder.

'Sorry. Ignore that,' she says. 'It's radio interference. Despite us having state-of-the-art cars these days, not all the tech is flawless.' She presses a few buttons on the dashboard. 'That's an improvement.'

He gives a noncommittal nod. His focus isn't to give an evaluation of the transport; he wants to get home. Cherie will have been looking after his father for more than two hours. The poor woman has no connection to his family, yet this isn't the first time she's been stuck with its problems. Hopefully, Hal will have had some lunch and then gone to his bedroom for a nap. Ash is more than aware of how much the chapel assessment means as far as Cherie's work is concerned, she's made it very clear. The sooner the investigation is over, the better it will be for all of them. It has a stranglehold on his life, and he needs it to end.

The afternoon is fading to evening. As they travel along the main road through town, many houses and shopfronts are decorated with festive trees and glittering lights. Christmas is usually a quiet, sombre time at Cemetery Lodge. Even before his mother left, there had been little in the way of celebration. His parents seemed always to dislike each other, and when this was mixed with a few days of enforced happiness, the situation imploded. Now, he and his father cook a decent Christmas lunch and watch television together, and are ready to return to normality on Boxing Day.

Ash was given a lot of information at the police station. DNA taken from the skeletons has revealed they belonged to people of eastern European origin, an adult female and a female child. The child's sample is much more stable than the adult's. Their bodies have been lying in the chapel for between forty-five and fifty years. Cherie had been correct on both counts; he was looking forward to telling her. The early seventies logs have not been returned to him, though Ginny Beck had to concede there was nothing in them that hinted at a chapel break-in or anything else to raise suspicion. She is now in possession of the rest of the logbooks from that era. 1970s police records have been checked through and revealed no recorded crime in the cemetery, or missing persons reports. When he'd asked if it meant his father was off their radar, Ginny Beck's answer had been clear: Hal was high on their list of suspects, and would be likely to remain so. Dale Scott had looked on uneasily when this statement was delivered. Ash caught his eye and saw his shrug. If anything came to court, Hal wouldn't be fit to testify. Should Ginny Beck want to pin any kind of crime on his father, she'd better be sure of the evidence.

When the lodge comes into view, a flash of emotion moves through Ash's body and startles him. It's a mixture of relief to be home and gratitude because Cherie will be there waiting for him. There's something else, too: he wants to see her. Which is ridiculous, considering he hardly knows her, and she's so far above him it's likely to remain that way. But he does have news that might please her.

She is sitting in his office, staring at her laptop. 'Hello.' She looks up and smiles, finger to her lips. 'Your dad is asleep.'

'That's a relief,' Ash whispers, then gestures towards the hallway. 'Can we talk?'

'Course.'

She clicks a few buttons then follows him to the kitchen. While she sits at the table, he busies himself with making a sandwich and explaining all that Ginny Beck told him.

'I pretended you hadn't mentioned the newspaper fragments under the skeletons. I think her timeline is clear now, and her prime suspect is Dad.'

'That's ridiculous,' Cherie spits. She puts a hand over her mouth and feigns shock. 'Sorry. But it is. What evidence does she even have, nasty woman?'

Ash tries not to laugh. 'I agree. And that's not all.' He brings over his plate. 'She says you can visit the mortuary and view the remains, if you like. They are struggling to find a definitive cause of death; even the mortician. The *nasty woman* thought you might offer some insights.'

'Me?' Cherie's eyes widen. Her hand flies to her chest.

Ash lifts one shoulder. 'That's what Ginny said.'

'But I've no medical training.' She frowns. 'How odd.'

'You've looked at recovered skeletons in your job, haven't you?' He's guessing, and with it comes the realisation once again, that he knows very little about her.

'I have, but–' She hesitates, chewing at her thumbnail. 'We'll see. In the meantime, I have news.'

'Oh?' Ash resists the urge to look at his watch. There are some jobs that can't be left. He hasn't hoovered the inside of the crem building for a couple of days. The last thing mourners want to experience is a scruffy reception hall.

'Yes. I've located Victor Hale. The clergyman who led services in the crematorium during the 1970s.'

'He's alive?'

'In a nursing home. If it's the right Victor Hale. Does your dad never mention him? They were together a lot, according to the logbooks.'

Ash stares at his teacup. 'Dad never mentions anyone from his past. He hardly has access to it, as you know.'

'I do know.' Cherie drops her voice. 'Sorry.'

Ash wipes his mouth and gets up from the table. 'It's late,' he says. 'There are things I ought to do before it's completely dark outside. Thanks for looking after Dad. I'll be backwards and forwards now, so you should be able to get on with your work.'

The last thing he wants to do is dredge up people from Hal's past. None kept in touch with him once he was diagnosed with dementia; none sought him out or checked up on him. Not that Ash has ever heard him mention Victor Hale. Hal had married in 1980 and there is never a word about it, never mind someone he worked with in the seventies. The past unsettles Ash's father; the present is all he's got.

Cherie takes the hint. She carries their cups and the teapot across to the sink. 'I'd like to visit this Victor Hale,' she says suddenly. 'If you wouldn't mind?'

Ash's stomach lurches. He's not sure how to react to her request. There's nothing he can say to stop her, and why would he? 'You're just going to rock up to whichever nursing home he's in and ask to see him? That's not how it works.' His patronising tone is fuelled by a flare of anger. Does this woman think she's a detective or something? If Victor Hale has family, they'd be infuriated, as Ash would be. 'It's hardly up to me, is it? But if you want my opinion, don't.'

She turns to face him. 'I thought you wanted to help your dad. You're the one who said the police aren't making progress. That they're treating Hal like their prime suspect.'

Ash snaps. 'You people are all the same. Thinking you understand everything, *know* everything. Let me decide what's best for my father; leave the police to investigate crime: it's their job. You'd best get on with yours.'

Cherie doesn't say anything else. She rinses their cups, then dries her hands on a tea towel, which she folds very neatly and deliberately. Ash can't find the right words to apologise for his outburst. He stands aside when she marches past him, out of the kitchen and into the hallway. Within seconds, he hears the front door slam.

His reactions are becoming uncontrollable. The more Cherie does for him, the worse they are getting. It's like he's an oppositional child, kicking back against constraints; making everything about himself. She can visit Victor Hale if she's a mind to, he can hardly stop her. The truth is, Ash is worried about what she might discover.

Hal

Hal is dumbstruck. He is not one for portents, and certainly has no faith to speak of, but the moment needs a herald. Something monumental is happening. Victor Hale: a name like no other; it stirs his heart.

They step into the reception area. Hal has painted it recently, retouched the walls in magnolia emulsion and glossed the tatty skirting. Victor casts around and smiles. His eyeteeth protrude slightly. It gives him a wolfish look. Hal's knees tremble. The new vicar has perfect manners, with impeccable diction, lacking northern twang or hard edges. In the office, he places his briefcase on the desk and requests coffee. It wouldn't have mattered if his request had been to spin straw into gold, Hal would have found a way. When they touch their mugs together, Victor salutes the future. He has plans. Whatever they are, Hal will fall in with them. This man has netted him as surely as if he were a fisherman with the most irresistible bait.

They talk of things Hal can only imagine. Victor has travelled. His descriptions of far-flung places, of warm white sand and jade-green seas, of mountains capped in snow and trees loaded with cherry-blossom, leave Hal breathless. He is an ordinary man; in Victor's presence he feels treasured.

CHAPTER THIRTEEN

Cherie

It has taken three days for the effects of Ash's anger to hit. Those words, flung in the most bitter tone, cut deep: *You people are all the same.* In some sense, he sounded like David. I can only conclude that there is some truth in what is said. I lean back in my seat and stare out of the carriage window. Whatever Ash Black might think of me for *getting involved*, I am heading in the direction of Victor Hale.

The morning is crisp and clear, with an eternal blue sky. The train is in no hurry to cross the estuary. I waited until after rush hour to make my journey, so there are very few fellow passengers. This route follows the west coast of Cumbria, with views across the Irish Sea and north towards Scotland. The trip should feel relaxing, but I'm grinding my teeth. The more I think about my treatment at Cemetery Lodge, the crosser I get. I've been nothing but accommodating, looking after Ash's father and helping in a police investigation that is nothing to do with me.

A more honest assessment would be connected to my

feelings: I was growing to like Ash and Hal. Now, I will have to collect my equipment and move out of the lodge. In the meantime, I am going to help Ginny Beck, and find out something about this Victor guy. There is little chance of me being admitted to Marsh House. The onus on these homes to keep their residents safe, especially since the pandemic, is heavy-duty. If I make it to the front door, it will be a bonus. What my training and the years of my job have taught me is that asking questions, however banal they might seem, often turns up something interesting. It is where I'm going to start.

I leave the train at the tiny station in Silecroft. It's in the middle of the village, and according to my trusty Google Maps, Marsh House is about a mile away, towards the beach. I slip my arms through the straps of my backpack and set off at a pace.

Silecroft is a higgledy-piggledy mix of whitewashed cottages and sandstone farm barns, similar to Biggar, where I encountered Ash and his motorcycling friends. He'd seemed so amiable on that occasion, relaxed and smiling. I shake away the thought. His dislike of what he thinks is my status would always cause a fracture in any shared understanding we reached. He's attractive but locked away in the same place as David, unfortunately.

Marsh House is a pleasant surprise. My Google search had shown the place as a dismal stone mansion with a backdrop of scrubby fells. In reality, the stonework is clean and sharply dressed, and the windows gleam. Sunshine transforms the fellside to a patchwork of vibrant greens and ochre bracken; a Christmas tree stands on the driveway.

As I peer through the wrought-iron gates, a woman comes towards me. 'Can I help you?' she asks. She has the ruddy complexion of someone who's outside a lot. Her hair is wild and blonde and held back with a paisley neckerchief.

'I was just looking at the house,' I reply, my mental list of white lies primed and ready for action. 'I've an old uncle who is wanting a placement. We've checked out Marsh House on Google and he loves it.'

I wonder if this woman is a gardener. She is wearing a khaki anorak over what look like salopettes in a similar colour. Her boots are clogged with mud. 'Do you have an appointment?' She rubs her hands on her thighs, then pulls back one of the gates. 'I'm Debbie, by the way. The owner's sister.'

'Hello, Debbie.' I give her my best smile. 'And, no. I don't have an appointment. The gardens are beautiful. Are they your responsibility?' I cast my eyes towards her boots. 'Just a wild guess.'

'They are.' Debbie surprises me by lifting my hand. 'Do I sense a fellow digger?'

I frown quizzically. 'What makes you say that?'

'State of those.' She points to my nails, then laughs. It is rich and hearty and makes me respond in the same way.

'I'm only teasing,' she says breathlessly. 'But you're wearing a Fjällräven jacket. Sure sign of an archaeologist.'

I'm about to disagree with her, then I realise she is still joking.

'Uncanny,' I say instead.

'Unkind of me,' she replies. 'I shouldn't be so judgemental. Would you like a cup of tea or something? You look cold.'

'Not in this jacket.' I give her a cheeky lift of my brows. 'And you're so right about the archaeology. Digging is in my blood. I'd love a cup of tea, by the way.' We shake hands, fingertips first. 'I'm Cherie, in case you were wondering, Cherie Hope.'

'As in *sherry*? The drink?'

'As in sherry, the drink. Though it's not spelt like that.'

I walk with Debbie along the drive. She points out various plants in the borders and talks about her plans for spring planting. Around the side of the house is a huge glass structure. It has been built in the old-fashioned way, to resemble an orangery, with a latticework of painted wood and panes. The inside is warm and tidy. Shelves of planted-up trays edge the space, and at the far end is a workbench with tucked stools.

'Have a seat,' Debbie says. 'I'll put the kettle on.' She disappears into what looks like a small cubicle. I hear water being run and cups knocking together. She pokes her head through the doorway again and asks if I take milk and sugar. It's a pleasant interlude and good to be out of the cold, but it doesn't get me any nearer to Victor Hale.

When we are basking in the filtered warmth of the sun and sipping our tea, I ask for more information about Marsh House. Debbie is happy to tell me about her brother, who runs the place, and has done for the past ten years.

'We don't take many residents,' she says. 'Since the blasted lockdown, we have to be so careful. Our folk need nursing care but there's nothing wrong with their brains. We're aiming for a *family feel*, rather than an institution. Hence the name: Marsh House.' She's quiet for a moment, then adds, 'This uncle of yours. Is he sharp?' She taps her forehead. 'Up here, I mean. If not, this isn't the place for him.'

'Oh, yes. He's sharp.'

'Might be worth getting in touch with my brother then, and getting an appointment. He'd show you round. And your uncle, if you like. Is he mobile?'

I've heard of lies spiralling out of control, and it's happening now. I try to stop the spiralling.

'Not really,' I say. But I'm also aware that our pleasant banter isn't getting me the information I want. 'He's got spinal problems and has almost lost his independence. He wants to come here because he's heard an old friend of his is one of your residents. My uncle isn't coping very well with his solitary life.'

'Shame. Are you both local?'

Debbie hasn't picked up on my comment about the *old friend*, so I reinforce it. 'We're kind of local.' I thumb towards an insubstantial south. 'From Barrow. His friend came from there, too. My uncle is dying to be reunited with him.'

'Yes, you said.' She drains the rest of her tea. 'So, who is he then? This friend of your uncle's?'

'Victor Hale. I guess you know him.'

'Not know, exactly. I don't get involved with the residents to that extent. But yes. Vic the vic, he calls himself.'

A burst of adrenaline shoots through my body. This has got to be the same guy. For a single second, I think about not telling Debbie any further lies. I already like her, and she doesn't deserve to be treated in such a shoddy manner. But I have to know.

'That's him,' I say with a smile. 'A local clergyman, wasn't he? That's how he and my uncle became friends. They worked together.'

'So I guess *unc* is a vicar, too?' Debbie picks up my cup and moves towards the cubicle. 'Another?' She glances at her watch. 'I've just about got time. Before the dreaded Duncan is on my case.' She laughs to herself. 'That's my brother, by the way.'

'I'd better not take any more of your time, then.' I get up from my stool. 'I have a bossy sibling, so I know what it's like.'

'No worries. I can handle mine.' She holds up my cup. 'Yes or no?'

'Go on then.' I gesture towards the shelves of seed trays. 'Then you can tell me all about what you do here. I almost became a gardener myself, you know.'

'But you liked the archaeologist outfits more?' She ducks into the cubicle.

There is something about Debbie. The woman has no need to offer me kindness, no need to be interested. I want to tell her the truth of my quest to find out about Victor Hale. If it comes up in the future, I'd hate her to think of me as a liar. We spend a pleasant half hour touring the glass house, joking about the snobbish tiers of academia. She studied at Myerscough College, but never thought her gardening qualification would amount to anything, particularly in the face of her brother's sociology degree.

'It's not that we don't get on,' she says. 'But he can be so high-and-mighty about who did and didn't go to university. Why the hell it matters, I don't know. There are some insecure people about.'

I'm reminded of Ash and his scathing comments. On the surface, he doesn't seem to have insecurities; perhaps I've made a misjudgement.

'My ex-husband being one of them,' I tell her, surprising us both. Debbie doesn't miss a beat.

'It's men, then. I could have told you that but didn't want to seem narrow-minded.' She tuts. 'Sorry.'

'Not all men. My boss is extremely supportive of everything I do. He appreciates my qualifications, but never uses them against me.'

Debbie gives me an appreciative nod. 'Now that's a guy who'll go far.'

'He's great.' There is a beat of silence between us. I feel like it's time I moved on. 'Thanks so much for the tea and chat. Does your brother have a card or something? Or a flyer for Marsh House? I'd like to show my uncle. He struggles to view things on a screen.'

'Sure. If you meet me round the front of the house, I'll see if Dunc has time to say hello.'

Debbie disappears down a thin pathway to the side of the glasshouse. I hadn't expected to find an ally at the nursing home. Especially not one who has swallowed every deceitful word I've told her. It won't be happening again. Now I know Victor Hale is still alive, I can share that information with the police and be done with it.

As I wander past the side of the house, I peep in through a large window. Lunch must be in full flow because there are a few elderly folk seated around circular tables, people wearing tabards moving between them. Plates are lifted, beakers filled. The ambience is relaxed and jovial. If I had an elderly uncle, he would love the place.

Debbie comes through the front door just as I arrive. With her is an older man. His hair is also wild and blond, but his navy-blue jumper and shirt collar mark the difference between him and his sibling. He is holding a large brown envelope.

'This is Duncan,' Debbie calls. 'Duncan Soames. I'm Debbie Soames, I forgot to say. Never did marry.' She gestures towards me. 'This is Cherie, Dunc.'

'Hello, Cherie.' He holds out the envelope. 'Pleased to hear that you're considering Marsh House. We don't have vacancies right now, but I can put you on our list.'

I'm not sure what to say to this. Being on a list would move my actions from despicable to fraudulent, and that was never my intention. I take the envelope.

'Let me talk to my uncle first,' I say. 'He can be a bit up and down.'

'Of course.' Duncan smiles pleasantly. 'Debs said your relative had a friend here. Our Victor. That's a lovely coincidence, isn't it?'

I nod. 'Thanks for this.'

'That's not a problem, my dear. Should I remember your uncle to Victor? He's as sharp as a tack and twice as bossy. He'd probably love to hear a name from his past. Not that he's short of visitors or anything. He has a lot of family. They're always here. He's quite a character, that's for sure.'

I'm trapped. If I name my fictional uncle as Hal Black, someone might sniff out my subterfuge; if I make up a false name, Victor Hale will not recognise it. My instinct is to tell the truth.

'My uncle's name is Hal Black,' I say. 'He'd love to catch up with Victor again. Anyway. Thanks for all your help.' I glance at Debbie and smile. 'Nice to meet you. I hope we can talk again, one day.'

'Let me have your number,' she says. 'Just in case.'

I think about giving a fake one. I'm already regretting the lies I have told. In the end, I tear a corner from the flap of the envelope and write down the landline number of Gillside. She thanks me. Before there can be any further conversation, I turn around and stride purposefully down the drive. I've a train to catch, after all. What Debbie or Duncan Soames won't realise, as they wave me off, is that my brain is zinging with possibilities: Victor Hale has family. If I could track them down and talk, what stories might they have to tell?

Ash

The day is clear as a diamond, but it doesn't lift Ash's mood. He hasn't slept well. The way he'd treated Cherie, the words he had thrown so bitterly, are playing non-stop in his head.

He is finding it difficult to understand his reactions. Explaining it away as a rise in his anxiety levels because of the upheaval in his life, seems too easy; he's usually good at handling stressful situations. When his father was first diagnosed, Ash had been the calm one. He had to be; there was nobody else. His implication, when he'd last seen Cherie, was that she'd taken on the persona of a *know-it-all*. The arrogance of this remark far outweighs any conceit on her part. She hasn't been near Cemetery Lodge since he'd made such an idiot of himself. He's expecting a phone call arranging to collect her things. A visit is unlikely.

He lifts the handles of his wheelbarrow and pushes it down the slope towards the shed. The car park has been gritted in readiness for the funeral happening this morning. A few mourners have arrived already, perhaps wanting to make certain they could get a seat in the crem building. One of the town dignitaries is being sent on his way, and Ash has been informed that there may be an attendance of more than 200. He wants everything to be perfect. Yesterday's bouquets have been cleared and the florist came in early. She has created a beautiful arc of silk flowers around the front door. Something caught at the back of Ash's throat when he saw it. He's never reacted like that before.

By the time he's put the wheelbarrow away and picked up the last pieces of litter, the car park is almost full. A queue of smartly dressed people winds around the perimeter of the crem. They huddle together, speaking quietly or staring at their phones.

Ash keeps himself at a respectful distance, helping cars to find a space and directing others away. It's a chaotic and tricky business, but it stops him thinking too much. When there's a lull in arrivals, he takes a moment to stretch out his back and survey the scene. Something is happening at the cemetery gates, just in front of the lodge. A crowd has gathered. They don't look like mourners.

Ash jogs down the slope, passing more sombre-faced people, dipping his head in respect. His heart is hammering against his ribs. Could something have happened to Hal? Has he got outside and onto the main road?

There is a white van, parked on the roadside outside the

lodge. Behind it are two cars, nose-to-tail. One has a BBC logo on the side. At the same time Ash realises what is happening, a woman approaches. She is small, with a wide grin and a yellow raincoat. What looks like an old-fashioned tape recorder is slung over her shoulder and she is carrying a microphone.

'Do you work here?' The grin widens. She eyes his high-vis jacket. 'By any chance?'

'I do. What's going on?' He tries to keep his tone even, but there's an anger rising. This is someone's funeral, not a soap-opera.

'We're running a story on the skeletons in the chapel. Can you give us some background?'

Beyond the van, a group of people have gathered. One has a dog on a leash. They watch as two men set up a camera and tripod. A third man is wearing a headset and carrying a black case. All three have jackets with the BBC logo.

Ash can't believe what he is hearing. 'Have you asked permission to run this story?' He's fighting to hold on to his *caretaker* persona, but it's slipping from his shoulders as easily as a loose coat.

The woman smirks. 'We don't need permission, sir.'

'From the police, I mean. Have you even mentioned it to them?' Ash is aware that the media have certain freedoms, especially if reporting a story is in the public interest. This one isn't, surely.

The woman ignores his question. 'I take it you're the janitor or something. Is there anything you can give us about what has happened in the–' She gestures towards the top of the cemetery. 'It was an old chapel, wasn't it? Where they were found.'

Ash glances at his watch. Within ten minutes, the hearse will be arriving. It will be followed by a car transporting the family of the deceased. The last thing they will expect to see is a film crew at the cemetery gates. The final threads of his temper snap. 'Unless you and your cronies step away,' he cries, 'I'm going to telephone the police. And they will respond; I guarantee it.'

'Do it,' the woman says, a half smile on her lips. 'I want to do a piece about them appealing for witnesses. As far as I've heard, they're getting nowhere with the investigation, anyway. They might appreciate a bit of publicity.'

Ash heads to the lodge. He has Ginny Beck's number on a card. If he can contact the woman, she'll have the authority to get something done about this media circus. It'll be quicker than telephoning the police directly. He knows this to his cost. Since the pandemic, money and resources have fallen away from public services: the last time he'd reported anti-social behaviour, the police had turned up five days later.

Hal is dozing in his favourite armchair. A newspaper is lying across his knees. Ash finds Ginny Beck's card and punches out the numbers on the landline handset. It doesn't take long for her to answer. She is not happy. It's Ash's comment about an appeal for witnesses that sends her over the edge of polite anger into seething rage. She breaks off their conversation with a promise to be at the cemetery gates, *all guns blazing*. What she means by this, Ash isn't quite sure, but it's a highlight in the solemnity of the day. Cherie would love it.

While he waits, Ash directs the funeral cortege by standing deliberately in front of the film crew and disrupting their work. The woman in the yellow jacket is still smiling, and he wonders if it is a prerequisite of her job; a smiling assassin. The atmosphere is thrumming with excitement. The gathered crowd has grown, catching the scent of something. A dog barks. If Ash was expecting flashing lights and blaring sirens, he isn't disappointed. Ginny Beck arrives in an unmarked police car, but it has a stick-on blue light and a high-pitched wailing alarm which makes the public cover their ears.

She hauls herself out of the car and storms towards him. 'Who's in charge of this *crew*,' she shouts, grasping at her swinging lanyard. Dale Scott is behind her, jaw tense.

Ash casts towards the woman in yellow. 'Her, I think.'

While Ginny strides across the scene, Dale comes to rest at Ash's side. 'All right, matey,' he says. 'It's not good this, is it?'

'No.' Ash has a long list of questions for this man. He settles on one. 'I need to ask you something, Mr Scott, if it's not too cheeky.' He waits for Dale's full attention. 'Did the logs turn anything up?' He raises his eyebrows. 'So to speak?'

'Ha, ha. Nice one, mate.' Dale pushes his hands into the pocket of his suit trousers. 'Sorry. That was flippant of me. Is that the right word? Flippant? Better ask your clever girlfriend, eh?'

'If you mean Cherie, she's not my girlfriend.'

Dale sighs loudly. 'Sorry again. And there's no joy with the logs. The boss has already concluded that whoever put those bodies in the chapel had access to the keys. The logs haven't changed her opinion.'

Ash wants to mention the name Cherie has come up with, Victor Hale, but something stops him. Better not to alert the police to an innocent man. Instead, he asks about the bracelet. Dale gives a sketchy response, once again.

'Those things were ten-a-penny in the seventies, boss says. And anyway, we have a pretty good idea of the ethnicity of the bodies. The bracelet adds nothing.'

'Other people had access to the chapel,' Ash reminds him. 'Other than the caretakers, I mean.'

Dale shakes his head. 'Think about it. The crem opened in 1962; that's when the chapel closed. It stayed closed right through the seventies and beyond. Whoever placed the bodies did it after 1972, but within a short timeframe.' Ash finds his insinuation slightly creepy. 'With no sign of any disturbance, break-ins or anything else, keys must have been used to get inside; *keyholders* must have known.'

'So you're convinced my dad had something to do with it. Thanks for the heads-up.'

'Don't shoot the messenger, matey.' Dale holds up his hands. 'The boss is pushing that. I'm a bit more open-minded. But you don't get to argue with her.' He winks. 'If you know what I mean. And here she comes.'

Ginny rubs her hands together in a gesture like she's cleaning them. Ash finds it immature. This woman seems to think she runs the world.

'That's put a stop to things,' she spits. 'They're packing up now. I've told them quite clearly that no story will run unless they get my say-so. The last thing we want are public do-gooders phoning in with stupid anecdotes about what they thought they saw or remembered fifty-odd years ago.'

To Ash, this is exactly what they *should* want, but he won't mention it. Keeping Ginny Beck on-side is important. Hal's name needs to be removed from her list of suspects. From what Dale has said, there doesn't seem to be anyone else *on* the list at this point, but she has nothing substantial to keep Ash's father pinned there.

'I could give you access to earlier and later logbooks,' Ash offers. 'There might be something.'

'I'll have that eventually, yes, Mr Black.' Ginny is distracted. She has hardly looked at him. He wonders if it might be appropriate to mention the name Cherie came up with.

'There is one thing, but you've probably picked up on it anyway.' He doesn't say anymore until she gives him full attention. Dale Scott is peering at him, too.

'A name, that's all,' he continues. 'Cherie noticed it coming up in the 1971 logs. My father wrote them, of course. But from the January of that year, he seemed to mention a man called

Victor Hale rather more than he needed to. A Reverend Victor Hale.'

Ginny's reaction isn't what he expects. She narrows her eyes, and moves her face close to his, so that he can see the catch of flesh-coloured make-up in her pores.

'I know what you're doing,' she says, her tone sharp enough to cause fear. 'Finding random names in the logbooks. And you can tell Cherie Hope to mind her own business. She shouldn't even be snooping.' Ginny pulls her head back. 'And here's another piece of news for you. I want to question your father again. He's the key to this investigation, you mark me.'

Hal

It has taken a death to bring life back into Hal's existence. His aunt has died and given him an excuse to be an attendee at one of Victor Hale's funeral services in the crem. He is waiting at the door of the reception area, immaculate in a dark suit and snowy-white clerical collar. Hal has to make do with his smartest corduroy trousers and a navy-blue blazer with brass buttons. He has worn a roll-necked pullover as his shirts never look clean. The weekly laundrette trip has moved to monthly, and he has even thought about installing a twin tub. Nothing seems important compared to finding ways into Vic Hale's galaxy: he is the sun.

Hal waits in the queue to shake the vicar's hand. Though people have come to mourn the passing of Hal's aunt, she is not the focus of their attention. Men and women, young and old, even a child, wait for a crumb of Victor Hale's attention. None look embarrassed, none leave the line. The personal touch will be worth it.

When Hal approaches, his thighs feel shaky. Victor is welcoming everyone, his tone low and smooth. He has an extra beam of attention for some people. They get a hand along their forearm, as though they are about to be pinioned and swallowed whole.

The hearse has pulled up in front of the swing doors. Only a few remain in the queue. Victor murmurs an instruction, and they move together into the main area. It is nothing like the inside of a proper church. It has lines of beechwood chairs that face towards what Hal always thinks of as a stage, complete with a microphone on a stand. A stained-glass window featuring a stylised dove casts a bluish-white glow. There is no evidence of anything religious, though there is a wooden cross that can be wheeled in if requested. It is at the front today.

Victor gives Hal what he classes as a special smile, then leads the bearers down the aisle. They lay his aunt's coffin on a pull-down dais. There are no flowers. As far as he can remember, this lady had never married and there was certainly no wealth attached to her life. He hardly recognises the relatives in attendance, and doesn't feel like one himself. The chance to hear Victor preaching is the only reason Hal is here.

The service is perfect, the delivery exquisite. Victor's voice is deep and melodious, his sympathies heartfelt. Hal closes his eyes and lets the sound lift him away from the mundane aspects of his life. This man has a gift. It inspires devotion. And he has agreed to visit Cemetery Lodge.

CHAPTER FOURTEEN

Cherie

The early morning sky is grey and heavy with rain. I hurry up the high street towards the Gillside office, peering into shop windows, hoping it's not too early to buy a newspaper.

Local gossip is an insidious but useful entity: I'd heard on the tendrils of social media about the scuffle between police and a television crew at the gates of the cemetery earlier in the week. I want to read about it myself. *The Gazette* is running a story, apparently. Ash must have been involved. Nothing happens at his place of work without him knowing. If this principle is applied to his father, it is transformed into a thread linked to the past. Pull the thread and it will tug out answers to the chapel mystery. Which is why I want to speak with Ash again, to tell him about Marsh House and Victor Hale. The sensible voice in my head is saying *don't bother*.

The only newsagents I find open has sold out of yesterday's *Gazette*. I buy a packet of local Christmas cards instead, not because I send them but because I feel awful about walking out with nothing. I chat about the weather with the young woman behind the counter, then flip up my hood and head outside.

Bill is unlocking the front door of the office as I arrive. 'Morning,' he says. 'You must have caught the *early* early train.'

'I caught the bus, actually. Picked it up on the main road.'

He gives me a sideways glance. 'Two-mile-walk before seven o'clock. You must be more unsettled than I thought.'

'Why are you saying that?' I slip off my coat and shake away the raindrops. 'Anyway, you've hardly seen me.' What I don't tell him is that he has it exactly right. What happened with Ash has left me troubled and edgy. Not least because my equipment is still at the lodge, and I need it back.

Bill interrupts. 'I'm talking about the whole situation: finding the skeletons then not being allowed to follow through. I'd find it difficult and I'm way past the springtime of my digging days.'

I try a sarcastic laugh, but it comes out as hysteria. 'That sounds like a line from a bad rock song.'

'Perhaps,' he replies flatly. 'But I'm right though, aren't I?'

'It doesn't matter either way. I'm not going back to the chapel any time soon. Let's just say I was more of a hindrance than a help.' I smile through gritted teeth. 'So, can we get the coffee on and look at what needs doing this week. I hate to be idle.'

We move adeptly around each other, firing up computers, riffling through post. I'd like to tell Bill more about what happened between Ash and me, but we don't have that kind of relationship. He knows about David and the hostile end to our marriage; he's offered words of support. I can hardly ask Bill if he thinks I really am *intellectually arrogant*, though. My view of how I behaved around Ash and his father doesn't match how they responded. Perhaps I ought to base my assessment on Hal's reaction, not his son's. Either way, I'm probably best out of it. That thought leaves a strangely hollow feeling in the pit of my stomach.

'Someone has left a message on the answer-machine.' Bill's voice cuts across my thoughts. 'A publican from over on the island. Darren something-or-other.'

Bill has my full attention now. 'Play it back, would you?' I lift my coffee cup and move to sit beside him. We listen. As promised, Darren Thompson, alias the Daz I met at Biggar, has been talking to his neighbour, the elderly man he named as Jakka. The wife he mentioned was indeed a traveller, and she left the clan to marry him. Her maiden name was Lovell, and her family continued to come to the site at Biggar until council bylaws drove them away. What I find more interesting is that the Lovells then set their sights on an area of Morecambe, and still have a semi-permanent pitch there.

'Mellishaw Park. I've heard of that,' Bill says as he flicks off the machine. He scratches at his chin and frowns. 'Let me think. There was an article about a traveller community on the local news. During the second lockdown, if I remember rightly – you know how we all watched too much telly back then. I recall they wanted a safe site in the north-west. Lancashire County Council set aside the park for them, but I don't think residents nearby were happy.' He pauses. 'Not sure how it ended. Google it.'

I do, and it doesn't take long. What I find out is that Mellishaw Park is a designated traveller area now. And it is in Morecambe, about forty miles away. My scalp prickles with anticipation; I want to visit, armed with the name *Lovell*, and the information I have about the chapel skeletons.

'Any joy?' Bill calls from across the room.

'Plenty. I'm going to visit this Mellishaw Park.' When his expression slides, I add, 'On my own time, of course.'

'No, I didn't mean that. Should you not just go to the police with what you've found out? If they haven't already discovered it themselves?'

I lean my chin on my hand and sigh. He's right, though there's nothing tangible yet, like there is with Victor Hale. What I really want to do is have a discussion with Ash. The whole point of my interest is to put a protective screen around his father. The one thing we agreed on is that Hal would not have been involved in anything illegal.

'Can you drive me over to Cemetery Lodge,' I say to Bill. 'I need to check on my gear.'

'Oh, really?' He gives an exaggerated nod. 'I thought you were never going there again.'

'Never say never.' I click off my computer. 'I am going to complete this chapel assessment, even if it kills me.'

Bill gets up. 'The council have already paid their fee, so it's hardly urgent.'

'It is to me.'

He sighs. 'Okay. Get your coat.' He pats the pocket of his trousers. The car keys jangle.

We drive to the edge of town, and divert to a road that skirts the coast. The *picturesque route*, Bill calls it. While he chats about the vista, and the landmarks obscured by today's grimy weather, I nod and smile, but my attention is elsewhere.

Ash will be working in the cemetery somewhere. It will be a simple case of finding him. Then I'll have to tread very carefully with regards to the words I use. There can be no moving forward with what I've found without his agreement; I've enough sense to realise that. What I won't accept is that Ash feels the same about me as David did. Perhaps when I share the news about Mellishaw Park and the Lovells, Ash will give me some leeway.

Bill drops me at the cemetery gates. All is quiet. As I walk up the drive towards the lodge, a car swishes past, headlights flaring, illuminating raindrops. If there's to be a cremation, Ash will be around somewhere, making things tidy. When I reach the crematorium, the place is in darkness. The car has parked, the driver still inside. It is raining heavily. I flip up the hood of my jacket and make a dash for the chapel. The police presence has gone. Around the perimeter, the safety fence has been secured with warning signs to potential trespassers. A few weeks ago, I'd been one. My only explanation is that I'm a compulsive scholar of old buildings and the chapel had snagged my interest even before I'd seen it. In the dank gloom of the morning, it has become more than just interesting; it's eerie.

I walk around the front. The main door has been resealed with the old padlock and new chains, and further warning signs. I can only presume the activity on social media, the messaging from Cumbria police, has been enough to warn people off. That, and the worry of hanging round in a cemetery, snooping.

The chapel has an aura; I can sense it. It is created for me by the thought of those two bodies, a woman and child, lying hidden for so long. Then there's the picture I have of Victor Hale: charismatic clergyman and possible murderer. What was the story of these three people? What, if anything, bound them together?

My archaeologist's brain is working overtime, weaving together every thread of evidence, hoping the fabric will be revealed. Did something grisly happen inside the chapel which resulted in death, or were the bodies dragged here under cover of darkness? And did Hal Black have a part to play? The thought gives me an edge of nerves. I close my eyes and inhale deeply, trying to distract my jangling brain.

Above the silence, I can hear footsteps, very light, to my left. I spin round. It's Ash.

Ash

She is in silhouette when he first sees her. The murk of the day has been pressing heavily on his shoulders, but now he is lifted.

'Cherie,' he calls. 'Fancy meeting you here. I'm starting to think you're a serial snooper.'

She smiles and holds up her hands. 'You've got me.'

Ash has so many things he wants to explain, but he's never been good with those kinds of words. His essay writing was praised when he was a student, but no one on his course knew how many drafts he'd deleted before he was happy. He wishes he could do that now, delete the previous happenings with Cherie, the unkind words he'd used. Instead he tells her about the big funeral earlier in the week, and about his argument with Ginny Beck.

'And she's threatened to interview Dad again,' he says. 'Can you believe it?'

They walk away from the chapel, towards the lodge. He wants to ask Cherie in. He was heading back to check on Hal, but hesitates over mentioning the pilot case and equipment in his invitation. Would she think he wanted rid of it – and her?

'I can believe anything of that woman,' she is saying. 'She's got a bee in her bonnet about your dad, that's for sure. Did you agree to her demands?'

Ash shakes his head sadly. 'What can I do? It's not a *thing*, is it, to refuse the police.'

'It is, if you think your dad isn't up to it.'

'You've seen him, Cherie. What do you think?'

While he waits for an answer, he slides his gaze sideways. Some of her hair has escaped from the hood of her jacket and is sticking to her cheeks. She is biting her bottom lip.

'He presents as an elderly man with nothing wrong,' she says. 'I'll grant you that. But if you have a longer conversation with him, he talks on a loop, says the same things many times. That's when you realise.' She catches his eye. 'Sorry if that sounds harsh.'

'No. You have it exactly right.' Ash pushes his hands into the pockets of his fluorescent jacket. Rain is dripping down the back of the collar. 'I'm soaked. Do you want to come in for a drink?' He gestures towards the lodge. 'I've got a bit of time. We can talk some more.'

Cherie gives him a wry smile. 'Go on then.'

Once they are inside, Ash hangs their coats in the porch and takes off his work boots. He wants to confide in Cherie, wants to bring up his overreaction the last time they met, but she is chattering into the space like she's more nervous than he is. When she asks after Hal, he reminds her that his father likes to have a snooze before his midday meal, and he'll probably be in his sitting room with the fire banked up. When Cherie comes back from checking, she is holding her finger to her lips.

'He's a creature of habit,' she whispers. 'Which is lucky for you. It's admirable, the way you deal with him.'

Ash doesn't have time to respond before she's covering her comment with an explanation. 'Sorry. I'm sounding patronising again, aren't I?' She lifts the kettle, and he nods. With her back to him, she continues. 'I know you think I'm an arrogant academic, but I'm not. Honestly. I'm very ordinary.'

'That sounds as bad.' He laughs lightly. 'It's not you, Cherie, it's how I see things. No way do I think you're anything other than you are.' He lifts two mugs from the cupboard. 'I guess I've got a chip on my shoulder – if we're talking in clichés.'

'Well, as long as you realise I'm not one of *those people*: you know, the ones you accused me of being. Whatever they are.'

'I don't even know. I'm sorry.'

She pours boiling water into the mugs. It feels so comfortable, so *homely*. He wants to make the moment last, then she brings up the subject of Victor Hale.

'It is the same guy we found in the logbooks, I'm sure,' she is saying. 'He lives in a nursing home up the coast in Silecroft. I went there.'

They move to the table and sit opposite each other. Ash isn't sure if he wants to hear what she is telling him; she persists. The guy was a clergyman in the seventies and working in Furness, it seems. He has a family. Cherie didn't get to meet him, which comes as a relief, but she did tell a lie to get the information. It makes Ash feel used. He can't ever remember his father mentioning Victor Hale. If Hal wrote about him in the logbooks it must have been because Victor presided over a lot of services at the crematorium; he would have got to know the guy fairly well.

'Where are you going with this?' he asks, when she pauses to sip her coffee.

'My thinking is that Victor Hale might know something about the chapel and what happened there. He's still very sharp, according to the staff at Marsh House.'

'You talked to the staff? How? Don't they have a duty of care to the residents?' Ash doesn't want to get into an argument with her, but she hasn't acted in a way that he would condone.

'Only the gardener. And she didn't tell me anything, really. I lied. Any breaches are on me.'

He shakes his head. 'So why do it?'

Cherie stares at her mug. 'I feel for your dad, that's all. You and I both know he shouldn't be on a suspect list. But someone should.'

'And you think this Victor Hale is number one?'

'Not at all.' She won't look at him. 'But there's something.'

'Whatever the something is, the police will discover it soon enough. Let's leave it to them. I'm not being negative; I just don't want any trouble.'

She lifts a shoulder and looks away. 'Okay. But there's one other thing. Can I tell you about it.'

'Go on.' He leans back in his chair, arms folded. Cherie is determined, and that is in her favour. He hopes it's nothing else to cause problems for his father.

She tells him about the phone call from Darren Thompson at the pub. Ash knows the guy quite well, but once again, he's astounded at Cherie's ability to probe for information. It's part of the archaeologist's psyche, she tells him. He has to laugh at this comment, because the more he gets to know her, the more he believes it is true.

'You can't object to me following up on the Romani bracelet, surely. That's nothing to do with your dad.'

'I suppose not.' Ash adds a sigh for effect.

'And didn't you say the police have no missing persons recorded at that time? It doesn't mean there weren't any. Traveller people have always slipped under the radar. It's better nowadays, but not perfect.'

He hesitates. 'Can I tell you one of my worries? It's small, but it's bothering me.'

Cherie agrees, then presses her lips together.

'There's something a bit off about the whole police investigation.' He holds up his hands. 'Don't get me wrong. It's not a green light for you to go snooping. But nothing much is happening, as far as I know. Apart from the guard at the chapel door being removed, that is. You'd think they'd have something by now. I want rid of Ginny Beck from my life, if I'm being honest.'

'I can't say I blame you.' Cherie takes one last gulp of her coffee. 'So I'm going to Morecambe when I get the chance.'

'I'll take you.' The offer jumps from his lips before he can think too much about it. Ash mentally scans through his routines. If he can arrange for someone to keep Hal company for a few hours at the weekend, he and Cherie could be there and back before he realises. 'Saturday okay?'

She stares at him, incredulous. 'On the bike?'

'On the bike.'

Hal

He has become the worst kind of curtain-twitcher. The nets are grubby, with holes in what was once a beautiful latticework of white. But if Victor doesn't arrive soon, Hal is going to think the promised visit a lie. Then the Datsun Sunny pulls up alongside the kerb and all is well with the world again. Hal stands back from the window and waits for the knock at the front door. Victor isn't a man to hide his presence; he calls and people answer.

Today, he is wearing a pale blue clerical shirt with a tweed jacket and brown slacks. He strides into Hal's lounge and leans in to embrace him. There is talk: Victor has come from helping parishioners in need; he's been visiting a poverty-stricken community on the island. Hal is only half listening. He is conscious of Victor's clean, lemon-scented smell, vying with that of the grimy lounge, the walls yellow with nicotine, the cushions faded and flat.

They pour beers from a bottle in the kitchen larder. Neither of them mentions the real reason for Victor's visit. He asks if there is a *Mrs Black*. Hal laughs at this comment and points out that he's hardly of an age to be married. He leans against the sink and waits, heart hammering. They sip beer and eye each other, while Victor talks some more. His voice has a musical quality; it is at once compelling and moving, then gentle and unnerving. When he puts down his glass and moves towards Hal, their eyes lock. A hand on his shoulder gives the strongest of clues about what is coming. Confidence is a powerful quality, and Hal is overthrown.

CHAPTER FIFTEEN

Cherie

Ash is wearing full leathers and standing on the doorstep of the cottage. A flash of desire floods my body. We've been working together in the last few days, and the wound he created with his words is starting to heal. Finding that I like his company and personality has come as a shock, especially after my recent assessment of him. When someone puts you down, it's hard to elevate your view of them.

'Morning,' he says as he lifts his crash helmet visor. 'Let's get going, shall we. It's dry just now, but the sky looks black.' He eyes my jeans and sweater. 'Put on your warmest gear, will you. And waterproofs, if you have them.'

I have fished out a knee-length macintosh used on wet-weather digs, and my waterproof over-trousers. Once they're on, I slide my feet into a pair of tall, lace-up boots, and wrap most of my face in a scarf.

'Have you borrowed your friend's helmet again?' I ask.

'No. This is my spare. It's old, but okay. Dad used to wear it. In the days when he wasn't too scared of the bike.'

I try it on for size. 'It's fine. Is Hal going to be okay this morning?'

Ash reaches under my chin and adjusts the strap. 'I've left him with the Age UK guy who sometimes visits. Weirdly, he's older than dad, but twice as fit. They're going to put up our ancient Christmas tree and cook some lunch.'

'Oh, that's nice. I didn't realise you could *hire* someone from Age UK. I thought they just did... well, good works, I suppose.'

'I didn't hire him. He's a volunteer. Dad was going to become one, then he got his diagnosis. He wanted to meet with like-minded people, he said.' Ash tuts. 'You never can tell how things will turn out.' He catches my eye. 'And on that note, what are you doing over Christmas? If you've no plans, why don't you come to the lodge for dinner on the big day. It'll only be me and Dad. We don't make a huge fuss, but you'd be welcome.'

He turns away and steps outside. The invitation surprises me, not least because I can't think of a reason to refuse. I've already told my parents and sister that I want to spend a solitary Christmas at the cottage. They have accepted my decision because they are presuming I've got a fabulous new social life now I am free of David. The truth is, I want to be by myself, to walk and cook and read, and not have to celebrate according to anyone else's rules. Bill also issued an invitation, which I have declined. The thought of being at Cemetery Lodge, the quaint cosiness of the place, and Ash's company, feels tempting. Whether it's tempting enough, I'm not sure.

'Nice garden,' he says as we walk along the path. 'Is it your doing?' His helmet muffles the vocals. My guess is that he's asking me about the cobbled front yard with its shrubby border and empty pots.

'It will be nice, come summer. I've not had time to do anything much with it yet. Not been here that long.'

'Hopefully, I'll come and see it in full bloom,' is his reply.

I'm happy to accept the offer, and I tell him so. He coughs lightly and suggests we get going.

Once we're on the bike and moving, I tuck in behind him and flip my visor down. There's a strange etiquette about riding pillion: is it hands on the waist of the driver or hands on your thighs and brace? I choose the latter, though I have to lean the front of my body against the back of his.

Motorway driving isn't something I'm looking forward to. There is a more scenic route to Morecambe, and I'm hoping Ash will choose it. He does.

Once the bay comes into view, we take a slower pace, chugging through villages and hamlets strung out along the road. I have no idea what will be waiting for us in Mellishaw Park. That thought feels as exhilarating as starting on a dig without a clue what will be waiting under the soil.

I'm good in situations like that. David said I could talk my way in – and out – of a paper bag. I don't think he meant it as a compliment.

There is a lot of intuition involved in my job; I'm feeling intuitive now. If we can leave the park with some knowledge of the families who travelled to Walney Island during the 1970s, the marine salvagers, it will set us on the road to identifying the chapel skeletons, I'm sure of it.

Mellishaw Park overlooks the River Lune and the city of Lancaster. Though I worked for the university here during the lockdown years, I rarely visited. I'd certainly never heard of the park. We join the flow of traffic on the main route between Morecambe and the city. Ash uses hand gestures to point out the signage and distances.

I stare across the river at what amounts to urban sprawl, and think about the difference between where we've come from and the landscape here. I'd assumed we would zoom along the coast, taking in a view of the bay. Seeing the city, feeling its anonymity, is making me nervous. What if the traveller community are not welcoming? Worse still, what if we can get nowhere near?

My musings are cut short when we pass a sign for the park, and almost immediately, we are there. We pull into a car park and find a safe space for the bike.

'That was weird,' Ash says over his shoulder as he turns off the engine. 'The park is almost in Lancaster. It's definitely listed as Morecambe.'

I clamber down from the bike and pull off my helmet. 'Do you know the area?'

Ash runs a hand over his face. 'I did a university course at Lancaster, believe it or not.'

'You did? There's a surprise.' As soon as I've said the words, I realise how they might sound. 'What I meant was–'

'I know what you meant.' He takes the helmet from me then locks both onto the bike frame. I want to apologise but realise that the more I highlight my words, the more they will seem significant. Is this what David sometimes experienced? My glib use of language? The simple truth is that I should think before I speak. I walk across the car park, and examine the *you are here* sign. Eventually, Ash comes to stand beside me.

'Is the traveller area nearby?' he asks. I search his tone for anything emotive but there is nothing.

'Not far,' I say, cautiously. 'We can walk. There'll be a gate, I'm sure, so we'll just have to see what happens.' Before I can stop myself, I reach up and touch the silver streak in his hair. 'I'm sorry if I offended you.'

'I guess we're equal.' He wriggles his shoulder, and my hand falls away.

'Ash, I mean it. Tell me a bit more about your university course. Please.'

He smiles uneasily. 'Another time, maybe. We need to get

going. I'm against the clock with my father, remember.' He strides across the car park. I run to catch up, falling into step alongside.

Mellishaw has neat borders and gentle slopes of grass. A light rain is falling, giving the tarmac paths and brick-paved steps a jewelled finish. We reach a pair of tall white gates, with an inset intercom. Through the bars, I can see a stretch of chalets and motor homes. There is barking somewhere in the distance. While Ash tugs at the zip of his jacket and shuffles his feet, I press the intercom button. In seconds, a response comes. With the minimum of introductions, we are told to wait, then a young man appears. He is wearing a baseball cap and short padded jacket. A rangy white dog is by his side.

'Sorry, fellas, I can't hear well through that pesky thing.' He thumbs towards the intercom. His accent is a mix of Lancashire and something else. 'Who did you say you were wanting?' He smiles, revealing perfectly straight, perfectly white teeth.

'I'm Cherie Hope,' I say. 'We were wanting to talk to Mrs Lovell. Or Mr Lovell.'

'Were you now. I'm Pat. Patrick Quinn.' He looks in the direction of the chalets. 'Are you wanting Nana Ena? Does she know you, like?'

Beside me, Ash sighs.

'No, she doesn't know us,' I tell Pat. 'But we're trying to track down the Lovell family who were travellers in the 1970s and sometimes worked on Walney Island.' I point in the direction of the bay. 'It's just up the coast. Have you heard of it?'

'I've heard of it.' Patrick reaches down and scratches at the white dog's ears. 'What's your connection to the Lovells?'

From the back of my mind, I pull a story. It's one where I'm researching my family history and know my grandfather married a traveller. I pad it out with facts which are actually lies, and try not to think about how this must look to Ash. I hope he's not appalled by my behaviour. When I glance at him, he doesn't appear to be listening. His attention is focused on his phone. I'm about to enlarge my story further when he interrupts, thrusting the phone towards us.

'We have one of these,' he says, enthusiastically. 'The only thing Cherie has left of her grandmother. It's a Romani bracelet.'

Patrick narrows his eyes and stares at the screen. 'I know what it is, fella. Be worth a tidy sum.' He sighs. 'If I let you in to see Nana Ena, you've to promise you won't go upsetting her. She's a tiny little thing. Very delicate, like.'

'We only want to talk,' Ash says.

Patrick sucks air in between gritted teeth. 'About the old days? It's her favourite subject, so it is. I'll be staying with you, if you don't mind.' He pulls back the gate and kicks the dog away in a playful fashion. We walk with him across the site, listening as he points out each chalet and tells us about the owners. If I expected negativity or lack of co-operation, neither of those are in evidence.

When we arrive at what he calls *Casa Ena*, he holds his finger to his lips and creeps up the three steps to the front door. It's a tidy white cube of a place, with frilled curtains at the windows and a cascade of plastic flowers down the handrail.

'Give me one second,' Patrick says, then he disappears inside.

'Who's the worst liar,' Ash mutters as the door closes. 'Me or you?'

Ash

By the time Cherie has thought of an answer, Patrick is back and beckoning them inside. Ash allows himself to imagine what being in a relationship with Cherie would be like. The sight of her, hair plastered to her cheeks and wearing oversized waterproofs with an elegance he can't quite fathom, sends a flash of desire through his body.

Then he remembers her comment about his university course, and the feeling shrinks away. She's keen to get answers for his father's predicament, and that is in her favour.

In the chalet, heat swirls. It reminds Ash of his one trip abroad. When he'd stepped off the aeroplane in Crete, the blast of hot air caused a physical reaction; he'd almost fainted. It was a stag-weekend with a difference; he'd stayed in the air-conditioned hotel while his friends – including the future groom – partied to excess. Ash hasn't left England since.

'Nan. Nana,' Patrick calls as they stand in the middle of a comfortable lounge, complete with plush pink sofa and huge television. 'Don't you be hiding. I know you're here; I heard you.'

A petite woman with black hair, white at the parting, shuffles into the room. She has the stature of a child, but her complexion is creased and weather-beaten. She could be anywhere from middle-age to ancient. In her arms is a tiny dog with a pointed snout and bulbous eyes. The woman glares at Patrick. 'Give me a chance, will ye,' she says, putting the dog down on the sofa. 'The old fella wanted to come in.' She frowns. 'Who are this pair? Haven't I told you about bringing in waifs and strays. Look at the state of them.'

Cherie apologises for their wet gear and the intrusion. She takes the lead in spinning a tale about the search for her lost grandmother, a Lovell by birth, but married to a non-traveller.

When she mentions Walney Island, the old lady holds up one hand.

'Stop,' she commands. Ash is startled by the shrillness of her voice.

'There's more than you're telling,' she continues, 'that's for sure. What do you know about my Elise? She's long gone, and I've not been told of any family.'

Cherie is lost for words. There is a certain amount of truth in the old saying, *beware your lies will find you out*. Ash has heard Hal use it; they've laughed about the fibs people tell. Cherie doesn't seem to have any fibs left.

'The woman we're trying to track owned a bracelet like this one.' Ash holds up his phone.

Ena squints at the screen. 'She did not. You're a pair of liars, you are. I don't know what you're doing here.'

Cherie is about to respond, but Patrick interrupts.

'Don't be rude, Nana,' he says. 'We have manners in this family, so you're always telling me.'

Ena's expression softens. 'This lad.' She rolls her eyes. 'Always bossing me around, and me always taking it.' She turns to Cherie. 'Well then. If you're desperate to know, I'll tell you. There were five of us girls. Sisters. The Lovell Girls, people called us. Daddy gave us all names starting with the letter E, so he did. Ena.' She pats her chest. 'Then there was Elise; Etta; Evelyn. And her.' The way she spits out the last words snags Ash's attention, despite his worries about what he and Cherie are doing.

'That's only four names.' He gasps. 'Who's the fifth? Sorry. I'm fascinated, that's all.

'Aye, *fascinated*,' says Ena in a way that makes him feel guilty for asking. 'One of my sisters left the family, abandoned us in the most terrible way, she did. Oh, not my Elise, no, no, no. We were happy enough that she married the *Jackson* fella. He was good to the family.' She peers at Cherie. 'You think my Elise was your grandmother. Unlikely. She had no children.'

Ash understands the need to give older people the space to recount their story. He flashes a look at Cherie; she takes his meaning and stays quiet. Ena sits on the sofa and smooths down her skirt. She pulls the dog into her lap.

'Sorry to say it, but you won't be a relation of ours,' she continues, giving Cherie a withering look. 'There's nothing of the Romani about you, and anyhow, it was only Elise that left the family. I can name every other of the clan, and you're not one.' She gives them an exaggerated sigh. 'Sad, but there it is.'

Cherie is about to say something, despite Ash's furtive warning, but Ena holds up the index finger of her left hand and waggles it at them.

'I don't say the name of my other sister,' she continues. 'So don't be asking me. She got with some man and got herself pregnant.' Her hands fly to her cheeks in mock horror. 'All that, and with no talk of marriage.' She shakes her head. 'Daddy wasn't having it, but she would never say who got her in the family way. Rather than do the right thing, she walked away. Broke faith. Left us all, and us never knowing where she was or if she was safe. And she was a thief, too. If we're talking about a Romani bracelet, she's the person who would have it.' The shrillness of her tone falters. 'We've never heard from her since, and most of us are gone now, without the knowing.'

'That's a sad tale,' Ash says when she is finished.

'So you never found out what happened to your sister and her baby?' Cherie chips in.

'No.' Ena's shoulders slump. 'You could be that baby, for all I know.' She turns to Patrick. 'I've had enough of this now, son. Talking about the family is one thing, but I'm loath to discuss *herself*.'

'You've been really helpful, Nana.' Patrick winks at Cherie. 'Hasn't she, now?'

'She has.' Cherie smiles and Ash almost falls apart. She is affecting him in the strangest of ways. He's up and down, liking her then hating what she says. It's making him jumpy. Ena is demanding they be shown out. What has the woman implied? Neither he nor Cherie are of an age to be *that baby*, and they've been lying about their relationship with the Lovells anyway. What he finds more interesting, though, is that the woman and child in the chapel fit the missing Lovell profile exactly. Cherie will have thought of this, too.

'If you want to be selling your Romani bracelet,' Patrick says as he herds them towards the door, 'get in touch, won't you?' He pulls a card from the pocket of his jacket. 'I deal in all sorts of scrap metal. Even gold.'

They call a thank you to Ena; she doesn't respond.

'Sorry about the lack of hospitality,' Patrick says wearily. 'Nana's a funny one. Sometimes she's up and sparky, sometimes she's flat. There's a café on the prom, if you're needing a pitstop. *Brucciani's*, it's called.' He runs his eyes over Ash's leathers. 'They cater for bikers and the like. It's only ten minutes away.' Then the door is closed.

They step into the dank and solid atmosphere of the day. Cherie whispers that she could do with a coffee and the use of a lavatory. She doesn't try to unpick everything they have heard. Ash's stomach is fizzing with anticipation as much as with hunger. They might have the first piece of tangible evidence as to the identity of the skeletons in the chapel.

CHAPTER SIXTEEN

Cherie

There is a cosy fug of damp coats and burnt toast in Brucciani's. Ash and I have studied the outside of the building and agreed about its art deco design and its original signage. We skirt around all manner of subjects and don't mention what happened in Mellishaw Park. It's as though we are saving that conversation until we can sit face to face and whisper. Once we've got a table, I excuse myself and search for the lavatory.

The café is long and narrow, lined with flat wood panelling and rows of circular Formica tables. There is a giant plastic ice cream in one corner and what looks like an American pinball machine in another. When I return, Ash has taken off his jacket and is smiling up at a waitress. She is writing his order onto a notebook.

'This place is unbelievable,' he says as I sit down. 'We've travelled back to the fifties, and we weren't even born then.' He points to a long stretch of chalkboard behind an even longer counter. 'They have twelve types of coffee.'

The waitress smiles pleasantly. 'What would you like, madam?'

'The same as him,' I reply.

'Macchiato.' She notes it down. 'Anything else?'

Ash asks for grilled cheese, which seems to be their speciality. I do the same. When the waitress has gone, he mutters about the place being a mix of American diner and Italian ice cream parlour.

'It's interesting though, isn't it?' I slip off my jacket and run a hand through my hair. 'Like our little visit to Nana Ena. I'm still trying to process.'

Ash leans towards me. 'Have we really just found what might be actual *evidence*? What are we doing?' His hand brushes mine, and I feel a frisson of connection. Judging by the look on his face, he feels it, too.

'God knows.' I give him a whispery laugh. 'I was right, though, wasn't I? About the Romani link. It's more than the police have, I'll bet.'

'That's what scares me.' Ash glances around the café. I don't interrupt his train of thought. I'm scared, too. We've moved beyond the realms of nosy investigation and into something that might require us to dig deeper. I recall Hal's words, how he should have held on to his love, but he let them go. I haven't mentioned this to Ash, but it seems more pertinent than ever. What if the adult skeleton in the chapel did belong to Ena's lost sister? Could she have been Hal's lost love? The connection is too close to ignore. There is no reason, as far as I can see, that Hal would have been responsible for her death, or the child's, and even less reason why he would have hidden their bodies. Even from the little I know about Ash and his father, my instincts are telling me they are honest people; they would not have been able to live with the consequences of causing a death, nor concealing one. The waitress brings our drinks. She tells us the food won't be long.

'As far as I know,' I say to Ash when she's gone, 'if Ena's sister disappeared in the 1970s, and no one reported her missing, only one person would have known about her death, and that would be the one who was involved in it.'

Ash sips his drink then wipes a thin layer of froth from his top lip. 'Did I tell you the police have no idea about *cause of death*?' He stretches his eyes. 'Their words, not mine.'

'You did tell me.' I lower my voice. 'Why put the bodies in the chapel, that's what I don't understand. It's hardly a good place to hide the evidence of your wrongdoing. There are a million other places. Why there?'

'You're saying there must be a connection between the chapel and those bodies? Dad, you mean?'

There is a snap of anger. In the midst of our new-found understanding, I'd forgotten how reactive Ash can be.

I hesitate. 'Not necessarily. What about Victor Hale.'

'A vicar? Are you kidding?'

'No, and it's unlikely, I grant you.' The waitress arrives again. We lean back and let her put plates heaped with wodges of cheese-on-toast in front of us. Ash tucks in straight away. I give him a few moments, then say, 'Unlikely, but possible.'

Between mouthfuls, he outlines his theories. Hal hadn't recorded any chapel break-ins during the seventies, which means whoever put the bodies there had keys. No one could have had keys, so they must have stolen them. The bodies had been hidden temporarily but whoever intended to move them again couldn't come back; they were likely to have been the Romani family members Ena mentioned, mother and child.

'Why the chapel though, Ash?' I nibble at my food. 'It had been chosen because it was all locked up and never used, in my opinion. Your average layman wouldn't have known this. Proof the culprit is connected to the place in some way.'

He wipes his mouth with the side of his hand. 'I don't like that word. *Culprit*. We don't know there was any *foul play*, do we?'

'Oh, come on.' I slam my hand down on the table. The move gets me some glances from other customers.

'Cherie. Shush.' A spread of pink creeps across his cheeks. I look at my plate and bite my lip. Ash is right, we know very little. My archaeologist's brain is letting rip again, without having any real evidence.

'Sorry. I'm sorry.' I tut lightly. 'I want to help your dad, that's all. Ginny Beck shouldn't be treating him as a suspect. I'm not sure what game she's playing.'

'Neither am I.' He glances at his watch. 'We should get back. And I think we might have to tell *Ms Beck* what we know. They'll be building a picture, and our info will feed into it, I'm sure.'

This isn't what I want to hear. There's a connection between Victor Hale and the bodies in the chapel, I'm convinced of it. But I have no evidence. Which means I need to keep it quiet.

'Can I say one more thing?' I ask as we get up from the table. 'It's a question, really.'

'Go on.' Ash slides his arms into his jacket and fiddles with the zip.

'When I was talking to your dad the other day. In the garden. He got all maudlin and told me to hang on to you, as he'd lost his love, or let them go, or something. What happened between him and your mother? Was it very sad?'

Ash's expression hardens.

'They hated each other,' he says.

The journey back is a wet one. I give up trying to enjoy a sea view: water and sky blend into one deep grey stretch. I tuck in behind Ash and watch raindrops congeal on my visor. Cold creeps down my already damp neck and across my shoulders. I shiver and slide my arms around his waist.

I'm suddenly feeling disorientated. What if everything we think we've discovered about the chapel skeletons is false? There are facts: I saw a bracelet and it is Romani; Hal and Victor worked together through the seventies; Hal would have had access to the chapel keys; the skeletons have lain in the chapel for fifty years; they are from the bodies of a woman and child and are of eastern European descent. Any other connections are tenuous and circumstantial.

I trust Bill's knowledge about the traveller community on Walney Island; I believe what Darren Thompson told me about his neighbour who married into it. Belief and trust; not fact. I have no doubt Ena and her family did visit Walney during the seventies, and I trust her story about the missing sister. That doesn't mean it has relevance; we're joining too many dots without first checking their numbers. The picture emerging isn't reliable.

Ash is correct in his belief that we should share our information with the police and let them create a meaningful picture. I take some deep breaths in an attempt to calm my overactive brain. Getting in touch with Ginny Beck is on my to-do list for Monday. What I won't be sharing are Hal's words about a *lost love*. According to Ash, his father wasn't referring to his mother. The situation would be far less clouded if only Hal had access to his own memories. Ginny seems to think the same, but I don't feel inclined to help her.

By the time we reach the main road into Furness, the skies have darkened enough for it to feel like evening. When we pull up at some traffic lights, I shout forwards to Ash, asking him to drop me off at Cark. He gives me a thumbs-up. We zoom along the A-road, splashing through puddles and weaving between lanes to avoid the spray from lorries and the occasional coach. As we approach the turn-off, Ash pulls into a lay-by. When he puts the engine into neutral and slides off his helmet, I panic. My village is three miles away and I don't fancy walking in this weather.

'Sorry,' he calls over his shoulder. 'My visor seems to be leaking and I need to clean up a bit.' His face is splattered with smut and dirty water. He reaches inside his jacket and pulls on the neck of his sweatshirt, then runs it over the worst of the dirt. 'That's better. Are you all right? It's getting cold now, isn't it?'

'I'm fine. I'll be home soon.'

The traffic swishes past. Our main problem now is to join it without getting ourselves into difficulty. I flip up my visor, as though seeing what we're up against will somehow make it safer. Ash lets the engine tick over, but there is no break in the flow. We wait. The stream of vehicles slows. Someone waves us out. A small car. Ash doesn't hesitate, he carefully chugs in front, lifting his hand in thanks. I've still got my visor up. I peer through the windscreen of the car. With a jolt of shock, I realise I'm looking at two women I know: Ginny Beck is driving and Ria Lace, the councillor, is sitting in the passenger seat.

Ash

It takes no more than ten minutes to get Cherie to her cottage. In that time, Ash mentally runs through how he'll respond if he's invited in. Having to rush back is about the best excuse; it's genuine and believable. She isn't to know the Age UK guy would be happy to stay on, if required. Not that Ash would ever leave Hal for a full day. Or overnight. If he became unsettled, as he sometimes does with changes of routine, it would be unfair to leave someone else to deal with it.

The day started with questions and has ended with them, but the biggest thing on Ash's mind is how Cherie expressed her surprise at finding out he'd been a university student. Her cynical smile had almost floored him. She'd covered it well, and he'd done even better, but he can't forget.

The next-door curtains twitch when he pulls the bike up at Cherie's cottage. She does exactly what he expected: she asks him in. He gives a quick apology, with an unexpected promise to see her soon, then leaves. As he bumps the bike over a line of street cobbles, he sets his mind on the journey home. One of the good habits he has developed is the ability to let problems slide off his shoulders, so he can focus on the present. He's going to give no more thought to the events of the day, and become nothing more than a biker doing his *thing*.

It is twenty minutes of escapism. He hunkers down and aligns himself with the tarmac. The engine's growling beat pulses through his body. With a twist of his wrist and a flip of his toe, he has control of the world.

The rain smashes against his visor but visibility is not an issue. He needs nothing more than a ten-yard-view. What he is seeking is a stretch of open road, traffic-free and straight, so that he can open the throttle and fly. The duel-carriage-way doesn't disappoint. When he finally hits the urbanity of his hometown it's like the end of a party; he's had the best time and is trying to drag it out for as long as possible. Then the cemetery comes into view and he's back to being Ash Black again.

His father is playing cards with the Age UK guy. They've

got a pot of tea on the table and plates littered with uneaten toast crusts.

'Hello, son,' Hal calls as Ash stands at the kitchen door. 'Good day?'

'It was, thanks.' He nods a hello. 'You all right?'

'I am. Greg's been a stalwart.' He peers at Ash's leathers. 'Is it raining? We've not been outside, so I've no idea.'

'We have,' mouths Greg.

Ash hangs his jacket in the outside porch, and unzips his boots. He fills them with some of the blue tissue-paper he keeps especially, then peels off his trousers. His inner clothing is dry, but he doubts Cherie will have the same experience. It's okay to occasionally take a motorbike trip wearing layman's clothing, but full-time riding requires the right gear. The thought of her stripping off her wet garments brings a flush of heat to his face. He takes a few deep breaths, then goes back to the kitchen and its stud-poker school.

Greg is tying up loose ends. He's not as physically able as Hal, but his brain is razor-sharp. They have been playing for small-denomination silver coins; he's clearly let Hal win.

'There's a pile of post for you,' Greg says as he gets up from the table. 'I put it on the desk in your office. It's a bit damp round the edges so I didn't leave it on the hall floor.'

Ash thanks him and wanders away. If he gets caught up in conversation, he's likely to be there for a couple more hours. What he really wants is to get a hot drink, close his office door and let himself consider the events of the day. He wants to write notes on everything he and Cherie have been involved in, every conversation, every finding. Then he can go to Ginny Beck and offload.

He flicks on the office light and half closes the door. Greg is in the hallway, laughing with Hal about something. Ash hears him leave. He calls to his father, asking if he is okay and Hal tells him he is going to lie down, that Greg has worn him out. In his father's shrunken universe, there is room for only one person. Ash smiles to himself.

He lifts the pile of letters from his desk. Greg was right; they are damp. Mostly, the envelopes are brown: bills and circulars. One stands out: white, and stamped with the logo of the borough council. Ash tears it open. He glances at the bottom of the single sheet of paper. It has been signed by councillor Ria Lace in lieu of the chairman. In the time it takes him to read the contents, Ash has to sit down. The council are not happy that Hal, who suffers from advanced dementia, is living, often unsupervised, at Cemetery Lodge. It is their property, and therefore they would be liable if anything were to happen. The suggestion is that if Ash wants to keep his job and therefore the lodge, he must find a secure nursing home for his father. The sooner, the better, is the implication.

Ash stares at the letter. He remembers the conversation he had with Ria Lace a few weeks ago, framed by the alarm Hal had shown when meeting the woman. She had been intent on getting a guarantee from him of Hal's innocence with regard to the chapel situation. He hadn't trusted her then and he doesn't trust her now. She wants his father out of the lodge, though her reasoning is flawed. There is no implication that Ash's job is at risk, and it certainly wouldn't be part of her remit to tell him so.

She must have taken it upon herself to report Hal's condition to the council leaders, perhaps pushed for a response. All thoughts of seeing Ginny Beck have gone from his mind. On Monday morning, he will need to contact the town hall and find out exactly what is going on.

CHAPTER SEVENTEEN

Cherie

Dale Scott is waiting for me in the gravelly car park of the train station. The window of his lime-green Volkswagen is open, and he is blowing a cloud of vape into the dank morning air. He lifts his hand in greeting.

'Morning. Thanks for doing this,' I say as I climb in.

'No problem.' He gives me a beaming smile. 'I'm off duty until Christmas, anyway, so a little jaunt is welcome.'

We're not on a *little jaunt*, but I don't point this out. My request must feel like work to him, surely.

'Nice,' I say. 'A few days off.'

He lifts one shoulder. 'I'm on duty all over the holiday to make up for it, though.'

'Oh, grim. Do you get any choice?'

'I don't mind,' he says, with resignation. 'It lets the boss have some time. She's from one of those big tight families that gather on every occasion; I'm not.'

Dale has agreed to meet with me and chat about what I have found out. I'd had a panicked phone call from Ash on the previous evening; he had something to deal with, so couldn't spare the time for Ginny Beck. He'd asked me to speak to her instead, to explain everything we'd found out from the Morecambe Lovells. I couldn't think of a reason why not, but when I'd tried to make contact with Ginny, I was passed over. Luckily, I had a phone number for Dale. His reasoning about Ginny's disinterest had been that she was extremely busy, and the cemetery investigation had been *put on ice*. I found his comments confusing. What could be more important than finding the reason why two bodies had lain hidden for fifty years without anyone's knowledge? Which is why I've added the question to my list of things to be discussed this morning.

'Where are we heading?' Dale asks as we drive away from the station.

'Turn right.' I point towards the main road. 'And over to Walney, if you don't mind. There's something I want to show you... and tell you.'

He gives me a sideways smile. 'Sounds intriguing.'

The car isn't clean inside. The dashboard is covered with a layer of biscuit crumbs and the footwells are full of fast-food wrappers and cardboard cups. A dried-up perfume sachet hangs from the rear-view mirror. I ask more about Ginny Beck's lack of enthusiasm for the chapel case, and Dale shakes his head. There's frustration in his answer: she's got a lot going on; there are no fresh leads.

'I might have some,' I tell him. 'Fresh leads, I mean. Thanks to the Romani bracelet. And my boss.'

'Oh?' He sounds surprised. 'I've been wondering about the bracelet. We've had to keep it in special conditions because it's fragile. What do you know?'

When I explain about the traveller community over on the island, he agrees and comments in the right places, but he isn't fully listening. We nudge our way through the town traffic and get snarled up in roadworks on the other side of the bridge. When we finally get free and I direct him towards Biggar, he sighs and says he hasn't been there for years.

'I'm not being funny, Cherie,' he continues, as we swish along the coastal road, wipers fighting with mist and murk. 'But it'll be common knowledge that there were gypsies visiting the island during the seventies. Being in possession of the bracelet proves nothing. Anyone could have owned it.'

'Don't say *gypsies*. It's not a recognised word anymore.'

He gives a fake cough. 'What should I say then? We both know how woke the world has become since Covid. Say it like it is, that's my feeling.'

'You should say travellers. It's nothing to do with being *woke*; it's more respectful, that's all.'

'*Travellers*, then. But if you're taking me to a traveller site, there has to be a reason.' He glances at me. 'Well?'

'Can we wait until Biggar? Then I'll explain everything.'

'Fair enough.' He takes a breath. 'There are no resources for jaunts like this anymore, you know. I hope it'll be worth the trip.'

'You offered,' I remind him.

'I did.' He smiles. 'That's me: job first, off duty or not.'

We park outside the pub. It's still early, and the village is quiet. There's a tinge of something pungent in the air.

Dale screws up his nose. 'This is too rural for me. I'm a town boy. I need pavements and bars and the sweet aroma of pizza dough.'

'The island's hardly rural.' I zip my jacket and pull on a hat.

'It is to me.' Dale is wearing a kind of waterproof hoodie, more fashionable than practical. He sucks on his electronic pipe, and puffs out a cloud of candy-floss smelling vapour. When I raise one eyebrow, he adds, 'Sorry. Policemen don't smoke anymore. *The Sweeny* it ain't.'

For a young man, he has some antiquated banter. When I tell him this, he laughs and says I should get a life. As this has been said to me before, I don't respond; his meaning is clear. I lead him through the village, hoping we will stumble across Turnstone Cottage eventually. I'm reminded, once again, of meeting Ash here while he was having a blast around the lanes with his motorcycling friends. The guy takes no prisoners, I have come to realise. It doesn't matter whether he *owes* me, when I say something that jars with his principles, he strikes back. It's honest, but it can hurt.

Dale and I come across the cottage at the edge of the village, not far from the road. It is single storey and whitewashed, with large Georgian windows and an authentic sandstone wall at the front. It's a conundrum of styles, exactly like Biggar itself.

'The man who lives here was married to a traveller,' I tell him. 'His wife was one of five sisters who used to come to the site during the seventies. I've spoken to the family; well, Ash and I have.'

Dale is interested, at last. 'And you know this because? Has this information come from Mr Black senior?' He peers at me. 'What have you been up to?'

'Give me a minute,' I say. 'What's pertinent is that one of the sisters was outcast from the family because she got pregnant. No one heard from her again. The family don't know what happened or where she went. A young woman with a child; no record of them, and they were travellers who worked right here. Do you see my point?'

'I certainly do. And one of the family lives in this cottage?' He frowns. 'Really?'

'One of the sisters did, yes. She's dead now, but her husband isn't.'

'You've spoken to them – him?'

'Not them, exactly.' I tell him about the pub landlord and

the connection he had discovered with the Lovells of Morecambe. When I explain that Ash and I had travelled there and met with the family, Dale groans loudly.

'You should have let the police know, Cherie,' he says. 'This information could prove to be vital, and it's something we haven't picked up on yet.'

'Not long ago you were bemoaning lack of resources. Haven't I saved you using some?'

He makes a clicking sound with his tongue and waggles an index finger. 'Fair point. What I can't understand is why this family haven't ever been in contact with the police, if they've been so worried.'

'They've never been worried. They're angry, more than anything, about one of their own walking away. The bracelet sparked more interest, if I'm being honest; they'd given up on the girl years ago.' I think about the skeletons, then add, 'Probably fifty years ago. We can walk to the actual traveller site, if you like. It's an atmospheric spot, that's for sure.'

There is no sea view when we get there. The paper-white sky and the water have become one. It's cold and bleak and Dale shivers in his damp hoodie. The vaping continues.

'It's really isolated,' he says. 'What do you think the travellers did for money? Same as now?'

'Marine salvage,' I tell him. 'So I guess it is kind of the same as now, if we're talking about dealing in scrap metal. It would have been a hard life, that's for sure.'

'And a poor one.'

'A poor one, back then. Definitely.' I'm not sure that Patrick Quinn showed any signs of poverty. Everything we saw of the Mellishaw Park site spoke of comfort and abundance. 'Things are better for the travelling community these days, thank goodness.'

Dale goes quiet. I ramble on about having the opportunity

to view the bracelet, and even the skeletons at some point, but he is evasive. Did Ash imagine the scenario of Ginny Beck asking for my help? When I ask about DNA matches from tests they have run, Dale shakes his head. The adult sample is more fragile than the child's, it seems, but neither has yielded anything of interest. I have heard of this fragility, evident during my own archaeological investigations. What I hadn't known, until he enlightens me, is that there are three levels of police DNA data matching: the universal one; the one where minor offenders' results are stored temporarily; the police personnel one. Most testing happens at the universal level only.

'Every officer provides a DNA sample when we're recruited,' Dale explains. 'In case we ever have to be eliminated from crimes scenes and the like.'

'That makes sense. Do you ever think of running tests at the other levels? You know, if you're not getting anywhere?'

'Resources again.' He gives me a grim smile. 'And DNA matches are just a small part of the big picture, anyway. If it was up to me, we'd have run an appeal by now. To the public, I mean. Asking for information.'

'Why haven't you? Same reasons? Resources?'

He shakes his head. 'Nope. The boss isn't keen, that's all. But I think we'll have to eventually. Someone must know something.'

I've just given him *something*. Has he taken in its significance? I hold back on the stuff about Victor Hale, because I don't want to get myself into any trouble. I don't tell him I saw his boss yesterday either, in a car with the woman who gave Ash and his father a bit of trouble. My brain has ring-fenced that information, though I couldn't explain why, even to myself.

'On the subject of the chapel,' I say instead, 'is there any chance I could get in there again, and finish my assessment?'

'Oh, yes, I meant to let Mr Black – Ash – know. He can

allow you to do what you need. Though I can't see much point, now, can you?'

'It's a paid commission, so there is a point.' I'm not sure what Dale is getting at.

He toes a patch of gravel, kicking some loose pieces. 'Repurposing the chapel is off the agenda, according to Ginny.'

'How would she know?'

'It's a small town. Everyone knows everything.' He pushes his hands into the pockets of his hoodie. 'Now, can we get back? I've a lot of stuff to write up. And follow up. I'll fill Ginny in with the main points, and see what she wants to do. Where shall I drop you? Back at the railway station?'

On the drive, I let him chatter about the police canteen Christmas lunch. Roast potatoes are mentioned, and the way he likes his gravy.

Does Ash's invitation to Christmas lunch still stand? What about Ginny Beck's attitude to the whole investigation? She is clearly in charge, a woman detective at the top of her game. Yet every time Dale speaks on her behalf, her intentions seem pliable enough for many different interpretations. It's like she's not interested.

Ash

He leans over the kitchen sink, taking deep breaths to steady himself. Hal is in the garden, so won't have heard the telephone row with Ria Lace. There's a day of work ahead and Ash is not sure he can face it.

When he'd confronted Ria about the letter, there had been no preamble; she'd not used pleasantries to cloud the issue. Her point was that when she'd visited the lodge, it was clear that

Ash's father, a man suffering with some kind of dementia, was residing there on his own for much of the time. Ash had tried to explain the truth, but she interrupted every sentence.

He'd asked to speak to someone with more authority. She'd laughed at this and told him he'd get the same answer: Cemetery Lodge wasn't a suitable home for an elderly and mentally disabled person. What had been baffling is that Ria seemed more focused on Hal than on the lodge. Strange, when a few weeks ago, she'd wanted the place for repurposing.

When Ash asked if his job was at risk, Ria had been clear that it wasn't. She was simply concerned for the elderly man's welfare. Ash didn't believe one word that came out of the woman's mouth, and he'd told her so. Then she'd broken off the call.

He wants to speak with Cherie. She is among the few people to have expressed genuine care about his father. Whatever she thinks of him personally, she seems to have empathy for them both. Her plans for today included meeting with Ginny Beck so that they could offload their findings about the Lovell family. Neither of them wanted to be in trouble for obstruction of a police investigation. Cherie had said she would send him a message, or telephone after it was done. He's not heard from her yet.

When he's settled Hal with a flask of tea and his radio, Ash hovers by the front door, thinking about Ria Lace and her unkind words. Did the woman have a point? Should Ash be heading out for a few hours of work leaving his father behind? He's done it so often as to be confident, but now he's not sure. In the end, he goes back into the sitting room and persuades Hal to accompany him. It will mean the jobs take twice as long, but Ash isn't in the right frame of mind to leave his father today.

They set off up the slope towards the crematorium. The first funeral of the day is at half past ten, and there are two more in the afternoon. The Christmas shutdown ensures that families take earlier slots rather than waiting until the gap after Boxing Day and before New Year.

Ash suddenly remembers the invitation he gave Cherie. It would be good to have her company over the festive period. Especially as she is so kind in her management of his father. If any emergencies come in, it will be easier to leave him with someone. Not that he wants to take advantage of Cherie, but Ria Lace has upended his conviction.

'Hey, lad.' Hal is tugging on his arm. 'Have you remembered the keys? There's a queue outside already.'

'Yes, Dad.' Ash pats the pocket of his fluorescent jacket. His father is correct. Though he's not had time to unlock the crem doors or put the heating on, people are waiting. The first funeral of the day is not going to be understated. A young man, a university student in his second year and beloved son, has died while away at college. His family have brought the body back for cremation in his hometown. Ash has been told to expect lots of students and a parade of rainbow-coloured balloons. Those, he can deal with; Hal pestering to see the roster, he cannot.

Inside the crematorium, Ash flicks on the lights and turns the central heating to full blast. He gives his father the manual floor sweeper and asks him to run it over the already immaculate blue carpet in the reception area. Hal stuffs his flannel cap in his pocket and gets to work. It's while Ash is giving the lectern on the podium a buff with lemon wood polish, that he notices a group of young men and women walking past the side window. They don't look like mourners. Something about their good-spirits doesn't seem right. If they are here for the funeral, it is respectful to wait by the entrance until the hearse arrives, not take a tour of the graveyard. Hal is immersed in his task, so Ash quickly exits via the back door, and heads in the youngsters' direction.

They are at the chapel when he catches up with them. Though it is a freezing winter's day, the women are dressed for high summer. They wear floral frocks, short cardigans, and have bare legs. The men are wearing pastel-coloured suits, and one has a straw trilby. The lightness of their youth makes Ash feel cumbersome and straight-laced. They appear to be taking photographs with their mobile phones.

'Can I ask what you're doing, guys,' he calls. 'This area is off limits to the public. If you're here for the funeral, you need to stand by the crem door.' He keeps his tone light and friendly.

'Do you work here?' one of the women responds. The others seem intent on taking photos, some of which they are in.

Ash grimaces. 'The chapel isn't safe: that's why there's a *safety* fence.' He points to the police tape. 'And you wouldn't want to break the law, would you?' His comment doesn't seem to bother her.

One of the men chips in. 'Is this where the skeletons were found, mate? We've read about it on our socials. Can't believe Gareth is getting buried here.'

'What do you mean?' Ash narrows his eyes. His tone isn't light anymore.

'The place is trending. Look.' The man holds out his phone. While he scrolls, Ash cranes and stares at the screen. There are hundreds of photographs of the chapel from different angles. Some haven't got the safety fence in, so he presumes they've come from years before, or been stolen from various local-interest websites. Some have been taken in the twilight or even at night. Many have been enhanced. He remembers how Cherie had got in that evening a few weeks ago. How has he not noticed these people prowling around the chapel, taking photos?

He runs a hand over his face. 'What's all this about? I don't get it.' Ginny Beck had created a huge fuss when the BBC turned up to cover the story. If the police have decreed the chapel private, do these photos constitute law-breaking?

'It's a popular story,' the man is explaining. 'All over social media, especially Instagram. Everyone wants a photo by the chapel.' He looks up at the spire. 'Creepy, isn't it? To think those skeletons had been inside for years. Well, bodies. Where are they now, do you know?'

There is something so upbeat about this group, Ash wonders if he's missed the point. They did mention a *Gareth* getting buried though, and he's fairly sure that is the name on his roster.

He directs an exaggerated sigh at the man. 'Look. You shouldn't be taking photographs of the place. Especially not on the day you're burying your friend. It's not right. Could I ask you to go back down to the crem entrance.'

One of the women is taking snaps of herself with the chapel in the background. Her stance is distinctly flirty and she's making a peace-sign with her fingers. She asks if Ash would like to come and stand next to her.

His patience is at an end. 'Right,' he cries. 'That's enough. Leave here or I will have to get in touch with the police. The chapel is still a crime scene, and you are trespassing.' His voice quivers but he stands firm, feet apart, arms folded, hoping for a confidence he doesn't feel. So much for Hard-boiled Black.

'Crime scene?' One of the men is typing something into his phone. 'Wow. So a murder did happen here.' He turns to the others. 'We're at a crime scene, folks. Hashtag that.'

Ash remembers his father, left cleaning the reception area. He will have completed the task by now and will be inventing another. In the early days, when Ash had been a small boy helping out, Hal made a point of using heavily scented cleaning materials to keep the place smelling fresh. There would be perfumed white powder for the carpets and upholstery, and cloying sprays for the air. Ash uses soap and water and opens windows. Left to himself, his father will be trying to access the utility room cupboards in search of his favourite products, though they no longer exist.

When Ash gets back, there is no sign of Hal. The Hoover is propped neatly against a wall, the carpet clean and striped like a manicured lawn. After a few seconds of panic, Ash tells himself there will be a logical answer to the whereabouts of his father. He finds him eventually, in a small office at the back of the building, chatting with the young man who keeps tabs on landline enquiries.

'There you are,' Hal says. 'Is there a problem outside? The queue's getting longer, and I wasn't sure what you wanted me to do next. Though I'd rather go home for a cuppa. I'm taking up too much of this youngster's time.'

Ash can't find any words. He's having a normal conversation with his father, after all the worries of the morning.

'It's sorted,' he says eventually. 'So, if you want to go back to the lodge, that's fine. Better to be in the warm. I'll walk you back down.'

'Okay, son.' Hal turns to the young man. 'Thanks for keeping me company, fella. Any time you need a brew, pop down. You know where I am.'

Ash leads his father out through the glass reception doors. He chats with some of the mourners, then gives a reverse wave. As they walk together towards the lodge, Hal slips his arm through Ash's, and he is reminded of his father's vulnerability.

Despite Ria Lace and the fear she had created, Ash realises his instincts are correct. With support, his father's condition is completely manageable. Leaving Cemetery Lodge would be the cause of deterioration, more than anything this woman could suggest. Ash glances at his watch. It's almost time for the first funeral. Once he's got Hal settled, he'll need to hurry back to the crem, prop open the outer doors and check the sound system is working. What he really wants to do is catch up with Cherie. He's sure she will have the expertise to find out how far the skeletons-in-the-chapel story has spread.

Hal

The sight makes Hal catch his breath. The way Victor strides down the hill from the crematorium, the skirt of his cassock blowing open to give a tantalising glimpse at the clothing below; the intensity of his expression. Hal watches from the bedroom window. The forsythia bushes in the garden hedge are ablaze with yellow blooms, a lilac crocus patchwork covers the lawn. Everything is more vibrant now that Victor is in his life. They meet when they can. He has a wife and children, a *cover*, he calls it, though Hal cannot understand what they need to hide. Their relationship would be frowned on, people would raise their eyebrows and look away, but there would be nothing unlawful. Victor insists the Church of England might have other ideas.

There is purpose now, to keeping the crematorium and cemetery in sparkling form. Hal had struggled with the job after the death of his father. A dark mood descended, and he didn't much care who thought what about him, or his work. Now he has Victor, it feels like keeping house for the man he loves. He has gained new skills from being around Victor: how to create conversation from nothing; how to *banter*. Hal thinks of himself as little more than a teenager, but in Victor's company, he is becoming a man.

Hal is concerned that Victor will leave him. So many people love the man that he loves; temptation is everywhere. It's not the archetypal vicar's family that bothers him so much as the beautiful men and women that throw themselves at Victor's feet, metaphorically speaking. He is ten years older, and so much more worldly; there must be other lovers. Hal tells himself he is the special one, but part of him wonders. If he could find out every aspect of Victor's life he would sleep more easily. As it is, he tries to be honest but isn't sure that particular favour is returned.

Victor barrels through the front door and brings with him the scent of spring. He takes Hal in his arms and all other worries flee away. The sense of urgency brings everything to a rapid conclusion. Hal wants to linger, to talk, but Victor has more pressing matters. As always, his departure is sweetly glazed. For the sake of normality, he wants to bring his children to visit the lodge; he wants Hal to meet them.

CHAPTER EIGHTEEN

Cherie

A watery sun filters through the branches of ancient trees along the main road. I pull down the windscreen visor and silently thank Bill for the loan of his car. He's gone to Scotland for Christmas and decided flying was the best option, considering the state of rail networks across the UK.

The final few days at Gillside have been a frantic round of getting project reports to clients before the festive shutdown. This will be my first visit to Cemetery Lodge for almost a week. I've talked to Ash, and we decided there is no reason to rush the chapel assessment. He sounded cryptic on the telephone, and I have my own reasons for saving the details of my conversation with Dale for a face-to-face meet-up. Which will be today, over a simple Christmas lunch at his home.

Something else I've kept quiet, even from Bill, is my accessing of further data on Victor Hale. I haven't used working hours for it, but have used the Gillside log-in codes. Victor was quite an enigma, it seems. He is eighty-three years old and a widower. There are two children somewhere, though I couldn't find anything further about them. He stopped presiding over the crematorium funeral services in 1980, and I could see he'd worked in a few other Cumbrian parishes until 1995. After that, there is no trace of him until he entered Marsh House in 2010. Mainly, he seems to have led a quiet life, apart from the one thing I discovered that almost made me go running to Cemetery Lodge in search of Ash.

Victor Hale had spent a good portion of his working life as an advocate, on the panel of a national charity for traveller families. Ash and I have accrued a lot of unconnected information. I hope this fact will blow his mind in the same way it did mine.

I feel like I'm going on a date. Explaining this is difficult, especially as although there are sparks between Ash and I, they are not romantic ones. He has, however, asked me to lunch, so there is something. I'm looking forward to spending the day with Hal, too. He is appreciative of my time, and that matters. One of the things which finally broke up my marriage to David was his loathing of us being together with nothing to do. He would never simply *hang out* with me. There had to be a plan. At first, it was fun, but after four relentless years, I sometimes wanted us to lounge around the house and just *be*. He didn't. Year five was our break-up year.

The roads are quiet. I pass family groups, young and old, and striding out together in festive finery. And the inevitable dog walkers, of course. I've dressed up enough to mark the occasion, in a sparkly blouse and velvet trousers, but I have my boots and a sweater on the back seat, along with my parka and a bag of gifts for Ash and his father. Nothing intimate, mainly food and drink, but I couldn't turn up empty-handed. When the cemetery comes into view, my stomach turns over. By the time I park outside the lodge, I'm trembling as though a job interview is about to happen.

Ash welcomes me inside and wishes me a happy Christmas, but it is Hal who leans in for a hug. There's an atmosphere of warmth and roasting meat.

An artificial Christmas tree stands in one corner of the lounge. Ash explains that it has been in the family for as long as he can remember, and apologises for its moth-eaten appearance. I like the tree. I'm a fan of family traditions in general; something else David wasn't keen on. Everything had to be new and swish, as far as he was concerned. People asked me, after the marriage imploded, how I had never realised the multitude of things waiting to cause the detonation. My answer is always the same: I balanced them all against sex, and the sex won. Not a mistake I will be making again.

'I've brought goodies,' I say as I hand Hal the gift bag. 'It's not much but you might enjoy them.'

Hal beams. He is wearing a patterned shirt under a tweed waistcoat, and his face looks freshly shaved. He takes the bag and peers inside.

'Whisky.' He pulls out the bottle. 'Glenfiddich, too. And Cartmel sticky toffee pudding; we'll have that for afters. You've spoilt us, hasn't she, son?'

'I live near Cartmel, so it seemed the right thing. It's the best pudding around, apparently. You have it steaming hot, with a dollop of ice cream. That's the tradition, anyway.'

'Good thing I ordered ice cream then.' Ash stands to one side, head tilted benevolently. He is dressed in a way I haven't seen before: neatly pressed shirt and grey jeans. The silver streak in his dark hair gleams.

'Who's the chef?' I ask. 'It smells wonderful.'

'Both of us,' Ash replies. 'Dad does the veg and I do the meat.'

Hal gives me a thumbs-up. 'That's it. We're a good team.'

He looks thoughtful. 'Did we get a dessert, son? A pudding? What are we having.'

Ash catches my eye, and we smile. I lift the sticky toffee pudding from the bag, and show it to Hal.

The meal is beautifully cooked and rustically served. We all chip in with the washing up, but it's clear that Hal is struggling. His cheeks are flushed, his eyes glassy. When he is sent upstairs for a nap, there is no argument. The atmosphere slides, as though the thought of being alone with me is making Ash nervous. He stops talking and we finish the tidying in silence.

'Shall I make a pot of coffee,' I suggest. 'Or we could take a walk. I've brought other gear.' I take a handful of sparkly blouse. 'This isn't really me.'

'You look nice, though.'

'Thanks.' A flash of adrenaline sets my heart racing.

Ash turns quickly away and fills the kettle. 'Coffee first,' he mutters.

While we wait, I lean my back against the sink and tell him about my conversation with Dale Scott. What worries Ash the most is the lack of interest Ginny Beck seems to be taking in the case. He wants things back to normal and Hal off her suspect list. When I explain that the chapel assessment can go ahead, he shakes his head.

'I had to chase a bunch of influencers away from there last week.' He frowns. 'What the hell, Cherie? Have people got no respect?'

'It's the times we live in, I'm afraid. Nothing and nowhere is off limits.'

He looks at me as though I'm spouting poison, like the words I'm saying are deadly. Does he think I was trying to capitalise on the creepiness of the chapel? On the night he'd caught me snooping? When I ask him this, he runs a hand over his eyes and sighs out his disenchantment.

'You must have known it wasn't the right thing to do, sneaking into the cemetery at night.' His tone changes. 'But you still did it. In a way, it would be better if the chapel became business units. Then it wouldn't have the same value on Instagram.'

'It's not likely to be repurposed now, is it?' I hesitate. 'But I think you already knew that, didn't you? You mentioned another row with Councillor Lace. Have you seen her again?'

'Not seen her. I telephoned. It was a good job there were screens between us because I wanted to punch the woman. She never mentioned the chapel. Her latest is that she wants Dad put in a home.' He shudders. 'How crass is that?'

'Extremely crass. And not her business, I wouldn't have thought.'

He grunts. 'You're right there.'

'I hope you told her what to do.'

'I did. But it was all very strange, Cherie, and I'm not sure what to make of it.' He fills the coffee pot and sets it on a tray with two mugs. 'Let's take this into the lounge and I'll try and explain properly.'

The fire has filled the room with a stifling heat. Ash opens the window and leaves the door ajar, encouraging a cool draft. I feel like taking the lead with our conversation, but I'm conscious of my imagined superiority; it crops up whenever there is tension.

'I'm confused, more than angry,' he says as he pours the coffee. 'One minute this Ria Lace is putting her energies into taking Cemetery Lodge for offices, and the next she's focusing her attention on getting rid of Dad.'

'Does she want you out, as well.'

He leans back, shoulders losing their tension. 'That's the weird part. She's now not interested in the lodge or my job; it's all Dad. It wouldn't be up to her anyhow, but why the change of tack? Stupid woman.'

'It's nothing to do with her being a woman,' I say, immediately defensive. 'You've said that twice now.'

'I know. That came out wrong, I'm sorry.' He slumps forwards. 'She annoys me so much, that's all, the bossiness, the dour expression and her–' He sweeps a hand over his hair.

I shake my head in a sarcastic manner. 'Grey is the new black, didn't you know?'

Ash huffs. 'Not funny. In so many ways, not funny.'

'I was being flippant. It was your *woman* comments. Negative personality traits don't just happen in women; it's a human failing.'

'I stand corrected.' He eyes me coldly.

I search my mind for common ground. Ash's overreaction is becoming difficult to navigate, and it makes me wonder if my hypervigilance is the cause.

'Anyhow,' I say, after a long sigh. 'There's something we're missing in this whole jumble, isn't there? Did I tell you I saw Ria in a car with Ginny Beck, when we were coming back from Morecambe?'

'No? What do you mean?'

When I explain about the car that let us out of the lay-by, and what I thought I saw, Ash doesn't respond straight away. He blows on the surface of his coffee and taps the mug on his chin a few times, but says nothing.

'And I've found something big about Victor Hale,' I continue. 'Apart from all the family stuff, he worked with a traveller charity for many years, as an advocate. That can't be coincidence, can it?'

Ash puts his coffee down and turns to me. 'What the hell is going on?' He stands up. 'I'll fetch paper and a pen. We need to write down everything we know, all the tangled threads.'

I agree. 'Like writing an essay. All the thoughts and theories you have, all the references, need to be combed through and braided.'

It is something I used to tell my online students, a way of making them feel they weren't alone behind the screen with their snarled-up thoughts. Ash gives me a strange stare. My promise to keep superiority out of our relationship has imploded, once again. He fetches the stationery. We list everything we know, grouping our information under various sub-headings: chapel, skeletons, Victor Hale. I suggest adding a *police* heading, and one for the Lovell family; Ash includes Hal, Ria and Ginny. What we end up with is a lot of scribbled ideas and no real links.

'Perhaps we should focus on what is fact and what is conjecture,' I say.

Ash jumps up again. 'I've got highlighters.' He rummages around in the drawer of a bureau in the corner.

I laugh. 'You've done this before.'

'I have.' He holds up a pink one. 'This is for facts.'

'Okay. So all of Victor Hale should be pink, then, because we haven't speculated about him.' I don't get to make any more suggestions. Hal is standing in the doorway, hair askew and wearing his dressing gown.

'Why are you saying that name?' he asks, voice shrill. 'Victor Hale? Why? Why that name?'

Ash

He knows immediately that something is wrong. Hal has pushed his hands against his temples and is making a low humming sound. Cherie tries to calm him, sliding her arm around his shoulder, but he shoves it away.

'Dad. Dad, you've had a bad dream by the looks of it.' Ash uses the soothing tone that he knows Hal can tune in to. 'We made some coffee earlier. The proper stuff. Do you want some?'

Hal continues to react, saying Victor's name over and over.

Cherie breaks the tension by changing the subject. It feels callous, but it works. She asks if he has fed the birds today, joking about them not understanding it is Christmas, but wondering why they haven't had their suet scraps and peanuts. Her comments grab Hal enough for a beat of distraction. Ash seizes it.

'We saved some turkey skin, didn't we? Remember last year when the jackdaws couldn't get enough of it? What was it you said, Dad?'

'Birds shouldn't eat birds.' Hal stares at him. 'Do you think we should do it again? Hang that skin from the feeder?'

'They did love it.' Relief washes over Ash.

Cherie grabs Hal's elbow and guides him gently towards the kitchen. He doesn't resist. All thoughts of Victor Hale have vanished. He is back in the present moment. Ash fastens him into a heavy coat and changes his slippers for the outdoor duck-boots he keeps by the back door. Cherie finds the turkey skin and cuts it into thin strips.

'Like this, Hal,' she says, too brightly.

'Good lass.' Hal shuffles across the kitchen. 'I'm such an idiot, aren't I? Forgetting things. Course the poor birds don't care if it's Christmas.' He takes the turkey skin, chuckling to himself as he wanders outside. Cherie washes her hands while Ash peers through the window at his father.

'I can't believe that just happened. Dad's never mentioned Victor Hale to me before. I'd never heard the name until we read it in the logs.' He passes Cherie a tea towel. 'Thanks for everything today. You handle my father better than I do, sometimes.'

'Hardly. You have Hal to deal with every day. I've only dipped in and out.' She turns to face him. 'But he knows Victor Hale, Ash. Knows him. This is the connection we have been looking for.'

'Dad mentioned the guy in his 1970s logs. It's hardly anything new.'

Ash is surprised when Cherie takes his hands in hers. They feel warm and soft.

'You don't get it, do you? Your dad had a lost love, and it wasn't your mother. He was obsessed with Victor, wasn't he? Victor was his *lost love*.'

Ash can't absorb what Cherie is saying: his father was in love with a *man*. There has never been a hint of this in his life. And if it was the case, why hadn't he taken up with Victor again, after Ash's mother left?

He pulls his hands out of Cherie's grasp. 'I don't see how my dad's private life has anything to do with the chapel fiasco.' He suddenly wants rid of her. 'Please explain.'

'This is what I think,' Cherie begins. 'If Hal was in thrall to Victor, he would have done anything for him. Including lending him the keys to the chapel. Victor is obviously connected to the traveller community in some way. It's not a coincidence that the bodies in the chapel were of eastern European descent. We know a young woman and her child, of similar ethnicity, went missing from a local traveller community at the time when Victor had safe access to the chapel. It all links.'

'You're saying this Victor Hale hid two bodies and my father was complicit? Why the hell would any of that be true? We know nothing about the guy. You know nothing.' These last words catch in the back of Ash's throat. His heart is racing. The whole situation is slipping from his grasp. He slumps into a kitchen chair and leans his head into his palms. He wants to go back a few weeks, when his life was divided into neat compartments, and he could manage each one. Since the day he met Cherie, nothing has been straightforward.

'We need to leave this alone,' he mutters, without looking at her. 'And you'd better go.'

There is silence. He expects to hear Cherie slam her way out of the lodge, but there is nothing. He's already vowed not to take his hands from his eyes until she has left. It is too confusing to be around her. He's surprised when she slips an arm around his shoulder and rests her head against his. She is close enough for him to pick up the warm citrus smell of her hair.

'I'm going nowhere,' she whispers.

Before he can think too much about it, Ash puts his hands on her waist, then slides them around her back. He leans his cheek against the sequinned blouse and lets the weeks of anxiety escape.

CHAPTER NINETEEN

Cherie

It has been raining all day and by the time I reach the hospital, the wet and cold has seeped through two layers of my clothing. I am trembling, though it might be because it's my chance to see the chapel skeletons. I've arranged to meet Ginny Beck in the reception area. It's that dreary period between Christmas and New Year, and there is no sign of her.

I've thought a lot about Christmas Day. When Ash had calmed, he'd once again made me promise to tone down my poking around in his affairs. I'd challenged his use of the word *poking*, but it made things worse. Though he had finally apologised for the outburst, his embarrassment had led to me leaving abruptly. Ash admitted to struggling with the complexities of juggling life, Hal, and the investigation.

What I realised, as he'd clung to me and wept, was his lack of anyone close. There were his biker friends, but from what he'd told me, any support that existed between them was based on who was best at *toughing things out*. Ash kept repeating the same thing as we'd talked: he wasn't sure his best care was good enough for his father, and what else did I think he should do. When I'd explained that I was no expert, that he should see a doctor and get Hal checked over, his response had been unexpected: I was *bound* to know more than him. That one sentence has convinced me there can only be friendship between us. Ash has made his mistrust of what he sees as my superiority clear as diamond.

So, I'm on my own. Bill will negotiate with the local council and transfer our assessment fee to another project. I am going to view the chapel skeletons for my personal interest only.

When the electronic doors of the reception area glide open, I am surprised to see Dale Scott. He is wearing a dark coat that glistens with raindrops. His expression is unreadable.

'Hello,' he calls. 'Lovely weather for ducks.'

I give him a confused smile. 'Hi. I was expecting Ginny. Is everything okay?'

Ginny has taken long-term sick leave, it seems. There are no details. Dale will be taking some of her workload, including the continuation of the chapel investigation.

'How is that going?' I ask, when he has finished explaining.

'Slowly. As I think I said when we met up before Christmas.'

'Did you follow up on any of the things Ash and I found out?'

Dale is ushering me down a long corridor leading to an area signposted as *pathology*. A person dressed in blue scrubs and short white wellies rushes past.

'Let's talk about it later, Cherie,' he says, with a glance at his watch. 'I told the mortuary attendant we would be there at noon, and it's two minutes past.'

We hurry down a flight of steps, feet rasping against the grainy lino, and through a set of swing doors. I think about changing my mind. Unearthing a Victorian skull or a bronze-age femur is one thing; this feels faintly voyeuristic. Dale is telling me about his Christmas, about the dinner his gran refused to eat and the drunken row it caused between his parents. He'd been praying for a call-out, or any other type of *out*. I try to listen, but an adrenaline rush is blurring my focus.

The mortuary has a small annex. There are metal lockers and wooden benches, much like the changing rooms in a school gymnasium.

'We have to take off our outer clothing and shoes, and get togged up,' Dale is saying. He points towards a tall cupboard, then pulls open the door. I realise he has been here before. Of course he has. He is a detective. Once we've put on the blue plastic overalls and matching bootees, he presses an intercom buzzer on another set of doors. A mechanical voice answers with a greeting and a promise to *buzz us through*.

The mortuary is sharply silent. There is a metallic tang and the recognisable scent of formaldehyde. A small woman, dressed as we are, is standing by a gurney. She beckons us over.

'Thanks for doing this,' Dale says.

'No problem, sir.' Her eyes meet mine. 'Madam.'

The skeletons lie side by side, one large and fearful, the other, tiny. The woman introduces herself as Bella. She reads aloud from a document that gives information about tests carried out and findings. There is nothing new.

While she is reading I take a first look. As far as I can see, there is no sign of trauma. Bella backs this up. The post-mortem age of the bones is between fifty and fifty-five years; they are not completely clear of fabric decay. When I ask about this, I am told that tests on fibre remnants have revealed very little. The adult skeleton, the youngish woman, had bad teeth; the bones of the child aren't particularly strong. The swathe of information runs on, but I don't hear anything that jars.

Bella sighs and blinks at me. 'As far as we've been able to

establish, the remains show signs of malnutrition, but not extreme. There is nothing *extreme* about either skeleton. This is why we are struggling. If a body is hidden, there is usually a sinister reason; a murder, perhaps. We can't tell that from what we've got.'

A deep wash of sadness comes over me. If this young woman and her child were relatives of the Lovell family, how would she have coped with expulsion. The traveller community seems bonded so tightly, it would be hard to find yourself on the outside. Where did she go? How did she manage? And what led to her death? I wonder if she knew Victor Hale. He was an advocate for traveller families. Had he offered her help? That makes him a good man, not a bad one. He would hardly have a reason to cause anyone's death, let alone conceal their bodies. But I want to know. It isn't possible to ask Victor himself, not without getting into a lot of trouble, but I could ask the Lovell family. Better still, locate a photo of Victor and show them. When I suggest this, Dale insists the police should be pushing the family for a sample of their DNA. This would at least give us an identification, perhaps even some kind of reconciliation.

'You could come with me,' he says. 'To liaise with these *Lovells*, I mean.'

'I could.' The thought of meeting with the travellers again sends my pulse racing. Photos of the bracelet might be helpful, too. The deceit Ash and I used on Patrick Quinn has been niggling away at the back of my consciousness. To see the real item might make him think less about its monetary value and more about its relationship to his family. If it did belong to one of them. Depending on the state of decay, the woman named Ena might recognise it. When I say this to Bella, she rummages around in an open file on her workbench, and produces two close-up images.

'This is the Romani bracelet,' she says. 'It has been expertly cleaned, and is being kept under special conditions. I haven't been allowed access.' She points to a disc of metal, embedded within the structure. 'We know this is made from pure gold, though it is tarnished. It's a coin, isn't it?'

I take a close look. 'Not a coin, exactly, though it is meant to look like one. Different families, tribes if you will, have their own motif. A close-up of this one would be invaluable.' I turn to Dale. 'Would that be possible?'

He is staring at me, brows furrowed. 'Course. Yes.'

'Let's get the photo, then we can go to Morecambe. You'll be busy, I know, so I will fit in whenever.'

What I don't tell him is that this will give me time to scour the internet in search of Victor Hale's photograph. If I can get into private ecclesiastical sites, there may be a record of some kind. Bill will give me access codes, I'm sure.

We spend a further twenty minutes walking around the skeletons, leaning in but not touching. I am itching to pick up the skulls and feel their weight, to examine the brow bones and touch the jaw line. When we've discovered bony remains on a dig, the first thing we do is meticulously brush away earth and rubble. The bones I am looking at have a stained and lumpen surface, from *open-to-air* decay. The process can't have been clean; there must have been a smell. When Ash and I entered the chapel that first time, there had been the whispered scent of rotting flesh, though fifty years had passed.

Once again, I puzzle over the reason no one had taken the bodies to a better hiding place. What had prevented such a move? Perhaps the chapel was secure enough in the end, though the crematorium incinerator would have been a more decisive choice. I shiver. Someone knows the answer to these questions, and the circle is getting smaller.

Leaving the hospital gives me the same feeling as escaping after a long day at school. There is freedom on my heels, though the insides of my boots are still damp, and the fur around the hood of my parka is as mangey as a wet cat. Dale offers me a lift to the station, but I politely decline. I need fresh air and exercise; I need to think.

Ash wants me to leave the situation alone. Am I supposed to leave him alone, too? The thought gives me a scooped-out feeling in my stomach. I'm still technically on the rebound after my failed relationship with David. Not the best time to become attached to someone else.

I catch a bus to the office. Bill is in this afternoon, and we have work to do. The journey takes me on a meander through housing estates, and past villages strung out along the main road. Rain teems down the windows. I wipe away a patch of condensation and watch the landscape. Colours run together in a blur of blue and green and grey. We are in for two named storms, according to the meteorological office. I smile to myself. Despite the weather, I'm falling for the Furness Peninsula. I'd love it to be more than a temporary home. My contract with Gillside is permanent, but when Bill took me on, he warned that the job might not be what I was used to, might not be *enough*. What he can't possibly know is that simply being part of a team, his team, is what I've been craving. I want to use my skills without constantly having to play a game of *how-do-I-measure-up*. The snobbery of academia was exhausting.

The office is warm with the smell of coffee and sausage rolls. I find Bill at his desk, tucking into a Greggs lunch.

'Hi, there,' he says. 'Wasn't sure what time to expect you.' He holds up a paper bag. 'Share my donut, if you like?'

I laugh. 'Don't worry. I could do with a hot drink, though. It's nasty out there.' While I hang up my parka and unlace my boots, I tell him about my morning at the mortuary. He listens with interest, especially when I mention the Romani bracelet.

'Did you ever think it was stolen?' he says when I have finished. 'Taken by someone who wasn't Romani.'

'And all the other stuff is pure coincidence? I don't think so. What I don't understand is why whoever put the bodies there didn't take the bracelet away. It's valuable, as well as being a hefty clue to identity.'

Bill wipes crumbs from his mouth. 'Perhaps it wasn't seen. Perhaps the person who put the bodies there had something against the bracelet, so left it where it was. Or they were rushing to get away? Who knows.'

I tell him about the motif. He wants to have a look himself. When I explain about Ginny Beck being away from the job, and Dale Scott taking over, Bill seems surprised.

'A detective sergeant has taken over the investigation? He must be talented.'

I hadn't thought of this. Bill wants to know what is so wrong with Ginny that she has stepped away from what might be a murder investigation. I can't tell him. Dale hadn't elaborated and it wasn't my place to ask. Now, I'm wondering what is going on.

'I have every confidence in Dale,' I say. 'He seems to know what's what. In fact, we're going to visit the Lovells again and see if we can get a DNA sample. That's a step forward.'

Bill flips open his laptop. 'You mentioned a local vicar, didn't you? Someone associated with the chapel. More information on him might be good.'

'I've got it, actually.' The outline I give doesn't include my illicit trip to Marsh House, but when I explain that Victor was an advocate for a traveller charity, Bill taps a finger against his temple.

'Ah, I see.' He winks. 'The plot thickens. I love a good mystery, if that doesn't sound too callous. There may be more information about this Victor Hale on the net somewhere, then.'

'My thoughts, exactly.'

We spend an hour browsing church records and the British newspaper archive. There is very little about Victor, aside from what I've already seen. Bill suggests one more search idea, reaching far back into the past. When archaeological services provide assessments, they have to be completed with pinpoint precision.

For accuracy, information must be referenced three or four times. Bill is at the top of his research game, and his knowledge leaves me breathless. He remembers that theological colleges often kept additional records on their students, and some of these have been digitised recently by a private company. Gillside has access. It doesn't take us long to scroll through the top six colleges and find Victor attending St John's York, from 1959 to 1963. The entry is accompanied by a grainy photo. When Bill runs it through his *Lightroom* program, the quality is unbelievable. I gasp. Victor Hale was an attractive man in his youth, and there is something about his smile that is very familiar.

'Can you get a printout?' I ask.

'Of course.' With the click of a few buttons, the printer on the other side of the room springs into action.

'Good-looking guy, wasn't he?' Bill says. 'One for the ladies, I'll bet. Theologian or not.'

I slide the printout into a plastic wallet and put it to one side. Victor Hale has taken enough of my time. Gillside has some *real-world* problems for me to work on. Access ramps need to be installed in strategic sites around the abbey ruin at the edge of town. We have been asked to partner with English Heritage to survey the site before any work can begin. They have requested Bill, as he's worked with them before, but he is happy for me to accompany him.

The irony is that although I've yet to set foot in the place, I feel I know it so well. One of my online students reimagined its narrative in such a poignant way, I could have been walking the ruin as a lay brother in the thirteenth century. I resolve to read the essay again before Bill and I visit.

He's right in his assessment of Victor Hale, too; he was a good-looking man in his youth. Which makes me wonder about him being *one for the ladies*. Was he really the love of Hal's life? And if he was, how did he become entangled with the missing Lovell sister and her child?

Ash

He is bone-tired and hungry, trudging through the rain to complete his perimeter checks. Ash doesn't want to think about his behaviour in front of Cherie on Christmas Day. She was a guest.

His life might be slowly breaking open, but he shouldn't have tried to drag her into the chasm with him. She'd been very kind, very understanding, but her embarrassment was clear. The only thing he could think of, to give her safe passage out of the lodge, was a fake response. She needn't come back again, he'd said, needn't involve herself in any more of his life. She'd left pretty quickly after that. The notes they'd made are still on the coffee table.

He wants to talk to Hal about Victor Hale, but it isn't the right thing to do. His father is already having more unsettled periods than has been normal; they hadn't even managed breakfast together this morning.

Perhaps Ria Lace is right, Ash should look at nursing homes. The thought makes him want to run over to the scrubby bushes by the gate and throw up.

He closes his eyes, and inhales the comforting smell of the rain. There are no funerals today. It will give him the chance to get on with the small winter jobs: clearing brambles from some of the oldest headstones; running a new water pipe to the lower slopes and installing another tap. He can't do this work in a dignified way if people are in the cemetery, grieving.

Working here has given him an understanding of death. Not in the scientific sense or even the spiritual. When a person has been loved, they hold a place in the world that can't be taken from them. The love they have generated is an energy that will never fade. He has seen this, felt it within the families he's come across in his work. If he can take away anything that distracts them while they are mourning, he will.

The afternoon is closing in around him, darkness pushing at the edges of grey. Ash collects a pair of pruners from the shed, and his thickest gloves. He makes his way to the furthest reaches of the cemetery, where the dank atmosphere and shadows encourage rambling plants to thrive. He should have brought his head torch. By his reckoning, there will be no more than an hour before it becomes too dark for working. He has four graves in his sight. One of them is so overrun by tendrils of ivy and blackened nettles that the white marble headstone is hardly visible. Though there may be no family left to care about the last resting place of this person, Ash does. He gets to work.

The silence is a blessing. Hal had spent the early part of the morning chatting furiously about a pair of rogue jackdaws that have joined the regular crew. The turkey skin was blamed, his father insisting this new pair got the scent of it from their friends.

Whatever the truth, Hal was going to spend the afternoon scouring his bird books and journals for hints about tackling off-comers. Ash doubts his absence will even be noticed, though Ria Lace's words still weigh heavily. As soon as the New Year shutdown is over, he is going to get in touch with his father's dementia nurse.

With the pruners poised, Ash yanks at ivy tendrils covering the marble kerbstones. He enjoys the popping sound as suckers are separated from the ground, then snips when necessary. It is satisfying work. The brambles prove more tenacious, their stems endlessly arcing from places unseen.

He senses the woman before he sees her. The back of his neck prickles, making him shudder. He straightens up and cranes into the gloom. She is wearing a dark coat, her pale face framed by a knitted hat. Ash stares at her, and his world tilts. A few seconds pass, but each feels like an hour.

'Ashley,' she says. 'Ashley Paul Black.'

It's not a voice he recognises, but there is something. She steps towards him. His heart pulses at the base of his neck; his breathing quickens. This is his mother.

'It's been thirty years since I've seen you,' she continues, reaching for him. 'My little boy.'

Ash wants to slap at her hand. He doesn't like her tone. It sounds false, *simpering*. He steps backwards. 'I'm not your little boy. Don't call me that. I'm a grown man who you know nothing about.'

'Ah, but I do.'

Ash can't work out her accent. He has no memory of how she sounded. All he can think is that she has no local twang, nor southern vowels. It is hard to make out anything about her, except that she is tall and long-limbed, like him. There is nothing of his face in hers. Her hair is hidden by the hat. She must be in her seventies, if she is from the same era as his father, but this woman could be much younger. Or older. He's about to say something that he hopes will cause her damage, but she interrupts.

'Saw you, didn't I? And this place.' She swings her arm in

the direction of the crematorium. 'I laughed. Seeing all this again.'

'Saw me where?'

'Don't you look at social media? That old chapel, the one up the hill, it's trending. Such a *spooky* story.' She wobbles her head slightly and matches it with hand movements that make Ash want to escape. 'How could I not come and find out what's what?'

'You've not been near for thirty years, not written, not telephoned.' The heat of Ash's temper is flooding his body. His face burns red. 'But a spooky story has brought you back? My God–' He doesn't trust himself to say anything else. 'Great to see you, *Mother*, but I'm going now.'

He kicks at the pile of debris his pruning has created, then stomps away through the darkness.

His mother follows. 'How is Harry?' she calls.

Ash doesn't answer. Moving away from her has lowered his anger just enough to allow curiosity to slide its way in. There are lots of things he could ask this woman, if he was on speaking terms with her. But she can't come to the lodge.

He wipes the rain from his face. 'Dad has dementia, if you really want to know. I've been his carer for a few years now. Not that you'll be bothered.'

'He didn't love me, Ashley. You must have realised that.'

'You had a son. Me.' Ash can't keep the emotion from his voice. Over the years, when his friends talked about their volatile, up and down relationships with their mothers, he'd wanted to say they should be grateful. Instead, he'd kept quiet and wondered what he'd done that was bad enough to chase his away.

'It was complicated,' she mutters. 'As I'm sure you know.'

Ash's mother launches into a story about Hal's little secret, his love for other men, one man in particular. It comes as no surprise when Victor Hale's name is mentioned.

'No doubt he's told you about his sordid affair with a clergyman. One that was married and went with other women, too. I couldn't be involved: it was vile.'

'It didn't make *me* vile though, did it? Yet you still left.' Ash feels faint. He wishes Cherie was here. She would put this *woman* in her place.

'I couldn't love you, son. I'm sorry. What happened with Hal turned me into someone without a heart. Escaping was all I could do. I had to save myself.' There is no charity in her words, no remorse; they shimmer with an icy selfishness. She thrusts a piece of paper towards him. 'I'm staying in town, at The Duke. Give me a ring and we can talk through a few things.'

Ash takes the paper. He won't be seeing this woman again. He feels less than nothing for her. 'Why did you marry my father, if you couldn't stand him?' He screws the paper up and shoves it in his pocket. 'Well?'

'He was so gorgeous in those days. Just like you.' She reaches for him again, and he grabs her wrist. There is an uncomfortable jostle, then Ash drops her hand as though he's touched the worst kind of poison.

'You are unbelievable,' he snarls. 'But thanks for showing up. It has helped me to realise my life would have been far, far worse if you'd been in it.'

'Ashley,' she cries. 'Don't be like that. I–'

He doesn't hear anything else as he strides away.

CEMETERY LODGE

Hal

While he waits to hear the Datsun Sunny's distinctive engine, Hal imagines what Victor's children will look like. Will they be striking and golden like their father, or something different? Meeting them will be testament to the fact that Victor has had sex with someone else. A woman. Maybe more than one. A flare of longing surges through Hal's body, but it is mixed with a newer feeling: jealousy. In the early days of their relationship, he'd been grateful for any crumbs Victor would throw his way; now, he wants the whole cake.

Cemetery Lodge has been spruced up in preparation, the table laid with high tea. Hal isn't used to girls, and Victor has two. He never refers to them by name, only using endearments such as *my darlings* or *my little birds*. Which is why Hal is struggling to create a human picture. When Victor's car pulls up outside the house, Hal lifts the corner of the net curtain and is surprised by what he sees. The girls are large and bullishly jostling towards the front door. Victor, dressed down in a white shirt and slacks, gives him a wave.

The children make themselves at home. They are wearing matching floral dresses and long white socks. Hal tries to smile and remember they are young, not yet attending what they are calling *big school*, but they sit at the table and make demands: their mother says they shouldn't drink blackcurrant cordial as it stains teeth; they hate fish paste sandwiches. Victor does nothing to control them. He sips a cup of tea, expressing his desire for Hal with his eyes.

When the girls have drunk a glass of water apiece, emptied the bowl of Chipsticks, and scraped the pink bit from every jammy mallow biscuit, they demand to be let out. Hal opens the rear porch door and they run into the garden. There is nothing for them, no swing-ball or skipping ropes. They perform handstands on the muddy grass while he and Victor watch through the kitchen window. There is no time for them to be together. Victor's wife has been told he and the children are on a visit to one of his needy parishioners. Hal will have to play along, though he doubts the girls can see further than the end of their snub noses.

After a short time, they are bored. They loll against the shed wall, and niggle each other. Hal wonders what they are saying, what they are thinking. There is no more than a ten-year age gap between him and the biggest one. She comes over to the window and flattens her face against it, making Victor laugh, though it won't be him that has to clean the snot and spittle from the glass.

If this was a test, Hal doesn't think he has passed. Victor is encouraging him to go outside and get involved in horseplay with his daughters. Hal is stalling. He doesn't want any involvement with this pair of large and noisy children; he wants their father. Relief washes over him when it is time for them to be taken home. He senses a cooling off from Victor.

When they drive away, Hal sits in silence at the kitchen table, and stares at the debris of the high tea. It can be cleared away, the half-eaten food thrown in the bin. It won't be so easy to deal with the detritus of his relationship with Vic.

CHAPTER TWENTY

Cherie

Dale's expression of exasperation tells its own story. While he is driving us to visit the Lovells in Morecambe, I make the mistake of asking after Ginny Beck. The woman is not only still off work, but is blocking much of what he is trying to achieve.

'She wouldn't let me access the bracelet remains, either.' His jaw is tense. 'Which means I haven't been able to get the photos you wanted.'

We've taken the motorway route, and I'm sure he is speeding. It is a blustery day, one which meteorologist have warned is a period of calm between storms. As we shoot past high-sided wagons, the car shakes.

'Can she do that?' I ask. 'Ginny, I mean? Didn't you say she'd handed over the investigation to your leadership?'

He huffs loudly. 'That's what was supposed to happen. It's like she wants to sweep the whole thing under the carpet because she can't control it.'

'I thought police had to be squeaky-clean.' I'm trying to be light-hearted, but Dale isn't playing.

'So did I, love,' he spits.

I press my lips together and stare out of the window. The focus of today is to persuade Ena that giving us a DNA sample would be in all our interests. It would be better if Dale didn't have to pull out his police ID and insist. I've explained the situation to Patrick Quinn, and he is expecting us. He's interested in viewing the photos we do have of the bracelet; I'm interested in showing off the print I have of Victor Hale. I've mentioned it to Dale, but he is preoccupied. We haven't talked about why Ginny allowed me to view the skeletons, though I'm happy she did, flattered that she thought I'd have a different perspective; one that might move the investigation forward. What she probably isn't aware of is how much I am doing behind the scenes. That Dale knows about it makes me feel easier. Despite his persona of affable informality, I like his focus.

'Nearly there,' he chimes, as we pull off the motorway. Our conversation goes no further than the safe zone. We chat about journeys and holidays, traffic lights and hold-ups. He is distracted and I am nervous.

Patrick is waiting for us by the gates. He pulls them back and we are allowed to drive onto the chalet park.

'It's a bit better than last time,' he says, pointing skywards.

I introduce Dale, and they share a joke about him being the first police officer ever to have set foot on this *sacred ground*.

'Dale isn't your average police officer,' I find myself saying, to cover the awkward laughing. I haven't forgotten his assessment of Ginny Beck: she wants to *sweep this investigation under the carpet*. Something is swirling through my unconscious mind, a wispy thread I can't grasp.

Patrick is keen to get us inside. He is in shirtsleeves today, though the wind is bitingly cold. We follow him to Ena's chalet, where he promises to make up for the inhospitality of the last visit. She is seated by the fire, the little dog in her lap.

'This is becoming a habit, lady.' She squints at Dale. 'You've brought a different fella this time, I see.'

'It's the policeman I told you about,' Patrick explains, while looking at me. 'We've had a good talk about the Lovell sisters, since you were here last, haven't we, Nan? Your sisters. And you want to know what happened, don't you?'

Ena harrumphs. She has been coerced: it's Patrick who wants to know.

'She's agreed to you taking one of them samples,' he says in a whispery tone, 'but it'll take a bit more sociable persuasion.' He winks. 'If you know what I mean.'

I do, and I think Dale understands as well. He crouches by the side of Ena's chair and makes a fuss of the dog. It snarls at first, but is soon coaxed into having its ears scratched. Ena talks to him about the breed, and he reciprocates with some dog stories of his own. Patrick and I head to the kitchen to make tea.

The room reminds me of my mother's. It is a perfect square of dark brown units, duck-egg blue tiled countertops, and has the same frilled net curtains tied neatly at the windows. The chrome taps gleam. Patrick fills the kettle and chats to me about the journey. He isn't impressed by what he calls Dale's flimsy car, and would recommend not taking it on the motorway again.

'You need a four-by-four at the very least to be safe, these days,' he says sagely. 'Nan will never go in anything else.'

When I point out the cost and green credentials of such a vehicle, he lifts his brows and says, 'Family safety before that climate change stuff.'

I don't want to get into an argument with him, so I change the subject. When I pull the bracelet photos from my pocket and take them out of their plastic wallet, his attention is captured. I go over the story again, about the chapel skeletons and some of the threads that are known.

The details on the coin motif are not clear, and Patrick can offer no help with identification, other than to confirm that every traveller family would recognise their own. He has a gold ring with the Lovell and Quinn crest, and offers to let me photograph it. I thank him, aware that it won't make a lot of difference to what we know. The key factor will be if there is a DNA match between the chapel skeletons and Ena; we mustn't leave without samples.

The other photo I have in my pocket is the printout of Victor Hale. I give Patrick a brief outline of his connection to the investigation, and he warns me that too much of the past can prove as upending as too little, as far as Ena is concerned. *Play it by ear*, is his advice.

Dale has smoothed the way. By the time we return to the lounge, he is holding Ena's hand while she tells him about the old days, summers on Walney Island, playing on the beach in between the chores all travelling families had to endure. Patrick sets down the tea and we listen, giving Ena room to relive her past.

'So, I'm about to speak her name for the first time in many years,' she says eventually. 'My *other* sister. She was Esme Lovell.' She puts a gnarled hand on her chest. 'Esme Lovell. I want to know what happened.' Her eyes are on all of us. 'I'm ready.'

Dale has a DNA swab kit in the pocket of his overcoat. I joke with Ena about me and my sister being called names starting with the same letter: I am Sheralyn and she is Suzanne, but it didn't work out because we became Cherie and Sue. Ena likes this story. As Dale makes an attempt at taking a cheek swab, she keeps her eyes trained on me, winking once.

'This reminds me of that blessed Covid testing,' she says breathlessly. 'I could never do it right. Those things never worked, anyway.' She thumbs towards Patrick. '*Me laddo* had the bug on two occasions and I never once caught it off him, despite the scaremongering.'

She makes Dale take a swab from Patrick too, the distinction between this and a Covid test blurring further and making us laugh. The printout bearing the face of Victor Hale is still in my pocket. The time to produce it has to be judged carefully. Ena is one of those people whose mood can flip in an instant: I don't want to be kicked out prematurely. Dale's professionalism creates the perfect opportunity.

'I don't want the adult skeleton to be your sister's, love,' he says, taking Ena's hand, 'but if it is, would it help the family if you could have it back? Because if it wouldn't, I will personally see to it that a proper burial is given. With something commemorative, a plaque perhaps, so that she wouldn't be forgotten?' He smiles. 'I'll help, either way.'

Ena gets teary. 'Oh, you're a good boy. Is there anything else I can do for you?' She turns to me. 'Either of you?'

I whip out Victor's photo before she can change her mind. 'Could you look at this?'

She frowns and scans the paper, then her expression changes. 'Him. The vicar fella. I remember him. Good to us, he was, and we were all a little bit in love, that's for sure, so good-looking he was.' She wafts a hand in front of her face. 'He'll be an old man now, I guess. Not as lovely as he was, I'll be bound. Why are you showing me?' There's a rise in her voice, and I flash a look at Patrick.

He responds instantly. 'If this fella ever helped your Esme, the police would like to know, that's all.'

'Course he helped her; he helped us all. But I don't think we saw him after she disappeared.' She screws up her eyes. 'Daddy never felt the same about Walney after that. A few of us kept in touch with Elise. You know, the one that married a *gadjo*.'

Patrick interrupts. 'Nan. We don't use that word.'

She waves him away, then picks up her dog and cuddles it. 'Are we done now? I'm tired.'

Dale stands up and stretches his back. 'You, Ena my love, have been a little star.' He turns to Patrick. 'Thanks for your hospitality. DNA analysis can take a couple of weeks, but I will be in touch the instant we have anything.' They shake hands. Patrick shows us to the front door, then we are outside in the buffeting wind. As we climb into the car, the electronic gates slide apart. I open the car window and wave my arm randomly, hoping Patrick will see it.

'That was productive.' Dale flashes a smile. 'The boss has got to be happy when she hears. Good job it wasn't her coming here, today, though.'

I am half listening. 'Why not?'

'She's struggling with her own elderly relative at the moment: her dad.'

His comment jolts me from my stupor. 'Oh? Why moan about the poor old guy. He can't help it.'

'She's not moaning,' he says. 'She worships him. She'd love to be like that Patrick fella, and have her dad at home, but she had to put him into care a few years ago, apparently. Mainly because of her job. She has a sister, but between them they couldn't manage him. They opted for Marsh House, which is up Silecroft way. It's a hell of a trek.' He lets out a long sigh. 'I think it's one of the reasons she's not coping. I'm glad my parents are relatively young.'

I nod, but say nothing else. In my head a picture is forming. No wonder Victor Hale looks familiar. He is Ginny Beck's father.

Ash

The house is silent when he gets up to make his first coffee of the day. The wind has ceased, leaving a strange and echoing void: the calm before the next storm. Ash has spent the night going over his mother's words. He can't let her disappear again without clarification. So, against his better judgement, he is going to meet her this morning.

He takes a mug of tea up to Hal and wakes him gently. The food delivery man will arrive at ten o'clock, a highlight of his Saturday, and Ash will return not long after. His father is perfectly content to be in charge. He has no idea that his son will be meeting up with the mother he hasn't seen for three decades.

Ash takes care over his clothing. He's not bothered what his mother thinks, but she won't be allowed to make any judgements based on how he looks. He chooses the same shirt he wore on Christmas Day, the same grey denims, teamed with his one good pair of boots.

In the mirror he sees a younger version of his father, longer hair and more defined features but he can imagine what Victor Hale saw. What does Cherie see? There have been messages from her, asking for him to get in touch but he can't bring himself to. There's a side to him that has no confidence, so unlike the organised and efficient caretaker who doesn't care what other people think. He wishes there was one level of functioning they had in common. Something that didn't make him feel so inadequate. Not that it matters now; he gave her the opportunity and she walked.

The hotel where his mother is staying occupies a busy block on the edge of the town centre. It is tall, with gothic spires and sandstone dressing similar to many local buildings. She is catching the train at noon, so he must be *brief*.

Ash finds her sitting at the bar in the hotel's saloon, suitcase at her feet. She acknowledges him with a wave. 'I've ordered a pot of coffee,' she calls, as he approaches.

'Thanks.' The word is hard to say; he owes this woman nothing.

She gestures towards a bar stool. 'Are you going to sit?'

Ash isn't sure what to call her. She wouldn't take Hal's surname, though they were married. She was always Cora Last. He quite liked the name: *Last* was more memorable than plain old *Black*. He perches on the stool and waits for her to start up a conversation; he's not going to make it easy. In his head is a list of questions, some of which he may not get answers to.

'Who's got your dad today?' she asks eventually.

'What do you mean *got*?' Ash tries to moderate his tone, but there isn't one scrap of sympathy in this woman's voice.

'You said he had dementia. Is he in a home or something?' She drums a gnarled hand on the bar. She is wearing no jewellery.

'I take care of him, as I think I told you. He's fine on his own at the lodge for short periods.' Ash looks at her face. He remembers her as pretty, but sees only hard edges now. She gives a breathy *thanks babe* when the barman brings their coffee.

'Tell me about dad's affair,' he continues as she fusses with the pot. 'You must know he's connected with what you've read online, about the chapel fiasco. Have you anything to add?'

'I'm not sure he is connected. Not in the way you mean. I won't slate your dad, Ashley. Naivety was his main problem.'

'I'm not asking you to *slate* him.' Ash takes a few deep breaths. 'The police have him pegged as their prime suspect. They think he was involved in the deaths and concealment of those bodies in the chapel.' He slams his hands against his thighs. 'We both know he wouldn't have been.'

Cora shifts in her seat. 'Don't start getting angry. You always did have a temper.'

'I don't have what you call a temper. You knew me for seven years, so you never really knew me at all.' He contemplates walking away. 'I'm angry: that's what you're seeing.'

'Look.' Cora gives a dramatic sigh. 'Harry was besotted with Vic Hale. Before we married. And after. That guy used to click his fingers and Harry would come running. Which meant he had to tolerate those awful daughters of Vic's.' She shudders. 'Teenagers are never good, but they were horrendous. They were the ones fixated by the chapel, if anyone was. Always pestering to look inside, expecting a ghostly tour, I don't doubt. Vic will have given in to them, I'm sure. He adored them.'

Ash wants to ask what his mother knows about teenagers. He couldn't bear it if she had another family and hadn't told him. Curiosity about these daughters of Victor Hale momentarily takes his attention away from the thought.

'Those bodies were placed in the chapel around 1972, Mother. Anyone being taken on a ghostly tour after that would possibly have seen them. *Smelt* them, anyway.'

Cora hesitates and screws her face into a wizened frown. Ash didn't think he could dislike her anymore, but he does.

'I met your dad in 1978,' she says eventually. 'And we married two years later. I put my foot down, after that, and Vic faded out of Harry's life. Those God-awful girls knew something about what was in the chapel, I'll bet. Nosy bitches. I pestered Harry constantly about why they were always hanging around, but he would never say anything bad.' She laughs harshly. 'As loyal as a pet dog, your father was. Pathetic, really.'

'My father is far from pathetic,' Ash sneers. 'He had to do the job of two parents because you walked away. He's actually the strongest man I know.'

'Whatever. It didn't feel like that at the time, is all I'm

saying.' Her hand trembles as she lifts her cup, and coffee dribbles down one side. 'A marriage should be about two people, and I felt there were three extras in mine, nibbling away at the edges, waiting to take a bigger bite.'

While she is talking, Ash thinks about Victor Hale. If, as his mother implies, Hal was being *controlled*, what was he made to do? What had Victor done? And if he'd been responsible for putting the bodies in the chapel, why hadn't Hal agreed to wrangle them into the crem incinerator? It would have been an obvious solution.

Not that it would be possible nowadays. The cemetery caretaker has no access, and undertakers tasked with arranging things need documentation in triplicate. Was there ever a conversation between Victor and Hal about this? Did Hal refuse? Once again, Ash's gut is telling him there wasn't any such conversation, but the thought is shaking him to his core. He needs to steer his mother away from such an incendiary subject.

'Why have you never been in touch, Mother?' He can't contain his emotion. Ash hardly knows this woman, but can't find anything to redeem her. Could any mother be that cruel?

'Your father trapped me. It made me loathe him.' She gives the tiniest twist of her lips and Ash wants to slap her.

'Dad would never have trapped anyone,' he spits. 'Don't you dare say anything against him. You know nothing.'

'I know this. Harry Black was trying to hide his... his... *that* from the world, and I was his cover.' Cora's shoulders sag. 'Believe me or don't. I'm long past caring about what people think.' She gets up from her seat and glances at the clock above the bar. 'I have to go, Ashley. I don't suppose we'll be in touch.'

'Tell me one more thing.' Ash's words catch in his throat. 'Have you got other children? Do I have half-brothers and sisters?'

Cora shakes her head. 'I trained as a teacher once I'd got

over leaving. It gave me a purpose, kept me busy. But it wasn't the best profession for forming long-term relationships. So, no. You've not got half-siblings.'

Ash is surprised to see her eyes glistening. This is the woman who might have stopped the shame he felt at not having a mother. He could have asked her how to fix his relationship with Cherie. Instead, he can only think about whether he can avoid walking with her to the train station. He decides that he can.

Hal

It is early morning, before anyone else is in the cemetery. The air is raw and makes Hal catch at his breath. With the coming of winter, Victor's ardour has cooled. They hardly have any time together. The wretched *girls* accompany him on weekend visits, and the crematorium is becoming so busy it takes away their opportunities for meeting. While Hal is feeling melancholy about this, Victor just seems edgy.

Today, though, they have arranged to meet before an early funeral. It is a Tuesday so all children will be in school. That includes the picky and exuberant Victoria and Virginia Hale. According to Vic, their mother is one of these *women's libbers*: she doesn't see her place as in the home. If he wants his freedom, she should have hers. Hal isn't sure what he thinks about this. Children should be loved, not seen as something to escape from, though he can see why this might not apply to Vic's girls. But they sit at the centre of his universe, and he worships them accordingly, so Hal keeps quiet.

His heart sinks when he catches sight of Victor strolling up the slope. He is holding hands with the oldest girl. She is wearing a navy-blue raincoat, and her face is pale. She is sick and cannot go to school, Vic explains, and her mother is away for the day. He speaks in a louder tone then, saying that he and Mr Black can still have their meeting, that Victoria can lie on the sofa with a blanket over her. She has been dosed with aspirin.

While they walk together down to the lodge, Hal takes some secretive glances at Victor. He is searching for the man he fell in love with, the golden man with the sparkling smile. Being a father should not blunt his appeal. Hal must try harder if he is to hold on. He smiles at Victoria. She screws up her nose and looks away.

The lodge is softly silent, filled with the smell of Hal's morning toast and coffee. Desire creeps through his body. He wants to kiss Victor, to be held against his broad chest and cosseted like one of his children. Victoria is whining for a drink. There is a bottle of orange cordial next to the taps on the kitchen counter. Hal doesn't like the child being in this room, helping herself. She seems well enough to be in school, not pulling open cupboard doors and letting them slam again. Once she has found the coveted flowery glass, she tips in the cordial and splashes in water, too much water, so that it overflows and floods the wooden draining board. If Hal doesn't clean it straight away, the sticky mess will stain.

Victor stands in the doorway, arms folded and smiling. He pets Victoria as she passes him on her way to the lounge, calling her *Vikki* and stroking her hair. Once she has disappeared, Victor takes Hal into his arms and presses him close. They will have to be quick. A shriek jolts them back to reality. The child has knocked her drink over, spilling the contents on the sofa, and on herself. She is calling for her father.

Hal surveys the mess, then goes to fetch a dishcloth and tea towel. He takes his time, wringing out the cloth carefully and searching for the cleanest towel. He wants to help, to get Victoria cleaned up and settled but his loathing of the child far outweighs any compassion he feels. At the door of the lounge, he hesitates. Victor is speaking soothing words to his daughter, but she is making loud demands. As far as Hal can make out, the child is complaining: she dislikes being called Vikki and wants a more grown-up name; she doesn't want to visit with another of her father's friends; she is sick of friends and wants to go home. This friend is called *Esme*, it seems, and Victoria particularly hates the smell of her baby.

Hal steps away from the door jamb and leans against the hall wall, trying to steady his breathing. A woman and her baby; a *friend* of Victor's. Over the months, Hal has become used to this euphemism. To outsiders, his lover must seem like the most dedicated patron. The truth is more vulgar.

CHAPTER TWENTY-ONE

Cherie

Getting to the top of the fell isn't as easy as I thought it would be. It's my last chance for a walk before the next named storm blows in, and after being confined to the house and working remotely, I need to escape. A short distance from my cottage is a footpath that passes the local church and leads onto a gentle green slope. There is a patch of woodland at the top, which I can see from my bedroom window. I've chosen to walk there today. Underfoot, the grass is sloppy, muddy water overflowing my boots.

I haven't spoken to Ash since Christmas Day, and that time has stretched to almost three weeks. He doesn't know about the Victor Hale and Ginny Beck connection; doesn't know I've met with the Lovell family again or viewed the chapel skeletons.

I realise now that I came on too strong the last time we met. He'd wanted the comfort of a supportive friend: I'd read more into it than that. I can't help thinking that my qualifications, my background in academia, will forever mean I have to forge relationships from that arena. It's a narrow-minded way of looking at things, but seems to be the truth. It was for David, anyway.

There's an ominous feel to the sky. It hangs low over the woodland, bringing an early gloom, though it's not long since breakfast. I wander between the winter trees, running my hand over their grey and scarred trunks. Early spikes of green are pushing up between the brown mush of last year's leaves, and I resolve to come back here in a few months' time, when the inevitability of spring will have beaten back the mud.

The first drops of rain hit me as I'm walking home. I pull up the hood of my raincoat and take a quick glance at my phone before the dash for cover. Dale Scott has left a voice note, requesting that we talk urgently and in private. I send him a message, suggesting he comes to the cottage. He responds instantly, and asks for directions. A call-out has taken him to the local motorway junction, and he will be passing my village in fifteen minutes.

My presumption is that the DNA results from Ena Lovell are in, and he wants to discuss next steps. Not that it has anything to do with me. If he has to make the journey to Morecambe again and let the family know whether or not their missing loved-one has been found, he will have to take someone more official. Not Ginny Beck though. Dale doesn't know about my theory. While his boss is safely tucked away in her sick bed, nothing need change. Eventually, I must tell him about her gigantic conflict of interests.

If it is likely the adult skeleton is Esme Lovell, I wonder what the family's reaction will be. Ena hadn't wanted to speak her name at first. Perhaps there will be some private animosity, something the Lovells want to keep to themselves. Then there is the matter of the smaller skeleton. Will any DNA matches be established there?

Thinking about that young woman and her child can bring

me to tears. No one ever missed them enough to find out what happened. How must that have felt? Why had this poor abandoned woman died? Was it even her child? Had she been trying to protect it? I'd seen no sign of trauma on the skeletons; the mortician had concluded the same. I feel compelled to find out what happened. What is the end of the story?

I am not home for long when Dale is knocking at the door. He holds up two cardboard coffee cups and a soggy paper bag. His rain mac is drenched, and he's only walked from the car.

'I stopped at that takeaway hut near the roundabout and got us these,' he says as he follows me into the hall. 'The main road is a nightmare. I'm sure I aquaplaned my way to your turning.' He glances at his shoes. 'I'm making puddles on your floor. Sorry, love.'

I take his coat through to the kitchen and hang it over the back of a chair. Hailstones are pelting against the window and I'm glad of the heat from the range. Dale leans against it, running his hands over the warming-rail.

'That's better.' He sighs. 'It's deffo climate change, all these different kinds of water coming down. I'd be worried, if I had the time.'

I give him a cocky tilt of my head. 'And so says everyone who doesn't want their own life disrupted.'

He huffs. 'Is that the reason you have to rely on the diabolical train company that is *Northern*?'

'That. Plus my ex-husband got the car.'

'I rest my case.' He lifts the lid from one of the coffee cups. 'Flat white for you, love? Espresso brownie?'

'Oh, go on then. We can save the world another day.' I'm itching to ask his news, though I know how important the banter is. 'But can you stop calling me *love*.'

'Why's that, love?' He gives me a mocking frown. 'And can you stop calling me Dale?'

'I don't think I've called you anything, have I? Apart from *sir.*'

'Funny. You've never called me sir, actually. I'm Scottie. People don't call me Dale. It's bucolic.'

I snort with laughter. 'What the hell does that mean? Have you swallowed a dictionary?'

'Have you?' He presses his lips together and peers at me.

We stretch the joke, suggesting his mother would have been better off marrying someone with the surname *View* or *Cragg*. He thinks she should have replaced Dale with Glen.

When we are seated at the table, wisecracks chased away with the coffee steam, he gives me the information I am craving. Ena Lovell's DNA is a probable match for both skeletons. I try to keep my emotions in check, but they well up in my eyes, and my bottom lip trembles. I look away, but Scottie reaches for my hand.

'I had the exact same reaction,' he murmurs. 'These things don't usually affect me, but it's such a sad story. A young woman and her baby, chased away from her community, and no one misses them.' He runs a hand over his eyes. 'I tell you something, Cherie. It's made me more determined to find out what happened. But there's something else, and I have to be careful, letting you in on it.'

My phone rings. I want to ignore it, and let Scottie finish. He tells me it's fine, he would appreciate some time to gather himself. I pull off a piece of paper towel and dab at my eyes.

There's an unknown number on the phone screen. My usual reaction to these is to press the red button, then try to locate who might be calling by using Google. I choose the green button today. It is the lady from Marsh House, Debbie Soames. I momentarily wonder if she is telephoning to offer friendship. There can be no other reason for her call. It was her brother who allocated the places, and I'm fairly sure my last words to him were that I would be in touch. Debbie briefly asks me how I am, then explains. The family of Victor Hale, the *daughters*, have found out that someone visited Marsh House and asked after their father.

Duncan had made an off-the-cuff remark about Victor being a good advert for the place, and they'd pressed for information. He'd tried to smooth things over, explaining there had been no breach of privacy or safety, but the women were *spooked*: Debbie's word. She wanted to warn me that no information had been given about who it was, no name or anything, but Duncan didn't feel that was the end of it.

I thank her for letting me know, keeping my tone dispassionate. A flush of heat is creeping up my neck and flooding my face. I have done nothing but lie to this woman, yet she is giving me a heads-up. I don't tell her there never was an uncle seeking a place at Marsh House, that she's been duped. To get her off the phone, my implication is that I will be bringing my *uncle* to visit soon. Debbie seems happy with this, and says she is looking forward to it.

We end the call. My embarrassment has no chance of survival when pitched against a tiny piece of information she had unwittingly relayed: Victor Hale had *daughters*? Plural? I think back to that rainy day, when Ash and I had visited the Lovells for the first time. Ginny Beck had been in the car with the obnoxious woman named Ria Lace. Could she be the other daughter? She was certainly fixated on moving attention away from the chapel. My heart lurches. Of course she was; they both were. My suspicions are confirmed. Victor Hale is inextricably linked with the chapel skeletons; so are his daughters.

Scottie is calling from the kitchen. He needs to know about my visit to Marsh House. He has probably made a lot of connections himself, but not had the full picture. He'd been about to give me some news of his own. I sit back at the table.

'Is all okay?' he asks.

'Fine.'

He shifts his weight, then rests his elbows on the table. 'As I was saying, Cherie, I have to tell you this but it's highly confidential. I'm not sure what to do about it yet.'

'Okay.' I stretch the word. Something doesn't feel right.

'I told you about the three sets of DNA information we store.' He waits for me to agree, then continues. 'Well, I ran the skeleton stuff through at the personnel level. Don't ask me to explain why, it was just a hunch. And a match came back. Between the baby's DNA and my boss: Virginia Beck.'

There's a silence in the kitchen that feels tangible. I want to jump up from the table, trap it and pummel it for the truth. I must go through with Scottie everything I know, every detail, every thought or conjecture. He has just given me the last piece of the puzzle. Even a layman would know that if Ginny Beck is a DNA match with Esme Lovell's baby, her father will have to be. Victor Hale was the person responsible for making Esme pregnant. Of course he was. Hadn't I found out, on numerous occasions, that he spent time with the Walney Island traveller community. The clues have been lying, like a pile of bricks in my head, and they are finally slotting into place as a wall.

'I need to tell you some things,' I say to Scottie when I find my voice again. 'And then I need to visit Ash Black. Can I come back to town with you?'

'Okay.' He pauses for a moment, and sits back. 'But let's get on the same page first.'

'It's a whole book,' I say grimly.

By the time Scottie and I have exchanged our information and created a picture of everything we know, it is past noon. The weather is bad enough that we decide to stay at the cottage, make lunch and check the roads via social media. I have tried calling Ash, but he isn't answering his phone. Or choosing not to.

Scottie has decided he must interview Victor Hale. According to Debbie Soames, Victor's brain remains sharp. If his daughters choose to block the interview, they will have to face the consequences. It is clear now that they are hiding something. Their father's infidelity must be known to them; Esme Lovell must be known to them.

The rest of the story is unclear, but as Scottie points out, hiding the bodies was a criminal act, never mind what else went on. I am certain Hal is out of the picture, and I want to let Ash know. If he gave Victor access to the chapel keys, it would have to be established by someone else. Hal's memory can't be relied on.

Our biggest worry is Debbie's use of the word *spooked*. What sort of lengths would Ginny Hale and her sister go to in order to protect their precious father?

'Check this out,' Scottie calls across to me as I butter toast at the kitchen counter. He is showing me his phone. On the screen is a site called *Cumbria Road Watch*. It is warning of standing water and marooned traffic on the A-road that would take us into town. I scroll through the comments motorists have contributed. It doesn't make good reading. There are shortcuts, what local people refer to as *the lanes*, but I'm sure these will be waterlogged, too.

'Can we just eat, and get going,' I plead. 'Ash needs to know what's happening. Ria Lace has been pestering about moving Hal to a nursing home. I'm wondering now if she's thinking he knows something.'

'He's got Alzheimer's. You've just told me.' Scottie is pacing the kitchen. 'It doesn't matter what he knows.'

'She's aware of that. Ash has told her. Ginny is, too. I'm not sure they realise the extent of it, though. Especially if Victor's health is what they're basing their experience on.' Once again, another piece of the story drops into place. 'Oh, God.' I put my hands over my face. 'Hal recognised Ginny and Ria. Of course he did. That's why he reacted so badly.'

Scottie moves to stand beside me. 'What are you saying, Cherie? Tell me.'

'Remember when Ginny first came to the lodge and Hal had that bad do?'

He frowns and nods.

'Ash thought his dad's dementia was deteriorating. Ria must have realised there was more to it. No wonder she wants Hal out of the way. There will be things he *can* remember. She can't have that.'

The whole time we are having this discussion, adrenaline is flooding my body. I need to see Ash. And Scottie needs to get Victor Hale's daughters under lock and key.

Ash

The wind gnaws, biting at the parts of his neck not covered by the knitted hat, and the rain beats down. Ash flips up his hood and strides towards the chapel.

A call has come in on the twenty-four-hour hotline. One of the window boards is loose and making enough noise to *wake the dead*. It's what the caller had said in the voice note. Ash hadn't found it funny, not least because the hotline was hardly ever used, but someone had bothered to ring it on a filthy evening like this. Cherie has been trying to contact him, but he can't face it.

Getting his head around Hal being gay hasn't proved as difficult as seeing his mother again. The word doesn't sit right: *mother*. She walked out of his life simply because she loathed his father. Is that what mothers were entitled to do? He shakes away the thought. Enough of his heartache has been wasted on the woman.

Cherie had been correct in her assessment of Victor Hale. He had a connection to Hal. When they'd spoken last, she was going to visit the Lovells and collect a DNA sample. At least that poor family might get some closure about their missing relative. Ash isn't sure he wants closure when it comes to what went on between his father and Victor. In his mind, their relationship is inextricably linked to the chapel skeletons. He doesn't want to know more.

Hal is safely settled in bed, claiming he felt sleepy after his squally afternoon in the garden, taking the bird feeders inside and generally battening everything down against the storm. Ash waits, trying to get a sense of the changing weather. There is the thinnest sliver of light on the horizon, and above it monstrous black clouds with the texture of wire wool. Night has come early.

The soonest appointment to be had with the dementia nurse is at the end of February. Ash has spoken to her about his worries, but resources are stretched. The fact that his father is well cared for and fairly robust puts him low on the priority list, apparently. As though suffering from dementia isn't in itself enough.

Ash has almost reached the chapel. He pats down his pocket, checking he has torch and keys. He'd somehow misplaced the main bunch of keys to Cemetery Lodge, which caused him to reach for the spare. It wasn't on the rack, and he'd spent ten minutes trying to recall if Cherie had it.

In the end, he'd found his own bunch at the bottom of his

laundry basket, with no recollection of how it got there. He feels disorganised and distracted; he's even forgotten to bring his phone or any tools.

A black mood has descended, and he is struggling to shake it off. He should get in touch with his friends, go for a blast on his bike. Take up his history studies again. Anything to get back his sense of who he is.

Having to look at this damaged window is a nuisance, and he'd almost decided to leave it until morning. Another thing he wouldn't have dreamed of a few months ago. He has lost interest in the job, lost his pride and work ethic. If there are no resources to help an old man with Alzheimer's, there certainly won't be any to help a younger man who is feeling depressed.

The temperatures have dropped, so that the rain has transformed into a mix of hail and sleet. Ash rattles the safety fence until he finds the weakest clip, then forces the panels apart enough that he can squeeze through.

He's reminded of the evening he first encountered Cherie. For a long time after he'd caught her sneaking around the chapel, he'd thought she had been concealing something. What he's realised now is that she'd had a genuine interest in the building, and it overcame all thoughts of propriety. If he hadn't been such an arrogant idiot on that evening, he'd have asked her why she was there. His actual reaction was one of assumed dictatorship. It's something he hides behind.

The board over one of the chapel windows is hanging off. Each time the wind gusts, it clatters against the frame. There are no houses from where he is standing, so he wonders who made the complaint. It would make more sense to pull the board off and fix a new one when the weather picks up. Otherwise he will have to go to the shed for his tools. When he reaches up to tug at the board, he isn't quite tall enough to get any traction. He scans around for something to stand on. There is nothing to hand.

The rain has found a way into his jacket. An icy trickle creeps across the nape of his neck. He wants to be back at the lodge. Without thinking too much about what he is doing, Ash walks around the building, to the porch door. The padlock and chains are in place, clogged with an oily residue after the police activity of the past few weeks. He carefully slides the key into the lock and lets the chains fall free.

Inside the chapel, there's an earthy smell. Ash flicks on his torch and pulls the door closed. The last time he had been in here, Cherie was with him. There had been nothing more worrying in his mind than how he was going to get rid of her from the lodge so he could have his office back.

It had been the day when Ria Lace first pushed her way in, demanding the chapel was left alone in favour of the lodge. Then her focus changed. Within a week of finding the skeletons, she'd lost interest in the lodge, wanting instead to be rid of Hal. Something isn't right with the woman.

His father seems to know her, when he has little recollection of the past. The swirling thoughts do nothing for Ash's mental state. He needs to focus on the task at hand: finding a box or chair or something so that he can reach the window board, tear it off, then get back to the safety of home.

His nerves are on edge. There will be a chair in the sacristy but he's not sure if he dares push his way through the door. He stands on the threshold, takes a couple of steadying breaths, then shoulders his way in. The air is icy cold, but a flash of his torch shows him nothing out of the ordinary. The cupboard is closed, the other furniture in exactly the same place as before. The police forensic team has done a good job of tidying up. He lifts a chair from the corner and carries it through to the main area. With one last pulse of light from his torch, he moves towards the porch. He has the chair hooked over one arm, so the other is free to let himself out. But the door is locked, has been locked from the outside. He rattles the handle and in his alarm, calls out for help. No one responds.

Hal

He is convinced Victor's children are stealing from the lodge. Each time they visit, Hal finds something else missing. It's never enough to bother telling their father, but it makes Hal dislike the Hale girls all the more.

Since Christmas, there has been a shift in his relationship with Victor, and he is sure the girls have something to do with it. What Hal had wanted was the romance of a first festive season spent with his lover; what he got was whining schoolgirls in blue velvet party dresses and patent-leather shoes. Which meant they couldn't play outside. The lodge has no facilities for entertaining children. Hal doesn't have even the most basic of board games, no Snakes and Ladders or Mousie-Mousie. Now that Christmas is over, the chapel has become the girls' focus again.

Hal keeps an assortment of keys on a rack in the kitchen porch. Many are antiquated; he has no idea what they unlock. The chapel keys are missing again. He has never needed to use them, the place being padlocked and boarded up for at least a decade. Now, they come and go, following the rhythm of the Hale visits.

Victor has set the girls free to roam the cemetery today. His way of squaring this is to say the eldest is twelve and she needs to taste freedom. Hal would rather she tasted it somewhere else. It does mean that he and Victor will have a half hour to themselves. A jagged relationship is developing between them; the soft edges have gone.

It is painful to see how Victor is losing his patina; the gold looks tarnished. He will not disclose what is worrying him, so Hal can only try and polish things up. The sex is over quickly. It is jarring and unsatisfactory. Victor doesn't apologise. The set of his jaw as he storms down the hallway makes Hal want to weep. He is losing his love.

CHAPTER TWENTY-TWO

Cherie

Cars are bumper-to-bumper, blurring into the distance behind torrents of water on the windscreen. Scottie's car hasn't the wiper capacity to keep it clear. The road is choked with vehicles. Drivers have attempted to drive through puddles which turned out to be pools.

I keep a check on social media updates while Scottie tries his best to get us through. For an hour, we have crawled with the traffic. There is no way forwards or space to escape. Being trapped sets my heart racing so fast I feel faint.

This has happened to me once before. I had the chance to excavate a site within a series of limestone caverns in Dorset. I thought nothing of it until our group was given hard hats and attached to ropes. Each step made me fearful, but I said nothing.

I was a trained archaeologist; I was used to the ground. Not going under it, though, as it turned out. By the time we had walked for five minutes, and squeezed into some awkward places, I could hardly catch my breath and had to be led out again by one of the guides while my junior colleagues looked on.

The experience was humbling. Which is why I would never do the thing David accused me of: look down on people.

I think about Ash. He has my admiration for the life he leads, holding down a challenging and vital job while caring for an elderly man with dementia. He will be holed up in Cemetery Lodge right now, watching the rain stream down the kitchen window while he gets supper for Hal. The thought calms me.

'Shall we just plough on through?' Scottie says as he tries to clear the windscreen of condensation. 'Or we can attempt a U-turn. It's the same distance both ways. What do you think?'

'Let's head to town. If I have to hunker down in the Premier Inn tonight, I don't mind. As long as we can see Ash and Hal and let them know what's what.'

Scottie tightens his grip on the steering wheel. 'Okay. I'll need to call them in next week anyway. Nothing is going to happen before then, is it?'

What I don't tell him is that my gut is working overtime. I feel compelled to get to the lodge. The meteorological office has issued an amber warning for floods in the next six hours, but after that, the storm is predicted to pass. I'd rather not be stuck at my cottage overnight with Scottie. It doesn't seem appropriate.

'Keep going,' I say, with a wave of my arm. 'What's the worst that can happen?'

'I get rescued by a policeman when I am one?' He laughs nervously. 'We have to be canoed out?'

'It'll be fine.' I turn up the car's heater and push my cold hands between my thigh muscles. 'I brought chocolate, just in case.'

It takes another two hours to reach the town centre. We pass a lorry with its front end in a ditch, and many vehicles stationary in deep pools. Two of them are Teslas, and I get a lecture from Scottie on how electric cars aren't capable of saving the world. It is almost five o'clock, but darkness presses against the windows as though it were much later. The streets are deserted. The traffic has thinned to almost nothing, so we speed up and head for the lodge.

Scottie pulls the car up outside the cemetery gates, and we sit quietly, decompressing from the journey. I snap the chocolate bar in half, and we share it.

'What's the plan?' Scottie asks eventually, wiping the corners of his mouth.

'Erm. Get out of the car. Run to the lodge. Knock on the door and wait to be let in. Not rocket science.'

'Not what I meant.' He sighs. 'I have to be careful what is said about Ginny. You're the only person with *that* information. I don't want it shared.'

'You've already said.' Police confidentiality isn't high on my list of priorities; I want to see Ash. 'The only information Ash will be expecting is the DNA match result. Let's start with that.' I click open the car door and haul myself out.

'Right you are.' Scottie follows me. We run through the cemetery gates and up to the lodge.

The place is in darkness. I hammer on the front door with the flat of my hand. There is no response. I try again. Nothing. It is too early for bed, at least where Ash is concerned, and he wouldn't have Hal out on an evening like this. Worst-case scenarios run through my head: Hal has had an accident and Ash has had to take him to hospital; Ash is inside the lodge, lying injured, and Hal hasn't been able to cope. I try phoning again, then ring the landline. I can hear the tone, but no one answers. Something feels off. I call through the letter box, but nothing changes.

'There is a spare key for the back door in the rear porch.' I peer at Scottie through the rain. He has no hood, and his hair is streaming. 'You'll have to give me a bunk-up over the fence.'

'Go for it.' He hesitates. 'Can I say one thing first.'

I shrug. 'Yep.'

'What if they are in and don't want visitors. Have you thought of that?'

I hadn't, but don't tell him. 'Well, they've got visitors, like it or not. We haven't made that journey just for the fun of it, have we. I'm going in.'

Scottie squelches across the patch of grass at the side of the house. He stops at the wooden fence. 'Here?' he asks.

'Here's fine.'

He shoulders the fence and links his hands together. I brace with my soggy boot and haul myself upwards. My stomach meets the highest plank, then I swing my legs over and hit the ground on the other side with a wet thud.

'That's a safe landing, anyhow,' I shout through the gaps. 'Give me a minute.'

The knees of my jeans are saturated with muddy water. I dry my hands on the insides of my pockets then move towards the kitchen window. There is movement. I peer closer but the room is empty. The spare key is where I thought. I try to unlock the door, but it won't budge. I knock a couple of times, and call, but no one comes.

'Scottie,' I call through the fence. 'Something isn't right. It feels like the door has been locked from the inside. I can't see anything through the window, which makes no sense. Ash and his father are always in the kitchen.'

'Let me try the front door again,' he says. 'Give me a minute.'

While I wait, I stare through the kitchen window and into the gloom. Where is Ash? His absence is worrying. I tap the glass and try to get some context. Is there a half-eaten meal on the table? Any sign of smoke or fire. There is nothing. Scottie comes back. He can't raise a response, either.

'Oh, God.' I remember the bolts. 'Someone has locked this door from the inside.' When I'd asked Ash about them, he'd joked they were protection from a zombie apocalypse. It occurs to me then that he is hiding. Had we parted on such bad terms, he can't bear the sight of me? That can't be the truth. Which means something bad is happening inside. 'I need to get back over to your side, Scottie. What should I do?'

The adrenaline of the day has heightened my anxiety and I'm starting to panic. I cast around but there is nothing in the garden that could help me scale the fence. I try the run-and-jump method but I've neither the height nor the strength.

'Take your jacket off and sling it to me,' Scottie calls. 'I'll tie it onto mine and see if it'll make a long enough rope for you to hang off the hood. I've seen it done. It'll give you a bit more to grab when you're trying to climb.'

It takes three attempts, and we are soaked to the skin, but Scottie's idea works. The *coat-rope* is just long enough for me to hold while I swing myself up. The muscles at the top of my arms are stretched to their limit, but I get over. I lean against the fence and take some deep breaths. We untangle our jackets and slip them back on. Mine is saturated inside and out.

'Do we just give up?' I say as Scottie glances frantically around. 'Perhaps you're right. The Blacks are hiding from us.'

'No,' he snaps. 'No they're not. I trust my personal radar in situations like this and it's screaming at me right now to get inside the house. I'm going to call for backup.'

He slides an arm around my shoulder, and we move close to the house for shelter. I can't see a good outcome to the situation. If Ash and his father are inside, an intervention from the police isn't going to end well. And if they aren't, where the hell have they got to?

'Can't you do another policeman trick, and kick the door in?' I ask as I stare up at the windows.

'I'd need a reason for doing that,' Scottie says. 'And it's not as easy as it's made to look, anyway. I'm in civvies, as it were, with no one in the force knowing where I am. Better I ring for backup. And an ambulance perhaps.'

I wipe the rain from my face. 'Good luck with that.'

'With what?' A voice comes from the shadows. Someone is striding towards us. Ash. 'Good luck with what? And I'm glad you're here, Dale. Something is very wrong.'

Ash

Relief washes over him. Cherie is here. Being trapped in the chapel created a wave of panic like nothing he'd ever felt. It was simple enough to rattle the door and slip his hand through the gap to free up the padlock; more worrying was the idea of Hal being alone in the lodge without knowing what was happening. Changes of routine needed explaining; the bad weather needed explaining. Ash gives himself time to think. Someone deliberately locked the chapel, knowing he was inside. He gives Cherie a nod, then tries to let himself into the house. The key turns but the door won't budge.

'What's going on?' His words fire out with a force he isn't expecting. Hal is in the house, and someone must be in there with him: he can't fasten the bolts himself; he doesn't have the strength.

Cherie puts a hand on Ash's shoulder. Her hair and jacket are drenched. 'The short version is that Hal might be in danger. Ginny Beck and that horrible Ria woman aren't who they seem. I'll tell you everything later. We need to get inside the house.'

There's an urgency to her tone he hasn't heard before. It sends a flash of alarm from his belly to his feet. What have Ginny Beck and Ria Lace got to do with any of this?

Dale Scott has moved away and is speaking to someone on the phone, barking out orders. Ash has the key to the garage on his ring. His hands are trembling as he lets himself in.

The thought of his father trapped in the house with some madman turns his fear to anger. He creates a mental picture of the bolts. They are sturdy and well-fitted, and the door itself is made from thick wooden planking. Breaking in would require expertise and time. Smashing the tiny plate-glass window at the side of the house might be a better option, though it will be dangerous. There is a reason why those kinds of windows aren't standard anymore.

He picks out a sledgehammer and a pair of motorcycle gloves. Within seconds he has charged around the side of the house and smashed the window. A few pieces fall inwards, and he uses the butt of the hammer to knock out the rest. Cherie is behind him, shouting that he should be careful. Then he hears Dale's voice. He ignores them both and decides that the best way to avoid the jagged edges he's left is to pull up the hood of his jacket and dive in. If his hands find glass, the leather gloves will protect him. He almost gets away with it, but his trailing leg is gouged as he pulls it through. It's painful but doesn't distract him. He unbolts the front door and opens it, then storms up the stairs, calling for his father.

In the doorway of Hal's bedroom, Ash stops. The darkly contoured scene makes no sense. Someone is standing in the corner of the room, another person cowering below them. On the bed is a further shadow. A prickle of fear creeps across his shoulders, and he's not sure what to do. He can't think, can't respond.

Cherie has come up the stairs behind him. 'Ash,' she hisses. 'Ash, switch on the light.'

Her presence snaps him from his trance. He flicks the switch, and the scene is transformed by harsh yellow light. It's his father on the bed. Ria Lace is somehow in the room. And Ginny Beck.

'Look after Hal.' Cherie pushes at his shoulder. 'Ash. What's wrong with you? Go to your dad.'

Ria Lace begins yelling at the hunched figure. It is Ginny, but not as he's seen her before. The grey hair is greasy and flat, the clothing looks more like pyjamas. She is clutching one of Hal's pillows and sobbing quietly.

Ash kneels by the bed. 'Dad,' he cries, shaking his father's arm. 'Hal. Wake up.' He tries to recall his first-aid training but there is a pounding in his head, a clouding of his judgement. His father is unresponsive.

'What the hell have you two done?' Cherie lunges at Ria. 'If you've killed him, you're dead.'

Ria takes a swipe at her. 'Get away from me. I hope he is dead, the trouble he's caused. I hope he's fucking dead.'

Cherie's hand flies to her mouth and her head goes down. Ash can see she's been thumped but he can't move. Ginny tries to stand up, but Ria knocks her down.

'You're going nowhere,' she snarls. 'This is your fault. I told you to bring that old duffer in, but you wouldn't have it. You're weak; you've always been weak.' She yanks the pillow from Ginny's hands. 'I'd have been better holding this over *your* face.'

'He doesn't know, Vikki. Harry doesn't know anything.' Ginny slides back into the corner.

Ria flings the pillow across the room, then punches at the top of Ginny's head. 'Don't fucking call me Vikki. I've told you. Don't call me–' Her voice breaks but she keeps on punching.

Then hands are on Ash's arms, and he hears Dale Scott

saying an ambulance is on its way, but he can't tear his attention from the three women.

Ginny is saying the word *daddy* over and over. Ria is screaming at her to grow up. Until the chapel skeletons unleashed their energy, these were two women Ash knew little about.

The high-pitched whine of sirens fills the room, and the curtains can't conceal flashing lights on the driveway outside. There is so much confusion and Ash is not sure what he should do.

'We know Victor Hale killed Esme Lovell and her child,' Cherie says to Ria. There is a hard edge to her voice he has never heard.

'You know nothing,' Ria shrieks, stepping towards her. 'There was no *killing*. Daddy would never kill. This is all Harry Black's fault. Harry the *girl*, we used to call him, all that long hair and eyelashes.' She grabs a handful of Cherie's sweater and rattles her head. Then she flicks a foot at Ginny's knee. 'Some decoy this one turned out to be.'

'Stop.' Ash yells so that his throat hurts. 'Stop this, the lot of you. I don't care about blame, whatever the hell you're blaming each other for. My *dad* could be dead and you're bickering. Shut. The. Fuck. Up.'

There is a beat of silence, then uniformed police officers tear into the room. An ambulance crew follow. Dale grabs the top of Cherie's arms and moves her away. He whispers something, and she kneels beside Ash. There is blood on her top lip. She takes his hand, and he lets himself be led from the chaos of the room.

CHAPTER TWENTY-THREE

Cherie

'Ria's excuse was family first.' Scottie leans against the wall outside the abbey ruin's ticket office, and rummages in his pockets for change. He's wearing a dark suit today. And a tie. 'She admitted everything but still insists she did nothing wrong. And she hates you, that's for sure.'

I run a finger over the scab on my upper lip. 'Why, though? I only met the woman once. Apart from that night, obviously.' We're waiting in a small queue for the ruins to open, and I haven't yet told him there is no need to pay. Since the stormy period of weather, it has been settled and bright, and people are venturing out again. Not Ash, though. He's been at Hal's bedside most days.

'Ria tried her best to get Ginny to use you, apparently. Another of her failed plans.'

'Use me how?' I ask, incredulous. 'I'm not much of a commodity.'

My comment causes a blast of sarcastic laughter. It's catching and leaves me breathless, perhaps because the solid anxiety of the past few months is finally vaporising, leaving my body each time I speak about it.

'Don't undersell yourself,' Scottie says when we have calmed down. 'You were key in the Lace and Beck plan to save their father. If anything had ever got to court – you know, about the hidden bodies and suchlike – the pair were going to say you tampered with evidence; that you had *ulterior motives*. Meaning your romance with Ash Black.'

'There was never any romance between us.' I turn away. Ginny Beck hadn't wanted my input; it was a ruse. The feelings of flattery had far outweighed my common sense. Ash would laugh at that.

When Scottie and I step into the museum area and move to the ticket counter, I flash my permit. It brings a raised eyebrow and reverence from the woman who is serving. She is small and wiry and offers us the use of her office. I decline politely. We step out of the museum and into a dazzle of spring sunshine. The ruin leaves us speechless for a heartbeat, with its tumble of carved sandstone slabs and its antiquity.

Then Scottie says, 'Talking of romance–'

I look sideways at him and tilt my head. 'What about it?'

'There was plenty between Harry Black and this Victor Hale guy, from what I can gather.' He pulls his electronic pipe from the pocket of his jacket, and takes a puff. Fragrant vapour fills the air: peppermint, I think. 'And Hale's lovely daughters were jealous. They went everywhere with him and hated it when others got attention. Including that poor lass, Esme Lovell.'

Scottie has told me as much of the story as he is able. Ria and Ginny are to be charged with attempted murder and obstruction. They had intended to kill Ash's father because he knew the truth. Except he didn't. No one had killed Esme Lovell and her child; Victor's child. When she became estranged from her family, Victor had arranged accommodation, a bedsit in a Victorian tenement block. He'd visited one day, as he often did, with Ria and Ginny in tow, and discovered Esme and her child dead in their beds. He'd blamed fumes from the decrepit gas boiler. Ria remembers the choking air and panic in her father's voice. Scottie feels some sympathy for Ginny, but not for her.

'I'd like to be involved when Esme is reunited with her family,' I say. 'Would that be possible?'

Scottie turns to me. 'Of course. You've been instrumental in bringing closure for them. That Nana Ena character would be cross with me if you weren't there, and I'm not about to make her angry.'

'Instrumental. That's a big word.' I give the top of his arm a mock-punch. 'Families, hey? In a way, Ginny and Ria were only trying to protect their father. It's not much different from Ash with Hal, is it?'

'Ash and Hal haven't tried to conceal a body; multiple bodies. When the Hales came across Esme and her daughter, they should have reported it, never mind Victor and his reputation. Ria told me, in a fit of pique, that they'd tried to get Harry Black to give them access to the crem incinerator. And if he had, no one would have been the wiser. That woman has no empathy or perspective. She's dangerous.'

'What about Ginny. Is she dangerous, too?'

Scottie shields his eyes from the sun and stares up at the ruin. 'I sat in on her interview and yet I can't answer that question. It makes me wonder if she and Ria went as far as plotting out their choice of career so as to fix things if this whole nasty story came to light.'

'That was a fail then.'

'It was.' He takes in a lungful of the soft spring air. 'And what about you? How's the battered lip?'

'Fine.' I laugh sadly. 'Ash got more of an injury when he climbed through that blessed window. He had to have six stitches, which didn't go down well.'

'I bet it didn't. Do you see much of him?'

I shake my head. 'Not really. But I am meeting him later for a catch-up.'

'That's good, then.'

I agree, but don't say anything else. The truth is that this meeting with Ash will be my last. We've exchanged a few messages, and I have been to see Hal, but I want to arrange to collect my pilot bag and equipment from the lodge. There isn't going to be a chapel assessment. The council have decided the place should remain closed. Too many ghoulish influencers have been trying to change its fortunes. The dignity of the chapel and cemetery need to be preserved.

Scottie and I wander the ruin, while I give him a rundown of the place. He is interested, but distracted. Not everyone feels bonded to the past: I understand that. The students I'd worked with online fell into three categories: the idlers who wanted results from minimum input; the intense academics who saw qualifications as stepping stones; the historic empaths. My best student would love to think I was walking his ruin, right now. We'd joked about how he felt an ownership of old buildings, particularly this one. Digital tutoring felt a bit like reading a fairy tale; all the beauty and angst were present, but not the gritty reality.

'It's been great, catching up,' Scottie says when we are nearing the end of our tour. 'I can't believe you get to work in a place like this. Is that soon?'

'It is. My boss, Bill, has cleared the decks of everything else, so we should be ready to start next week. I can't wait.'

'Well done, Bill.' Scottie looks skywards. 'Can't beat the outdoors on a day like this, can you?'

'Don't pretend you're an outdoorsy type. I remember you at Biggar.'

He elbows me. 'Fair point. I like a bit of sun, though. Me and Cindy – that's my girlfriend – have booked to go to Crete this summer. She reckons I can afford it now, with the promotion and everything. She's spending my pay rise before it's even hit my wage packet.'

'Wage packet? What the hell's that?'

Acting Detective Inspector Scott: it suits him. When I point this out, he blushes.

'The show must go on, love,' he says as he kisses my cheek.

'Sorry I'm late.' Ash hurries towards me. The brisk weather has brought a glow to his cheeks, and he has had a haircut. A motorcycle helmet hangs from his hand.

'No problem. I've only just got here.' I touch the neat strands that lie across his shoulder. 'Nice hair. I'm glad you've preserved the jackdaw streak.'

'That will never go,' he says. 'The barber asked me if I bleached it. As if.' We laugh at this. Ash is a man with no affectations. He wouldn't have the first idea how to use peroxide.

We push our way into the café. I cast around for a table and spot one in a distant corner, away from the throngs of Saturday families and children. Ash drapes his leather jacket over the back of a chair and goes to the counter. While he chats to the assistant, I watch with a mixture of interest and regret. He is wearing a rough striped shirt and faded jeans. There is a quiet confidence about him that I've fallen for, but I can't acknowledge my feelings. Today will probably be the last time our paths cross.

When he comes back balancing a tray of drinks and some cellophane-wrapped biscuits, he is smiling.

'What?' I love his smile.

'I was just thinking.' He puts down the tray. 'Remember that café in Morecambe. Brucciani's or something. We were soaked to the skin and filthy, weren't we? Like proper bikers.' He fluffs up his hair. 'Today, I'm what we in the business call a *holidaymaker*.'

I take my drink and some packets of sugar. 'What does that mean?'

'It's a local term. Taking the mickey out of people who aren't genuinely into what they claim to be.' He shrugs. 'I haven't explained it very well.'

There isn't an answer I can give. My hope is that I'm not included in his generalisation. Does he think I'm just playing at caring about him and his father?

'Well, holidaymaker,' I say, 'sit down and have your coffee. I've got my boss's car today and I want to collect my stuff from the lodge. Would that be okay?'

He is suddenly subdued. 'It would.'

'How is Hal?' I ask, looking for common ground. 'Any sign of coming home yet?'

Ash tells me that his father is now able to get out of bed and is driving the nurses mad with his endless loop of demands. Arrangements have been made to bring professional carers to the lodge, three times every day, so that Hal won't be alone for any long stretches of time.

'He's had a shock, but doesn't remember much of it, which is a blessing. I'm not sure what Beck and Lace did to him. There was bruising to his shoulders and around his mouth, but thankfully they didn't have the guts to finish what they started. Why they thought Dad would tell on them is a mystery. They'd both seen how ill he is. And I don't think he ever knew the full story, anyway.'

'Is there to be a trial?' I'd like to listen in on how the Victor Hale epic was going to be spun.

Ash shakes sugar into his coffee. 'I'm not sure. I don't want to think about it. What those two did to Dad means they are off my radar for ever.' He peers at me and raises his eyebrows. 'One good thing came out of all this, though. If you can call it good.'

'What?'

'I met my mother again, after thirty years.' He lifts his cup in a fake salute. 'What do you think of that?'

'What do *you* think?'

I sense tension. Ash takes a sip of his drink then puts it down. 'I felt very little when I saw her, if I'm honest. She called me Ashley Paul. No one calls me Ashley Paul. Not even her, Cora Last. She never wanted to be Cora Black, even though she and Hal were married. That is so typically *her*.'

Something jolts in my brain. He continues, telling me about this woman, and how she blamed Hal's homosexuality for her abandonment of her son. I try to listen, but my focus isn't there. It's on an entirely different subject, if only I could articulate it.

'She knew there was something off about Victor Hale and his daughters,' Ash is saying, 'but never thought to say. In all the time she was somewhere else, living a different life, she felt uneasy about those bloody people, but was happy to leave Dad with it. What do you think of that, Cherie? Cherie?' He touches my hand. 'You were miles away.'

'Sorry. Yeah. What a bitch. Who abandons their son? It's cruel.'

My words make him laugh. I use a few more to describe this woman that I've never met. Ash seems to appreciate my support.

'Anyhow.' His shoulders relax. 'I can honestly say there

were no sentimental feelings from me. Or her, actually. She's gone back to wherever she came from.' He goes quiet, then breaks the silence with, 'What about you?'

'What do you mean?' I feel like I've missed something.

'What's next for you? Once you've moved out of my office.' He stretches the word with a wink. Is he flirting? Would Ash even know how to flirt?

'Gillside has lots of other projects for me, starting with that hulking abbey ruin. Immense, isn't it?'

'Oh?' The flirty attitude slides. 'Furness Abbey? What's happening with the place?'

'EH are wanting to install access ramps, so certain areas need surveying, that's all.'

'EH? I'm sure they love being called that.'

His mood has dropped, once again, and I wonder what I've said. He's acting like English Heritage are his family. When I point this out, he gives a sharp and sarcastic lift of his brows and changes the subject.

'My instincts were right about Ria Lace, weren't they? Do you know she actually stole the spare front door key to the lodge? Bold as you like, and I had no idea. That's how she and Ginny got to Hal, once they'd padlocked me in the chapel.'

'Oh my goodness. You're going to have to get your locks and keys under control.' The words hit the table with an awkward *thud*. 'Sorry. That was meant to be a jokey reference to the whole chapel fiasco. Not to you personally.'

'I know what it was.' Ash unwraps a packet of biscuits and breaks one in half. 'Share?'

'Thanks.' We lock eyes. 'I need to learn to *shut-the-fuck-up*.'

'You make me laugh,' he says softly. 'And you're right, you do.'

I pull a face, then say, 'I'm going to visit the Lovells again, by the way. With Scottie.' I pause. 'Dale Scott, that is. He wants to reunite the skeletons with their proper family, and he let me telephone Patrick Quinn with the latest news. Poor guy was very emotional. Esme would have been a great-aunt of his. Scottie says we can return the bracelet remains, too.'

'*Scottie*, eh.' Ash tuts very gently, but I hear it. 'Is there something I should know?'

What he is getting at, I can't fathom. These comments aren't on a par with how he usually communicates. I've never once heard him use innuendo. Before I can stop myself I snap out yet another caustic response.

'There are probably lots of things you should know, but I can't help that.'

His shoulders sag; his gaze follows. 'Right you are,' he mutters, then pushes his cup away. 'Better get back, anyhow. Then you can collect your things. The police have given me back my spare key. The one Ria stole.' He passes me a key ring. 'Here. Let yourself in and I'll catch up with you later.'

Ash

He runs a hand through his hair and wonders what it is about him that women don't like. Even his mother left. Ash has been trying to process this all his life, and thought he'd managed quite well. Then he'd met Cora again, and his feelings have been upended.

It's the same with Cherie. They've been through a lot, but whenever he tries to make something of it, she pulls rank. That's the only way he can describe it. She often reminded him, unintentionally, that they weren't and never would be operating in the same lane. He should have been more careful before allowing his feelings to develop into something tangible; he can recall her smirk when he'd mentioned his university history diploma. He's probably doing her a disservice. Not that it matters now. In an hour or so, she'll be gone from his life.

Cherie's car is already at the lodge when he arrives. The boot is open. He parks his bike and pulls it onto the stand. It has been strange not having his father at home. There hasn't been a day in his life where they have been apart. Even the training courses for his caretaker job had taken place locally and were never residential. Staying away will never be an option now; Hal needs him.

Cherie is in Ash's office, pulling cables from her computer. The pilot case is open on the floor.

The police have told him that the chapel will have to be monitored for a while. They don't want people snooping around, trying to get stories for social media platforms or newspapers. Especially since there will eventually be a trial for Ginny Beck and Ria Lace. Ginny's situation must be handled with the utmost care as she was a serving police officer at the time of her offence. Ash may well be called to give evidence, though it is not certain. Ginny's mental state is such that she could escape severe punishment. Her sister had been the main perpetrator, forcing Ginny into actions using emotional blackmail.

Victor Hale must have been worth the trouble. Hal thought so at one time. The end of that story isn't clear, and it would be pointless asking his father about it. Cherie had it all worked out. Her brain must be far superior to his.

'I'm not happy about leaving,' she is saying. 'I really wanted to do a full assessment of the chapel. You know what I'm like about old buildings.'

'I do.' He drags the office chair to one side, pulls his foot up so that it rests on the opposite knee, and watches her work. 'The lives they've contained create a story, don't they? Give the place a soul. Almost like they are human.'

Cherie gives him a strange look. She's about to say something then changes her mind. He's tempted to leave her to it, and find some work of his own. There's plenty, but it's a Saturday; he's not paid to work the weekends, apart from emergency calls. The last time he took one of those, Ria Lace had locked him in the chapel. It's an experience he doesn't want to repeat.

He's still trying to come to terms with the fact that she and her sister have lived a relatively normal life, yet for the past fifty years have been covering up something horrific. How do people live like that? That they expected to escape the lodge after getting rid of Hal, and hoped to get away with what they'd done, sends a shiver across the back of his neck. What does anyone really know about anyone else? Perhaps Ash is better off staying in his own *lane*, caring for his father and not getting involved.

Cherie zips her case and pulls up the handle. 'That's about it, then. I'll get going.' She bumps down the hallway. Ash follows behind her trying to put together a goodbye speech. Will there be the offer to meet up again? It wasn't so long ago that he was hoping for a return to the mundanity of life before the chapel skeletons. Now, he wants more for himself, though he's no idea how to ask.

There's the smallest breeze, and it lifts the ends of Cherie's hair and flaps at her anorak as she puts the case in the boot. He watches, hands in the pockets of his jeans, wondering if he should give her a hug. She walks towards him.

'Thanks for everything,' he says. There are more words, but they catch in his throat.

'No worries.' She holds out her arms. 'I'll let you know how it goes with the Lovells. Give my best to Hal. I will pop by once he's home. You've got my number.'

'I have.' Ash lets himself be embraced. He wants to give a huge and meaningful speech, but his throat feels clogged.

They step apart.

'Bye then.' Cherie moves around the car to the driver's door and climbs inside. Ash is trembling with unspoken angst. He lays a hand on the roof and as she starts the engine, slaps his hand down a couple of times. Then she drives away.

Hal

A jackdaw has landed on the patch of scrubby grass he calls a garden. Hal remembers his father calling them vermin and chasing them off, but they've come back to Cemetery Lodge, and are nesting in a nearby clump of beech trees. This bird is peering, head tilted in defiance. The creature can have no idea how welcome it is.

Hal is missing human interaction; any interaction. There have been polite conversations with patrons using the crematorium and cemetery, but nothing real. Victor is about his business, but as distant as the stars. Since Hal hinted he should not bring the girls on his visits to the lodge, there have been no visits.

Hal throws some toast scraps through the open kitchen window. The jackdaw makes a startled dash for the high boughs of its tree. It waits at first, then drops to the grass again. The scraps don't last long; it probably has a fledgling to feed. Hal closes the window and thinks about his jobs for the day. There is a graveside service at noon and another in the crematorium at three. He will need to water the grass at the top of the cemetery, where the scorching weather has caused unsightly brown patches. Working stops him thinking. He hasn't looked up the identity of today's clergyman; he'd rather not know.

Outside, the heat is stifling, though it is nowhere near midday. Hal has left his donkey-jacket hanging in the porch. He is supposed to wear it at all times for protection, but not today. He rolls his shirtsleeves as high as they will go, and heads up the slope. The sea has matched its colour to the sky. Both are unbroken blue, too perfect for him to contemplate in his broken world.

Victor is standing in the shade of the chapel. He is wearing a black cassock, and appears to be praying. Hal steps aside and watches. This is the man he loves. It shouldn't matter if he has a family; it doesn't matter. They will be together, despite the difficulties. Hal leaves his hiding place and strides towards him.

The reaction he gets is not expected. Victor will not look at him. He wants to know about the chapel, who uses it, who has access. Hal answers to the best of his ability, while wanting to call his love from its rooftop. When he lays a hand on Victor's arm, it is brushed away. He tries to apologise, but Victor cuts him off. He will see Hal when he can, but there is no future for their relationship, no stability, no *love*. He is setting Hal free.

CHAPTER TWENTY-FOUR

Cherie

'Give Ash Black a wave.' Scottie points in the direction of the water. 'He'll be right over there, stressing about something.' He wiggles his fingers. 'Yoo-hoo, Mr Black.'

'Stop it.' I won't join in with Scottie's teasing. We have journeyed around The Bay again, and have stopped on Morecambe prom for a walk before we meet the Lovells. We've travelled in Scottie's car, and the mortuary transit van is due to meet us in the Mellishaw car park at noon. Esme Lovell and her child are finally coming home.

'Sorry.' Scottie turns up his collar against the bite of the wind. 'Just trying to lighten the mood.'

'Ash has had a tense few months. You and I might be at ease with dead bodies, but he certainly isn't.'

My comment causes Scottie to splutter. 'He's a cemetery caretaker, for goodness' sake. Of course he's at ease with the dead. The guy is a stress-head, pure and simple.'

This is not a conversation I want to have. We are early, so I suggest we walk down to the promenade. The tide is halfway out, leaving an expanse of wet yellow sand and a thick line of bladderwrack along the edge of the pebbles, and the tang of *seaside*. It reminds me of the day Ash and I visited here before. It was fun; we were friends. He felt something for me, I know he did. The time I'd spent with Ash and his father had an authenticity that was lacking in my life. It has helped me realise what I need; it isn't people like Scottie and his pigeonholing.

'Imagine.' I stretch the word. 'If you were a full-time carer as well as a full-time policeman, Scottie. Would it make you a stress-head?'

He thinks about this, but I don't give him time to answer.

'Of course it would. So don't be bad-mouthing Ash.'

Scottie stops walking and leans on the promenade's lengthy iron balustrade. It is painted in blue gloss and is interspersed with seabird sculptures. 'I've told my mum I'm putting her in a home if she ever loses it.'

'That's cruel.' I nudge his arm. 'You don't mean it.'

'I do.'

A group of people are flying rainbow-coloured kites below us on the sand. The adults are more enthusiastic than the children. I wonder if this is a family, wonder what creates that label. Is it simply an accident of birth? Ginny Beck and Ria Hale were prepared to do anything that would help the father they loved. Ash's mother wasn't prepared to sacrifice anything of herself for a son who needed her love. Had Victor Hale loved Ash's father? And what does Ena Lovell feel now she is about to be reunited with a sister she tried to write out of her life?

Scottie interrupts my thoughts. 'Oh, to be ten again, with nothing more to worry about than kite flying.' He takes an exaggerated breath of sea air.

I lean into him. 'Speak for yourself. At ten, I was worrying that Rick Astley might not marry me.'

'Was that a guy at your school?' He pulls a wide-eyed smile. 'Come on. It's nearly time. Patrick Quinn awaits.'

When we get back to the car park, Patrick is leaning against the passenger door of the transit, chatting through the window. He gives us a mock-salute. The sporty clothing and peaked cap are missing today; he is wearing a sharp black suit and shiny shoes. I had discussed protocols with Scottie, and our conclusion had been that we would dress for a funeral, though we didn't expect to attend one. We have it exactly right.

'How are you both?' Patrick asks, offering us a handshake. We accept.

'Happy to be doing what's right,' Scottie says, 'at last.'

'Would you walk with me to the park?' Patrick gestures at the van. 'These guys say they'll follow at a slow pace. I think it's the right way to do it. Nana Ena and the others will be there to meet us.'

He leads us away with an outstretched arm. My stomach is performing somersaults at the thought of meeting more of the Lovell tribe. Families are at the heart of history, I've always thought. These people will be a direct link to a time when Victor Hale was pedalling his charm. I'm glad I never met the man. His dishonesty created upset for many; his position in society should have meant the opposite. Patrick had sobbed quietly on the end of the phone when I'd informed him of the DNA matches. He'd no idea who Victor Hale was, yet the guy fathered a child who would have been his relative.

The electronic gates are open when we arrive. About fifty people, dressed sombrely, stand in a horseshoe by the chalets. They join together in a slow hand-clap. Ena sits amongst them in a wheelchair. Patrick hurries to her side and she grasps his hand.

'Hello,' I say, and can't help myself kissing her cheek. Patrick escapes and she clutches at me.

'I owe you some thanks, for sure,' she whispers in my ear.

Scottie and I stand by her side as the transit drivers, wearing long grey overcoats and downcast expressions, move to the back of the van. The level of gratitude I feel when they wheel out one small wooden casket, is echoed in gasps and sighs from the gathered crowd. There is nothing macabre about the spectacle, no waiting around for two bodies: Esme and her child are making their final journey together. The drivers behave as though they are delivering a most prized possession. Ena leads them away.

We gather in a large chalet at the back end of the site. It is clearly someone's home, but the main room is empty of furniture apart from a table, draped with a white cloth. Once the casket is placed, Patrick brings Ena to the middle of the crowd. It falls silent.

'You've come here today,' she says, as she's helped from the wheelchair, 'in support of a family member. Esme Lovell was my sister, her child my niece. The past is the past, and best left to do its festering there.' She lays a hand on the casket. 'Regrets aren't something I admit to, as most of you know.' A murmur of agreement zips around the room. 'But I will own this one: I should have helped my sister, not shunned her. We all should've.' Her voice crackles with emotion. Agreement comes from the gathered crowd.

Patrick steps forward. 'Our community is different now,' he says, emphatically. 'Old values have died with those who held them. Nana here,' – he places a hand on Ena's shoulder – 'she's a twenty-first century girl.' He stoops to embrace her. 'Aren't you, Nan?'

'I am, and my Benny would have been proud of you today, if he was here.' Ena and Patrick continue with the love-fest, and others join in. Past events are mentioned: past struggles and past highs. Names are spoken with the utmost reverence; noisy tears are shed. It is then that I realise this is tradition, not a spontaneous outpouring. I wish Ash could be here to see it. He has made a career out of supporting families at their most vulnerable time; he would enjoy this. As soon as it's possible, I am going to get in touch with him and paint a picture.

Ash

When Cherie messages, Ash is sitting in a booth at the Biggar pub, and listening to his friends recount their most recent brush with death.

'What about you, Blacky?' one says. 'Where were you when our Jan almost got mashed? Mooning after that lass you gave a lift to? One of the anorak brigade, wasn't she? You're going soft in your old age.'

Ash is smiling and nodding in the right places, but he's only half listening. He'd rather be with Cherie at Esme Lovell's reunifying ceremony; he'd rather be with Cherie anywhere, if he's honest. He denies the accusation of *mooning* by explaining that he's had a lot to deal with, which brings more guffaws and nudges.

Hal's physical health is improving every day, though his mental state remains unchanged. He's due to be discharged from hospital in a few days. Being on his own at the lodge is giving Ash plenty of time to think.

Had his father been involved in covering up the deaths of Esme and her daughter? This Victor Hale character certainly had him in thrall. The police have visited Marsh House and spoken to Victor, but Dale Scott is yet to share information. Cherie has his ear, perhaps she is the one to ask.

Ash's flare of jealousy at her involvement with *Scottie*

hadn't gone down well, and now she's backed off. They exchange phone messages, the tone upbeat but with no depth. Ash wants to tell her about real things that are happening in his life, to speak about his feelings, but he's no fool. A woman like Cherie wouldn't have time for him. He could invite her back to the lodge, ask her to become part of his life, and Hal's; let her know how much he misses her company. Instead, in answer to her message about Esme Lovell, he sends a *thumbs-up*.

It's the first day of spring. Ash steps out of the pub, and takes a moment to breathe in the beauty of the morning. The tide is high. A brine-soaked breeze tugs at the ends of his hair, and flicks the silver strands into his mouth. He scrapes them away with his thumbnail. Cherie was fascinated by what she called his *jackdaw* streak; he was fascinated by her ability to *spin* people. His friends have decided a blast along the road to Walney Lighthouse might be fun, and Ash agrees. It will be five miles of flying free. He can loosen the woes from his shoulders and let the slipstream carry them away.

Within minutes, they are chugging out of the village in a noisy, gleaming convoy. Ash is leading. He relaxes his spine and hunkers down, ready to open the throttle. When he catches a first sight of the empty road, he lets go. Inside his helmet is the sound of muted engine whine and scattering air. The bike roars beneath him, but the thrill isn't there. Meeting Cherie changed things, changed what he wanted from life. And now she's gone.

Hal

Hal stands in front of the bathroom mirror and drags the razor across his foam-covered cheeks. It is important he looks his best tonight. His hair is washed and brushed and falling in a dark sheet on either side of his face. A handsome face, he thinks, despite what Victor has sometimes told him.

Hal isn't mistaken, Victor is using him. Almost a year has passed since he ended their affair, but he still turns up, pushing his way into the lodge, demanding sex then asking questions. Hal is not strong enough to refuse but Victor's obsession with the chapel is off-putting. He has even insisted the roof is looked at and repaired, despite it being none of his business. At least the horrid daughters don't visit much. It's mainly the older one, the self-styled *Ria* Hale. He's never heard of such a name, but on the one occasion he dared to call her Vikki, she flew at him, fingernails poised. Victor thought it hilarious, and petted her for showing strength of character.

If Victor is still living with the girls' mother, Hal would guess it isn't going well. Something about him has changed. He has lost weight and vigour. His clothes have taken on a shoddy, slightly seedy appearance. It could be that Hal is seeing things differently, seeing Victor through less naive eyes. Either way, the relationship is becoming painful.

Hal wants to be settled, to have a family perhaps; a son. Victor will never give him these things, but Hal has a plan. He is aware of his attractiveness in the eyes of women. They take sly peeks at him while he is working around the cemetery. Some go out of their way to greet him, despite their status as mourners.

He has never gone into public houses with the intention of meeting them, but he's going to try. It's not that he dislikes women. He finds them soft and forgiving, and extremely caring, but there is never that frisson of sexual desire. He can easily fake something, he's sure. It will make him respectable in the eyes of the community, if he is seen with a pretty woman on his arm.

He has purchased a new pair of trousers, flared and with a wide waistband, and a bri-nylon shirt. Hal is slim around the hips and has well-muscled shoulders, and when he examines this new appearance in the mirror, his throat tightens with tears. This is the life he must lead now, a life that isn't authentic, a life that's a lie. Perhaps there will be a time when men like him are nothing more than ordinary. Until then, he will take everything Victor taught him, and use it to his advantage.

CHAPTER TWENTY-FIVE

Cherie

Saturday mornings are the hardest. In the early days of my marriage, David and I would use this time to decompress from our working week, enjoying the humdrum of shopping and laundry. I don't miss him, but sharing those tasks built our relationship in a good way at first. He soon decided they were beneath us as a couple, that some of their mundanity might rub off on him, so he'd hired a cleaner.

I stand in the kitchen of the cottage and wonder how to fill the empty day. There is my Gillside work; there's always that. What I crave more than anything, is company. It's a beautiful day. The sky is high and blue and layered with back-lit clouds that look like they belong in a Constable painting. I want to share that with someone; I want to share it with Ash.

I've been offered one day a week working for the university again. Not remotely this time, but face to face. Bill has agreed it would be good for the company to have these links, and he can realign my pay structure to suit. I haven't decided yet. It would mean buying a car. Getting from Cark to Lancaster by train is doable but a long journey. Commuting was another thing I was happy to leave behind when I finished with David. He didn't see anything wrong with a daily commute: *follow the money* was his motto.

Ash has been in touch a few times, to update me on his father's progress. The messages are friendly and precise, but nothing more. I'd love to meet up with them both again, but remember how much Ash hated having his routines upended. Scottie is still working on the chapel case, and sends updates now and again. Sometimes we reflect on the short and sad life of Esme Lovell; sometimes we get angry at Victor Hale's arrogance. Scottie never mentions his ex-boss.

My brooding is cut short when the telephone rings. It is Bill.

'Hi,' I say. 'Happy Saturday.'

'Happy Saturday.' He gives the word a spin of joviality. 'And on that note, Disa has tasked me with asking you for lunch tomorrow. Would you be interested? Nothing formal, but the weather has turned, and we always celebrate with a first meal in the garden.'

I have heard about Bill's legendary garden. And his partner's culinary skills. 'I'd love to come. Thanks.'

He fills me in on timings and reminds me of how to get to his house. Then he says, 'You sound a bit down. Is everything all right?'

'Course. I've just been pondering the whole Esme Lovell thing, and it's making me sad.' It's a lie but it's all he's getting. I don't want him to think my efforts at starting a new life and new job have not been worth it. They have; I adore working with him at Gillside. 'Old bones and the stories behind them can cause that effect, can't they? Bring a perspective on life you might not want to face. Your own mortality, that is.'

'Tell me about it,' he says with a long sigh. 'I meant to ask you about the Romani bracelet. Did you find out if it belonged to the family?'

'Patrick Quinn thinks so. He's doing a bit more research, now he's got the remains. He thinks it held monetary value as well as sentiment.'

Bill, sharp as always, asks why it was left on Esme's body, if it was so valuable. He knows something of the Hale girls and their wants, knows that they took things that didn't belong to them: keys for example.

'Why not the bracelet?' he asks.

'Ginny took the bracelet,' I explain. 'I presume she was going to keep it, but at the last minute, when she and her sister and Victor walked away from the bodies they'd hidden, Ginny slipped the bracelet over Esme's wrist. That's what she's saying, anyway. Perhaps it will get her sympathy. Who knows?'

'Do you – I mean the police – believe her?'

'I'm not sure. Dale Scott, the guy leading the investigation, gives me updates but doesn't comment on conjecture. Which I think is fair enough.'

'Course it is,' Bill says brightly. 'Fair play to him.'

'He's been brilliant. The guy is on the fast-track ladder, and he deserves it. Even if he did keep referring to me as *love*.'

Right-o, I hear Bill say to someone in the background, which sounds like his cue to end the call.

'Okay, *love*,' he says, then laughs at his own joke. 'We'll catch up tomorrow.' He pauses then adds, 'Can I say one more thing?'

'Go on.'

'You can bring that caretaker bloke to the lunch, if you like. If you're seeing him, that is. The more, the merrier.'

'I'm not *seeing* him, but thanks for the offer.'

Bill says *bye* three more times before we end the call. I think about his words. Had it been so easy to spot that I was keen on

Ash? Did I talk about him a lot? I wasn't aware of this, but Bill is a highly trained researcher; he has the nose of a spaniel. Either way, I'm not and never was *seeing* Ash. The thought brings back my melancholy mood, once again.

I've considered trying to get in touch with Debbie Soames. She is the kind of person with whom I could easily strike up a friendship. The leaflets her brother gave me on the Marsh House facility have a mixture of contact details. It wouldn't be too difficult to locate her. But I lied to the woman, and I'm sure if she doesn't already know, the truth will come out eventually. Lying is no basis for a friendship, so I ditch the idea before it really has a place in my list of valid friendship options.

I make myself a pot of tea, then sit at the kitchen table and flip open my laptop. There is a local ramblers group in the next village, and they have a website. I'd like to put my name down, and join them. It will give me a bit more human interaction, if nothing else. Like most people, I lost connections after the pandemic. I communicated with friends via FaceTime and Zoom when we were banned from contact, but when it came to meeting up again, things had changed. There would have been a natural cooling of friendships, I'm sure, but no one wanted to sever connections during a time when we needed each other. Once the last restrictions were lifted, we walked in separate directions.

It looks like I will be walking in the direction of Cat Bells if I join this group. It's a mid-level fell near Derwentwater, about an hour from the cottage. Lifts are being offered for next weekend.

I'm about to introduce myself in the group chat room, when I hesitate. Is this really what I want? My fitness is up to the walk, but I'm not sure if my sociability will stand the test. What if this new set of people find me as superior as Ash did? Perhaps I would be better off saying yes to the university job. I would be a definite fit for my colleagues there.

I pour a mug of tea and close down the ramblers tab. Walking by myself might be easier. I've spoken to a few people around the village, and they're friendly enough, but distant. I want discussion, debate. Laughs.

On a whim, I open the folder which contains the essays of my previous online students; those are always good for a *laugh*. One or two showed promise; most were short on detail and rather pompous.

My favourite had been written by a guy who didn't want face-to-face tutorials, so we'd worked on everything via the university Moodle platform. His prose was lyrical enough that I decided he must be a poet, but his essays were academically rigorous in a strangely naive way. He obviously loved old buildings with a passion; my kind of passion.

There was a sentence at the end of his last essay that I want to read again. Thinking about it snags at my memory: *the lives contained in buildings give them something akin to a soul.* Someone has said this to me recently. I was kneeling, tidying, while they spun back-and-forth on a chair, sardonic smile across their lips.

I click rapidly through the file names, and find what I am looking for: *Paul Last*. With trembling hands, I open the document. There are references to buildings in the town where Ash lives. Of course there are, he and Paul Last are the same person. I have no idea why he didn't register with me using his real name, though I'd welcome the chance to ask him.

Everything is falling into place. Ash had mentioned his history studies on numerous occasions, even naming his university. I can't remember the conversation going anywhere. He talked about buildings in a way I found familiar. Why had I never made the connection? How insulted he must have felt at my lack of interest. I put my head in my hands and take a deep breath. Ash is in the same position, I realise. He doesn't know me as Dr Sheralyn Smith. He won't have any idea I was once his tutor. A plan is swirling through my brain. It will be a bit of fun, but I'm sure he'll appreciate it.

I retrieve his email address. There is nothing to suggest it belongs to Ash Black. I'm hoping the address is still active. I put together an amusing and flirty message, signing myself off as Sheralyn Smith aka Cherie Hope. I check and recheck it, leave it and drink more tea. Then I press send.

Ash

Hal is having his first outing since coming home from hospital. It is a simple high tea at Greg's house, some five minutes' drive away.

One of the recommendations from the dementia team had been that Ash's father get out more. As long as a suitable care plan is in place, a risk assessment of sorts, he can mix with people outside Cemetery Lodge. Not for the Alzheimer's, but for his mental health – no one ever asks about Ash's mental health.

So, even though it is a Saturday morning, and he is free to go where he chooses, Ash finds himself sitting at his desk sorting through invoices. They could wait until Monday. He should be out on his bike with his friends. There had been an offer of a blast up to The Lakes, or a longer haul to Devil's Bridge. He can't face either. The last time he'd tried had felt like a chore. He switches on the computer, then leans back in his chair and waits.

There are five notifications on his works email account. They weren't there when he had tied things up yesterday evening. This is one of the downsides of the digital age: people expect instant access to services, then aren't happy when the service provider doesn't magically appear.

He's about to work his way through, giving advice and finding solutions, when he notices a flag on his university email icon. He hasn't looked at the account for almost three years. The presumption had been that it was closed down; he never checked. The Moodle tab is still on his computer, too. He should perhaps see what is going on there as well. In his attempt to be coy, he'd called himself Paul Last while he was an online student. The pandemic made people into a facsimile of themselves. During the hours he was working with his tutor and fellow students, he felt like someone else. Looking back on this now, it seems an immature thing. It felt quite cool at the time.

He gasps at the contents of the email. It is from his tutor, Sheralyn Smith. When he starts reading, his eyes flee to the final lines, then everything makes sense.

> Hello, Paul. Ashley Paul.
>
> I've been looking over the final grades I gave my 2020-2021 students, mainly for reasons of quality control. What I have realised is that your last essay, entitled 'I am no ruin', is deserving of more recognition than it previously gained. I have thought of a suitable reward, but you would have to claim it in person. I wonder if this would be possible. I look forward to hearing from you, perhaps even seeing you, very soon.
>
> Regards,
>
> Sheralyn Smith (aka Cherie Hope)

Ash reads the email again, picking apart the words, wondering if they are meant for him. He looks at the date. It was sent two hours ago. He peers at the screen, thinking he has picked up the wrong gist. Cherie was his online tutor.

How could he have not known? They never met, never spoke, simply communicated as many did at the time, via an electronic platform. From behind a screen. Had she ever mentioned using a different name? Was she married? Separated? The flirty tone of the email sounds nothing like the Cherie he knows, but did he really know her? They never talked about important things; he never asked.

He is aware, from the comments his tutor made, that the work he completed for his diploma was of a high standard. He'd wanted Cherie to know that about him, but it never came up. A tangle of confused thoughts clog his brain, but one manages to break free: Cherie wants to see him. He doesn't need to read that part of the email again. She wants to see him and she's going to. Hal won't be back until the middle of the afternoon, and Greg has a key. Ash is free, and he is heading to Cark.

Within minutes, he has dragged his bike from the garage and is zooming through the cemetery gates. He's hardly given himself time to fasten his jacket. It's a day of dazzling sunshine and diamond-clear air, one he wants to share with someone. It sounds like Cherie is thinking the same.

The traffic is heavy, chugging towards the edge of town in no particular hurry. Ash wants to put his head down and open the throttle. When it is held back, the bike can be noisy. Pedestrians are staring, grabbing on tightly to their children. Eventually, a duel-carriageway looms, and Ash lets fly.

Within fifteen minutes he reaches the edge of Cark. He brings the bike to a halt and turns off the engine. His plan is to arrive on foot, rather than alert the whole of Cherie's street to his presence. The cottage is in the middle of the village, as far as he can remember, and it sends a quiver of excitement through him that she will be there and waiting. He locks the helmet onto the bike frame and sets off.

She is standing nonchalantly in the cottage doorway. He waves a greeting.

'I heard the bike,' she says as he walks towards her. 'I think we all did.'

A wash of heat spreads across Ash's cheeks. He smiles. 'I got your email,' he says with more confidence than he is feeling.

She pulls back the door. 'Better come in then.'

Something about her is different. He saunters past. Cherie directs him to the kitchen. He unzips his jacket and slides it off. She hangs it over the back of a chair.

'Well,' she murmurs, stepping towards him. 'Small world, isn't it? Paul Last.'

'It is, Dr Smith.' He lifts her hand and kisses the palm.

The butterflies in his stomach are threatening to escape through his mouth. Paul Last might have been cool and in control, but Ash Black is far from it. Cherie must feel the tension, too. She looks up at him with a surprised expression.

'You're definitely after favouritism.' She hesitates. 'That's against the rules.'

Ash's mouth is so dry, he can't speak. Somehow, Cherie senses this. She moves gently away, lifts the kettle, and waggles it at him. His relief comes out with a puff of breath.

'What are we like.' She laughs softly. 'All that time together and we never made the connection. I've stood in your kitchen so many times, but we never really talked, did we? Let's talk now.'

Ash is grateful for the distraction. He settles himself at the tiny table, and smiles at Cherie across the room. It's a moment he's been desperate for, a moment when he can be honest with the woman who helped him so much, but he's nervous.

'You talked,' he says, 'but I rarely listened. And I never asked. That's what I'm most embarrassed about. I was curious about you, Cherie, but I never asked. You'll laugh at this, but that first day when we met properly, I was expecting Gillside to send a grey-haired man who favoured arran sweaters and coffee from his own flask. Then you turned up and I was miffed.'

'Why? I'm perfectly qualified to do the job.'

Ash shakes his head. 'It wasn't that. I didn't want to engage... and you're very engaging.'

She blushes and he gives himself a metaphorical pat-on-the-back. The only way forward is to be honest. He isn't one for being open about emotions, but is aware this will be his last chance with Cherie.

'You thought I was superior and snobbish,' she says in answer. 'Don't deny it. I knew I wasn't, but the issues I've had with my ex-husband made me think twice about having to explain myself.'

'Sorry. I've only just realised you must have been married or something.' He grits his teeth so that she sees. 'Not my business. I don't want to be nosy.'

'I thought we were being.'

'Tell me then. I am quite nosy, where you're concerned. I know nothing about this ex-husband of yours and I already want to kill him.'

'You'll definitely want to do that once I've told you.' She looks at the ceiling and puts her hands together as though she is praying. 'Sorry, David, but you are an arse, pure and simple.'

She gives him a brief account of her time as Mrs Sheralyn Smith. The husband sounds like a complete joke, but Ash doesn't pass comment. He's feeling guilty enough that the way this David guy treated her had parallels with his own actions.

'The worst of it is that I'm very ordinary,' she says, 'and he made out I was something else. He was probably looking for a reason to break up, but it caused a lot of heartache, as you can imagine.'

'I can.' Ash accepts the coffee she's made, and keeps staring at her as she sits at the table with him. He wants her to know when her *ordinariness* first rocked his world.

She frowns. 'What?'

'This is really embarrassing, but can I tell you it anyway?' His heart is hammering against his ribs, but he remembers his promise to himself about honesty.

She lowers her gaze. 'Go on then.'

'I fell for you when you said you were perfectly used to sharing toilets.' He smiles and waits for her response. It isn't what he expects.

'I can beat that,' she says. 'I fell for you when I saw your silver streak.'

His hand reaches up. 'This bloody thing. Pardon my language. I tried to cut it out when I was a kid, but it kept coming back.'

She leans across the table and touches his hair. 'I like it.'

A rush of desire shoots through Ash, and it would be dishonest not to act on his feelings. He pulls back his chair and moves to where Cherie is sitting. She tracks him with her eyes, then stands in greeting. He doesn't move as she puts her hands against his chest and slides them upwards.

'I think we know where we're going with this,' she murmurs, then presses her lips against his. 'Not to bully you or anything.' He puts his hands on her waist and pulls her closer.

'I might need to lie down,' he stammers. 'You're far too scary for me to handle.' He winks. 'Dr Hope.'

Cherie sighs lightly and takes his hand. She leads him up the stairs to a tiny bedroom under the eaves. It has flowery curtains and a patchwork quilt, and he thinks he might have fallen into a parallel universe. Her hands slide under his shirt, and his thoughts are confirmed. He can do nothing else but give in to what is happening.

Afterwards, when Ash is lying in the narrow bed with his feet hanging over the end and Cherie in his arms, he lets himself think about the future. Hal's illness has taken away almost a decade of his life. What if the same thing happens to Ash? He doesn't want regrets, doesn't want to spend time lonely and wondering what Cherie is doing and how her life is going, he wants to be her life.

'It's funny to think we spent a year communicating behind a screen,' he says. 'I still can't quite get my head around it. There was no way to make sense of the other person, was there? All the normal cues were missing. I didn't have any mental picture, or any idea you were a real person.'

Cherie props herself on her elbow and traces his silver streak.

'It was the same for me. The poignant words you used in your essays, the sentiment. The whip-smart observations. I didn't attribute them to Paul Last, whoever he was. When Ash Black started quoting the same content, it felt very weird, like you and Paul had been reading the same textbook. There was still no connection to, as you say, a real person. That's the digital age, for you.'

'It has goods and bads, I guess.' Ash kisses her fingertips. 'Were you even married then?'

'I was. Just about.' She frowns at him. 'Why?'

'I'm trying to get a handle on who this Sheralyn Smith was, that's all. I invented another version of me at the time: Paul Last. He was everything I wasn't.' Ash runs his fingers across her cheek. 'Cool, clever. Sophisticated. It embarrasses me now, but it felt like a way to escape. Did you do the same? Was Sheralyn Smith secretly trying to get away from this lousy bloody David character?'

'Deep.' She brings a mocking tone to the word. 'Sorry. I don't mean to be flippant. It's just that I've always been Cherie.

To my friends, anyway. There's no elegant, stylish and misunderstood twin. But I think I understand what you're saying.'

'You would.'

She gives him a playful thump. 'Don't start that again, or I'll downgrade you.'

'Before you do, can I put in a request? You did say my academic work deserved a bigger reward.' He wriggles his brows hopefully.

'Go on then. What?'

'Come and stay at the lodge with me and dad for a while. Not for good. Just to see how things pan out.' He takes a deep breath and exhales slowly. 'I want to throw myself into a relationship with you. I want to break all the rules about taking things slowly and being respectful of personal space. Can we just do it? What do you think?'

Cherie goes quiet. She slides away from him and sits up, and he thinks he's just made the biggest mistake of his life. How can she come and live with a cemetery caretaker and his elderly father? She has a doctorate and a sharp brain and years of academic training and work. A minute passes, and it's the longest one he's ever experienced, then she turns to face him.

'I can't think of anything I want more,' she says with a smile. 'Can you give me ten minutes to pack a suitcase?'

Ash watches as she slips on a fluffy dressing gown and opens her wardrobe. Cherie is coming with him to the lodge; coming with him into a new life. He won't think of how the future might look, and he can't dwell on what has happened between them in the past. To get a sense of past and future, as a tutor of his once commented, he should simply *get his feet wet*.

THE END

ALSO BY PAULA HILLMAN

Halfmoon Lane
The Cottage
Blackthorn Wood
Chapel Field
Seaview House

ACKNOWLEDGEMENTS

On a foggy evening in December 2023, I found myself taking a short cut through Barrow cemetery. It's a 66-acre site, spread across the western flank of the town, and is a nod to Victorian gothic. Three separate chapels once stood here: the modern crematorium swallowed two of them. One remains, boarded up, dropped from use in the 1970s. Walking by the chapel on that evening, peering through the safety fence, gave me the first sparks of a story idea.

During the pandemic, I gained two qualifications from Lancaster University. My studies were undertaken via a virtual learning platform called Moodle. The second qualification, a history diploma, required no human contact whatsoever. In the end, some of my fellow students set up a working group and we would meet via Zoom. It was a relief to connect names to faces, believe me! However, many other students and tutors chose to remain anonymous. This weird way of interacting gave me the other part of my story, and Ash and Cherie were born.

Lots of my readers were anticipating *Cemetery Lodge* when I was completing the final edits. They would stop me in the street and tell me stories of their connections to Barrow cemetery. I received messages from across the world, from ex-Barrovians eagerly awaiting the chance to walk the slopes through my words, and revisit their hometown. I hope they are happy with the story.

As always, I must thank Betsy Reavley and Fred Freeman for their continued support of my writing. The Bloodhound team are first-rate, particularly my editor Clare Law, and production manager, Tara Lyons. Thanks also to Hannah and Lexi for their clever marketing strategies. My husband, Steve Hillman, read Cemetery Lodge in its early stages and picked up some rather daft plot holes. We were once bikers ourselves, before children and the inevitable family hatchback came along. When I wrote Ash and Cherie's motorbike journey to Brucciani's in Morecambe, it reminded me of the good times!

A NOTE FROM THE PUBLISHER

Thank you for reading this book. If you enjoyed it please do consider leaving a review on Amazon to help others find it too.

We hate typos. All of our books have been rigorously edited and proofread, but sometimes mistakes do slip through. If you have spotted a typo, please do let us know and we can get it amended within hours.

info@bloodhoundbooks.com

Milton Keynes UK
Ingram Content Group UK Ltd.
UKHW042117201024
449912UK00004B/109